RED

THE AUTHOR

Frank Palmer gave up journalism to write the now-completed 'Jacko' series, highly acclaimed on both sides of the Atlantic. He then embarked on the Phil 'Sweeney' Todd series of whodunnits, of which this is the second.

Red Gutter

Frank Palmer

a&b

This edition published in Great Britain in 1998 by
Allison & Busby Ltd
114 New Cavendish Street
London W1M 7FD
http://www.allisonandbusby.ltd.uk

First published by
Constable & Co Ltd in 1996

A catalogue record for this book is available from the
British Library

ISBN 0 7490 0336 7

Printed and bound in Great Britain by
Mackays of Chatham Plc
Chatham, Kent

In memory of my wife ANN,
with whom I discovered these wonderful parts of the world –
and much, much more besides.

The East Midlands Combined Constabulary and its cases are fictional. So, too, are the characters, companies and all the events in this story.

My gratitude goes to Mr Rupert Vinnicombe, Newark District Librarian, for historical background, not least the title, Mr Michael Sheldon for access to the battleground, and the Rev. Graham Firth, rector of East Stoke, for his help.

The staff of Hunting Cargo Airlines (though they took no part in the trade described) provided valued advice in setting up the aviation company, as did Flight Lieutenant Mark Robinson. Brian Waldram gave expert help on cold stores and Tony Knowles on sewers.

Special thanks to Brian Dixon, my host in Normandy, and Steve Panton, who did all the driving.

1

D-Day minus two

POLICE CHIEF
IN DEATH
PLUNGE RIDDLE

Any cop above the rank of inspector is a chief to a tabloid, so it's not the headline, big and black though it is, that jolts me, but the single column photo half-way down the front page.

Silent Knight's.

My chief.

Is he heading up some new and major inquiry, called in, perhaps, by another force? Or is he the dead police chief?

For a moment, I gaze at him, feeling my brow crease, then lean forward cautiously. 'Excuse me.'

A man sitting diagonally to me on a soft pink L-shaped couch peers over the top of his newspaper, frowning, disturbed.

'May I take a quick peek at the main story?' I shuffle closer.

'Help yourself.' He tightens his grip, straightening and stretching the outer pages. His head drops back inside.

The photo is a few years old, when he looked more dashing, boyish even, but the story is about Knight all right.

Dead.

Yesterday.

In a fall while bird-watching. Head injuries. Major investigation launched.

So stunned am I that a soft 'Christ' is all I can manage.

The man, mid-twenties, casually dressed, rustles the paper together and turns it to read what provoked my profanity. 'A friend of yours?' he asks in a soft, concerned accent from the south.

'A neighbour,' I reply, the truth only in that we worked in the same building and then not very closely.

He reads what I've already scanned: Andrew Knight, aged fifty. Assistant chief constable of one of the biggest provincial forces. Top man in the field of anti-terrorism. Responsible for some major coups, including here in his Ulster days.

'You a policeman, too?' he finally asks.

Even nine months into the peace I'm not about to admit that I'm Special Branch. I shake my head and pat my right leg and flex it stiffly, hoping to give the impression that I'm too lame to be plodding any beat.

A pale red head approaches, saving me from further interrogation. 'Morning.'

He smiles up at her. 'Sleep well?' Both look so washed out I doubt it.

'Yes,' she fibs. Then: 'Ready?'

Not for more of what I'm increasingly getting less of, but for a country house grill with fried soda bread which I've already had.

He nods goodbye, gets up, taking the refolded paper with him.

From beyond the long reception desk, where a printer is rattling out our bill, Emma strolls slowly, slightly splay-footed in blue loafers, across the patterned carpet towards me. She's rehearsing her walk for a couple of months hence when her blue jeans and white T-shirt will no longer fit.

Her brown eyes sparkle like early morning on the Lakes of Killarney. For four years now I've known that the shine in them has as much to do with contact lenses reflecting a brief and unaccustomed burst of sun as with love for me.

In bed, she wears granny specs for reading – mostly Shakespeare these days since last year's 'Bard on the Box' prompted her to give a second chance to works she left behind at school.

Now she's hooked, reads me extracts from books propped on her ever-enlarging stomach. Last night I went to sleep to a sonnet:

> From fairest creatures, we desire increase,
> That therefore beauty's rose might never die . . .

It's not morning sickness that made her skip breakfast. She never eats it. She nibbles at nearly all other times, except mealtimes. She flops into the low seat that's just been vacated. I tell her what I've read.

'Je-sus.' She strings it out. Her face registers mild shock in the way that people do when they hear of the death of someone they know of, but don't really know. 'Let's get a couple of papers.'

We didn't order any when we checked into this out-of-the-way hotel last night, having come inland to look at the loch on our way to Ireland's northern tip.

We've been here, west and north, just pottering, for ten days. She didn't want to travel too far or go anywhere hot. We've motored more than a thousand miles since we left home, but her second wish came true – rain every day; not those Irish softs you hear so much about, stair rods.

She didn't want to see any papers either now she's on maternity leave. Once she was a news junkie. Now she's addicted to sonnets.

The rim of Ireland had been one misty, rugged view after another, white waves crashing on sheer cliffs and golden deserted beaches, and what the weather lacked in warmth was more than compensated for by the people, everyone so pleased to see us. Peace and perfection. I have a sinking feeling it's coming to a premature end.

The nearest town nestles in a green valley, a dozen or more church spires in the foreground, blue mountains in the distance.

Such was her sudden craving for news, Em bought all the papers from the only shop that was open down the narrow main street. A couple in their Sunday best, the only couple in the street, eyed with disapproval my ice blue travel-stained windcheater when I stopped our new, silver Volvo, safe and sensible for a couple about to be a family, to seek directions.

Now we've found the only other place that seems to be open, apart from churches: an ivy-covered hotel with a Union Jack hanging limp and bedraggled on a pole above the flat-roofed entrance.

We are sitting at a round table on a black stand going through the pile of papers, me sipping coffee. She of odd eating habits is nibbling toast that came with Marmite (substituting for the smooth pâté on the menu), served by a cheerful waitress with an arm in plaster.

9

Each paper has its own angle on the story. Piecing them together, it amounts to this:

Knight left his home in a village, only a mile or so from force headquarters, yesterday morning.

He told his wife he was going bird-watching, a pursuit he'd only recently taken up on medical advice which hints at a secret illness; but then almost everything about Knight was cloaked in secrecy.

His wife phoned headquarters when he didn't return for lunch, wondering if he'd dropped in there. She expressed concern, but didn't officially report him missing.

Like any sensible officer with half an eye on his pension and a chief overdue for lunch, the control room inspector launched inquiries.

It was a holidaying historian, pictured in gumboots in some papers, who found him. He was visiting the scene of the last battle in the Wars of the Roses.

He'd photographed a stone marking the spot where Henry VII raised his banner in victory, then walked through a wood to take a photo of a deep gully in which thousands of fleeing rebels were massacred.

All the papers record the gruesome name of the ravine: Red Gutter.

Knight was lying at the foot of it. He had head and other unspecified injuries. CID officers were treating his death as 'suspicious'.

All the papers report that he was in charge of a nationwide hunt for a gang of animal lib terrorists who had sabotaged a cattle boat in an increasingly violent campaign against livestock exports that had waged all year.

Em says what I'm thinking. 'You'd better phone in.'

'Superintendent Todd on an outside line, sir,' announces the switchboard operator.

'Ah, Philip,' says the chief constable. He's rarely about HQ on a Sunday. I guess the mystery death of his No. 3 is rare enough. 'Good of you to check in.'

I tell him where I am and what I've read and he says how shocked everyone is. 'His heart, you know.'

Never realised he was ill, I respond. Only he and his family did, he says. 'Angina.' The chief had visited his widow. Daughter and sister were with her. 'Coping well.'

What about the head and other injuries the papers were reporting? I ask out of professional nosiness.

'Cracked his head on a rock and there was a friction mark on his
chest, both consistent with a longish fall, the pathologist reports.
No doubt about cause of death. The arteries were badly diseased.
Nothing suspicious.'

He's issuing a full statement, he goes on, with the coroner's
consent, to damp down the media speculation. I'm losing a bit of
interest.

OK, it's desperately sad for his wife, daughter and a small circle
of friends who were really close to him. It matters not to them
whether he died suspiciously or naturally, won't lessen their
shock and grief. But, to me, cranking myself up for the hue and
cry of an old-fashioned murder hunt, a cop-killing to boot, it's
something of an anticlimax.

'You'll take over his caseload, of course,' the chief continues.

I don't know whether he means just the sabotage inquiry or the
whole department. There's a chief super between Knight and me,
above me in the pecking order of rank. I can't ask outright if he's
being bypassed, so obliquely, 'Is Mr Dale otherwise engaged?'

Yes, he replies, lots of protection duty coming up, by which he
means guarding royals and VIPs like cabinet ministers when they
visit the patch.

'You'll be acting chief super with immediate effect,' he adds.
'Makes sense. You know the story so far.' He pauses. 'Andy was
anticipating an imminent breakthrough. We spoke on Friday. He
was working hard on a good lead. Wanted to clear it all up, then
retire on health grounds.'

Before I can ask more questions, he hurries on, 'Full briefing on
your return, eh? We'd all like a good result for Andy, wouldn't we?'

He expects me to say 'Yes' and I'm not about to disappoint
someone who can give me a mighty shove up the promotion
ladder.

All this I report back to Emma who breaks off from leafing
through a magazine's pages in the otherwise deserted lounge.

The chief talks in code, I explain. He is setting me up against
Dale with Knight's job as the prize. By 'immediate effect' he
means come back straight away.

11

'Do I see the gleam of vaulting ambition in thine eyes?' she mocks.

A weak smile hides the fact that she's seen right through me. Acting chief super could soon become substantive and then what? Acting ACC. At thirty-nine. And then? All the way to the top? Why not?

I tell myself that with another mouth to feed and a wife undecided about going back to her well-paid job in television the salary hike will be useful. I don't kid myself that I've never felt like this before, experienced this urge. Many times in private moments, driving, gardening, in the bath, I've day-dreamed about how differently – and better – I'd run the department if I was in charge.

'Ah well,' Em sighs theatrically, 'the mountains and the glens will still be here when all three of us return in our chauffeured Roller.'

2

'The story so far . . .' The chief's words echo in my head. My stomach churns.

I blame Em for this queasiness, having just watched her devour a Sealink bacon sandwich that oozed fat. She has put on her thick blue jumper and left me now to take the air on deck with its view of the mountains we never visited slipping into the murk of a grey, still afternoon.

The last thing I wanted, I told her, was to be reminded of Irish breakfasts. I've taken off my windcheater, reclined the airline-style seat and, with a two-hour voyage ahead and a seven-hour drive on the other side facing me, close my eyes to nap. Sleep won't come.

'The story so far . . .'

It's, what, fourteen months since I made super and joined Special Branch after a year off sick with a shot-up leg.

Never speak ill of the dead, my old gran used to say, so I'd like to say that I enjoyed working under Knight. In this honest moment, I can't.

They don't . . . (he's past tense so better get used to it) . . . They didn't call him Silent for nothing. Nothing's what he told you. In the canteen they said he treated everyone like mushrooms – kept 'em in the dark and fed 'em shit.

I came from Special Operations, the fire brigade of the force, and, before that, CID, used to the openness of being part of a team, one of the boys, lots of fun.

There was no openness, not much fun, working for Knight. He ran every inquiry on a need-to-know basis, as if still operating down the coast in Belfast.

And I was foisted upon him; recompense, no doubt about it, for a permanently gammy leg and a thank-you for taking time off from sick leave to go undercover to clear up a case of political corruption. Not being a Freemason, I know that I was not his personal choice.

Special Branch was once an élite posting. Its great days – catching Iron Curtain spies and Irish terrorists – are over.

Nowadays we spend much of our time monitoring drug traffickers, commercial extortionists, eco-terrorists, Fascists and anti-Fascists while bosses like Knight fight internal turf battles against MI5 and the National Intelligence Bureau who, with peace breaking out all over, are touting for new business, our business.

It was almost a year of file updating, weeding and occasional watching before I got a decent job and what a cock-up we (correction: I) made of it. I sweat every time I think of it. I'm sweating now.

It started six weeks ago, the day after Easter, one of those spring days that can't make up its mind between summer and winter, so gives you both – warm, sunny spells and showers of snow that doesn't settle.

A woman on the switchboard of a big shipping line got a phone call at their wharfside offices: 'Animal Salvation speaking. Take a look next to the wheelhouse of your cattle boat. Fifty thousand pounds to our fighting fund or it goes up. Details of the drop within the hour.'

Knight dispatched me with a woman sergeant; a fast run, due north alongside the river, not too much traffic about with half the workforce adding an extra day to its bank holiday. Even so, the locals had easily beaten us to it.

A keen young patrolman had already been on board. He'd found a smallish sports bag. Inside were plastic bags of cream crystals which gave off a diesel smell. On top of them were wires, a battery and a wrist-watch ticking away.

He didn't stop to note the time, cleared the area and alerted the bomb squad. 'Name of *Lindum Castle*,' he said, pointing down a long concrete quay to a stout, single-funnelled boat painted dark green where rust and salt hadn't left their colours.

The vessel, about two hundred feet long, was tied up front and back and rode high on the tide. 'Less than a seven-foot draught,' the patrolman said, showing off recently acquired knowledge. 'Under three hundred tons unladen. We can get closer if you like.'

'No, thank you, constable.' No need to tell him that since my leg got shot I don't run that fast any more. 'Well done.'

A sergeant from the army bomb squad defused it. 'Ten pounds. Ammonium nitrate-based. Primed to go off in four hours.' Coolly, he added, 'Plenty of time.'

My sidekick, Hazel Webster, manned the switchboard and took the second call. He gave precise instructions on where the money should be left – in one of those boxes containing sand to grit accident blackspots in the winter, this one at a busy junction in a tranquil town twenty or so miles south.

Hazel gabbled into a prepared piece about cattle boats not being like long distance lorries to keep him listening, if not talking. They had open pens, bedding, plenty of feed and water, the humane way to travel to some Continental slaughterhouse and so on. A waste of breath. The line had gone dead.

Knight ordered a strictly covert operation, and not a penny of public money to be gambled on the pay-off. Instead, a parcel of cut-up newspapers was placed in the yellow grit box. A traffic video was installed at the junction. Observation posts were set up in shops and a comfortable old hotel, me in charge, running things from the hotel, booked in overnight, naturally.

The operation was called off the following evening when, with no advance warning, an empty cattle boat, the *Lindum Castle*'s sister ship, was holed in an explosion in a Wash port a long way away from the wharf and the grit box we'd staked out. A replica bomb, the army sergeant reported later.

Hazel, who'd had the cushy job of temporary operator in the offices, got another call: 'We'll be back next month. And next time, no tricks.' She passed the message on to me at the hotel, busy with homeward-bound racegoers.

I walked out and opened the lid of the grit box. The parcel had gone. So had the salted sand. So had the cover of a manhole to a sewer we didn't even know was there.

A hundred yards down the street, alongside the cathedral, we found another manhole cover, freshly prised up, judging by the disturbed debris around it. The water board was summoned. It was a two-man job, using steel keys shaped like Ts, to lift the square, cast-iron cover.

My guide loaned me black waders with an elasticated waist and went in first. At the bottom, ten feet down, he checked a black meter on his belt for methane, called, 'All clear.' I took half a dozen staggered iron steps down to join him.

Remember that scene in the Vienna sewers where Harry Lime got his in *The Third Man*? Like the London Underground with a waterfall clear as a salmon stream, wasn't it? Remember? Well, it wasn't like that at all. It was pitch black and so was the sewerage.

There was a sweet, sickly smell, not at all rank or overpowering. Ahead of us, the odd rat swam against the tide, only two feet high. 'Just as well there's been no heavy rain or we'd be up to our necks in it,' said my guide.

It was the cloying heat, the blackness and the claustrophobic feeling I'll always remember, the way every word echoed, so your voice didn't sound like your own.

The tunnel was lined with bricks that glistened in the torchlight. It wasn't round or even oval, but egg-shaped, upside down with wider room for heads than feet, and then not much for either. It was six feet across at its widest, the same in height. I could have walked upright, I suppose, with two inches to spare, but didn't fancy the idea of my blond, almost white hair being used as a toilet brush.

A steepish walk, with neck plunged into shoulders, took us to the next set of steps. With the lid of the grit box open, I looked up into the worried face of a surveillance sergeant framed against a cold, cloudless blue sky.

One smart-arsed remark – like, say, the old Irish joke 'You on time and a turd, then?' – and he'd have finished up as humus in the treatment works down near the racecourse. He was smart enough to say nothing.

'What a shitty job,' I grumbled, trudging back.

'Hurry before the commercial break in *Coronation Street* or we'll be up to our eyes in it,' said the guide, not joking.

A big internal inquiry followed, of course. Didn't you check if there was a sewer under the road? Knight wanted to know. Nothing overt, you ordered, I replied. Didn't you check the grit box with the council? No, I confessed, but locals reported two men, one dressed as a fireman, had resited and refilled it a week ago.

The sinking of the boat got a big show in the media. Knight took charge of public relations, playing it close to his chest, not ruling out arson, but not mentioning commercial blackmail either.

Next day, the media got a call from Animal Salvation, spilling the lot, every detail. It got an even bigger show, the headline writers having lots of fun. POLICE OP DOWN THE PAN, said one.

To give him credit, Knight didn't attempt to pass the buck and took all the flak. He appeared, grey-faced, on TV explaining that details had previously been withheld because publicity spawns copycat crimes; all too true in the weeks that followed.

There was a spate of calls to supermarkets. 'Take a look at the baby beef broth.' One can had been opened, ground glass sprinkled inside, and the lid resealed in a microwave.

No call with ransom demands was made, but when baby broth was removed from the shelves, amid precautionary publicity, a couple of mothers turned up at hospitals with babies with bleeding gums.

Now, no one would ever dream of saying this officially and certainly not publicly, but we wrote them off as hoaxers. The caller, we suspected, got cold feet and the mothers gave their infants slivers of glass to chew – either for the insurance or to have a bit of a fuss made over them, some excitement, fifteen minutes of fame in their bleak lives. We never charged them with wasting our time. Not out of compassion. We just couldn't prove anything.

The first Thursday in May was the local elections. I didn't vote, not after my experience of both sides in that corruption inquiry. Em did. She floats between Labour and Liberals, never Tory. Not many people were Tory that day, not even coppers.

The natural party of law and order wasn't the only thing to

suffer meltdown that Thursday as the saboteurs struck much nearer home – Knight's in-laws.

In his university days, he'd married young and well, his bride's family big landowners on Trentside.

With a whizzkid degree, he gained fast-track promotion in his first force, then a posting to Ulster. When the four shires of the East Midlands merged into the Combined Constabulary, he came back to the mainland as an assistant chief constable, aged thirty-eight, among the youngest in the service.

They bought a rambling old house on the east side of the river, close to HQ – 'like being above the shop,' he once said – on the opposite bank to her family's estate.

His father-in-law died three or four years ago. According to the canteen grapevine, he left property on the west side of the river to his younger daughter and the cash equivalent to Mrs Knight.

The sister and her husband introduced modern methods to the old estate. They got out of livestock, apart from a herd of pedigree cattle, and built up the long-established meat storage side of the business, using their married name: Thorne Meat Depots. They formed a consortium to turn three hundred acres no longer needed for grazing into a country club with two golf courses.

That Thursday, a beautiful day with temperatures in the unseasonably high seventies, Knight got a panic call from his brother-in-law. 'Just had a chap on. "Animal Salvation," he said. "Your prize bull's dead. Anthrax. Fifty thousand pounds to our fighting fund or the whole herd goes the same way." '

There was to be no waiting for follow-up instructions this time. 'Put it personally in a plastic container you'll find in the grass on the river bank to the left of your depot's jetty. You've got thirty minutes.'

As the helicopter flies, it's about half a mile from HQ to Thorne's place. Ours was having an airworthiness test.

It was fifteen miles and as many minutes on bad roads. By the time Hazel and I arrived, Thorne had diverted his manager by mobile phone to their bank to withdraw the money. They'd only let him have ten thou at such short notice.

Thorne was for handing it all over. 'The bull's dead. Foaming at the mouth.' He was close to it himself, gibbering that anthrax would make his land a no-go area for generations, like some Scottish island where they'd conducted germ warfare experiments in the forties.

Much fast talking persuaded him to put only a couple of grand into the box with a note, the usual stall, saying: 'All I can raise immediately. Give me more time. Please phone with further directions for the balance.'

We couldn't talk him into letting me make the drop. Dripping sweat, he insisted on doing it himself. I was still setting up observation posts, binoculars on the drop, when – God, will I ever forget this – the box just took off. Out of the long grass it flew, through the reeds, cutting a silver trough across the river.

From beyond a high hedge of hawthorn, dotted with white bloom, on the opposite bank came the roar of a vehicle setting off down a dirt road leading to the A46 Fosse road only a mile or two from the headquarters I'd just left. Trailed on a link chain behind was the money box.

A clean getaway, bloody brilliant.

That balmy evening we set up an observation post on a weir, white water noisily cascading down angled steps that did remind me of Harry Lime. We watched over his herd.

The sun set prematurely and disappointingly behind the only cloud that gathered all day, leaving no afterglow. Within an hour it was as dark as a sewer.

The clap – no, wrong word – the crump came from the north. The black sky glowed red, like a belated sunset. The black river seemed to go against the natural flow.

Thorne's cold store had gone up, thawing thousands of tons of frozen meat. In the smoke from the fire, thicker than a November pea-souper, melted blood flowed down gutters and through slatted drain covers. My reputation, my adult life's work, seemed to be following it into the gutter and down the drain.

Sweating, I was; much more than Thorne in his initial panic. Not from the half-mile run to the scene or from the heat of the fire; much, much hotter than at the height of that hot day.

Twice now they'd outwitted me, struck while I was watching the wrong target. Flatfoot left flat-footed. I could see the headline above my picture.

'Ten times the size of the boat bomb,' the army sergeant briefed us, 'with fuel added. Very professional.'

Next morning, a stolen car was found in a riverside council car-park. Its tyres matched the tread on the dirt track behind the flowering hawthorn.

We discovered that fertiliser had been stolen from the green staff's stores at Thorne's country club. And the bull? Not anthrax, the vet reported. Strychnine mixed with molasses.

Knight's grim face went greyer still when I briefed him. The chief constable wisely barred him from giving interviews because of his family connection and deputed me to handle media queries. In response to phoned questions about the fire, non-committal stuff was trotted out. 'Open mind as to the cause. Arson not being ruled out. Neither is an electrical fault.'

I waited for the sky to fall in, the full media fall-out – a police chief's family bombed, the ransom snatched from under my nose for a second time, the makings of a scandal as big as the wholesale jail farces that brought in the New Year and almost brought down the Home Secretary.

I lost sleep over it, wondering what a fool the media would make of me.

Yet nothing leaked. Not a self-congratulatory word or a single crowing peep came out of Animal Salvation.

It was a huge relief, admittedly, not to have your incompetence exposed. But it's there, always, at the back of my mind. One day, I fear, it will all come out. And sometimes I still lose sleep over it.

With no baying MPs and leader writers or copycat hoaxes to distract us, we got down to the real business of police work – the routine.

Hazel homed in on a former employee of the cattle boat company – an ex-clerk called Richard Stone, aged twenty-four.

He'd been born with a physical deformity which left his back twisted. He'd worked for Lincsline, his first job, for a year or so but had been fired.

His sister had threatened action claiming the firm breached all sorts of laws, including disabled employment acts. She was twenty-one, a drop-out from university where she'd studied chemistry. Her name – Zoe Stone – was in Records for a conviction for obstructing a policeman during a riotous blockade of cattle transporters at a ferry port on the south coast.

They lived on a houseboat. An older man was a frequent caller in a green truck. I argued for a warrant for both barge and truck, seeking traces of fertiliser.

Silent Knight held fire, ruling that links between the Stones and

Thorne's business had to be established first. I'd left him still silently pondering tactics and sailed away on this holiday.

That's the story so far. My story anyway. Less than half of it now, I expect.

Eyes lightly shut, thinking it through, I've come to accept that my seasickness has nothing to do with breakfast or Em's bacon butty. It's indigestion of a different sort that comes with biting off more than you can chew.

3

D-Day minus one

In the police service, possession of the executive chair is nine-tenths of promotion, so it's no surprise to find Chief Superintendent Dale sitting at Silent Knight's desk.

In the canteen, they call him the Professor and apparently have done so throughout his service of a quarter of a century. He delights in it, attributing it to high marks on his training course. To live up to it, he's allowed his silver hair to grow long at the back and curl over the collar of fancy, rumpled suits. Today's is Prince of Wales check.

It's a nickname that's always mystified me because he has none of the wit, warmth or wisdom of anyone who taught me at college. Once I queried it with an old constable who joined at the same time. 'Yeer,' he sneered. 'He was the only cadet with the technical know-how to change a light bulb in our billet and it just stuck.' Thus are legends created in the police service.

Dale looks up from his VIP duty rosters, but doesn't thank me for cutting short my holiday, just grumbles about his workload, which included a stint on Saturday, standing in for Knight at some presentation.

He talks a good game without the track record to prove it, making an empire out of a doddle of a job. Security strategy is worked out by a sergeant. Dale gives the briefings, presenting the plans as all his own work. Everyone knows it. So, too, must have

Knight. The fact that he's never been shunted sideways has less to do with ability, I suspect, than membership of the same lodge.

First the formalities. 'Shocking news,' 'Very sad,' and so on. Then he pointedly asks if I've spoken to the chief. I plan to see him later, but don't want Dale in on it, so I tell him, 'Only on the phone.'

'Then you'll know you've got the sabotage,' he says, rather pleasurably.

I request to be brought up to date, but he says Sergeant Webster has the file downstairs.

I inquire about Knight's family. Bearing up, he informs me. A downward glance tells me he's not been round to pay his respects. He leans slightly sideways, dropping his right shoulder, reaching for something on the maroon carpet. A fist reappears, clenching the string handles of a brown carrier bag with the initials EMCC of the East Midlands Combined Constabulary.

'When you go, drop these off.' He lowers the bag on to an under-used desk. I finger it open, peer inside at clothing.

When you go, not if, I note. He's giving me an order, pulling rank. He's also putting as much distance as possible between the sabotage job and himself.

I lift the bag and turn back to the door, pirouetting to close it. Dale has both elbows on the padded arm rests and is screwing himself deeper into the cushion. Behind him is a picture window view of parkland, trees hardly stirring on a windless day, the clouds beginning to break up, but the sky still more grey than blue.

Don't make yourself too much at home, Prof, I think moodily. It won't be your seat for long.

Hazel Webster gives me a white dazzling smile and a little wave across the branch office downstairs from the executive floor.

I flick my head towards the door to my office, windowless if you discount the glass door, a cubby-hole really. She follows me in, carrying a thick yellow file clutched to the double breast of her pale linen suit. She sits across a desk half the size of the berth Dale has commandeered. When we've both put our loads on it, there's not much spare space.

Formalities first again. 'Shocking news.' 'Yes. Sorry to hear it.' 'How's Em?' 'Fit and fat.' 'Happy hols?' 'Terrific.' 'You've drawn the short straw?' 'Yes.'

Hazel loves to natter and has a lovely way of telling a yarn in a classy southern accent. A great old mate of mine, now retired, reckons her wide mouth, highly kissable, comes from talking so much.

I met her through him four years ago, just after falling for Em. A month or two earlier and I think I'd have offered to run away with her.

Knight's death will have been a blow to her, a far more personal loss than mine. Four years ago, my mate and Hazel teamed up to track down a bomber hired to blow up an over-inquisitive camera-man poking his nose into the affairs of a corrupt industrialist. They got held hostage in a lorry at a gravel pit. Knight saved them by dumping a load of sand on their heavily armed kidnapper. It was one of his coups the press were talking about yesterday – perhaps his best in his twelve years on the EMCC.

A narrow squeak like that forges unbreakable bonds and Hazel has become sort of extended family to my mate and his wife.

She often pops round to see them. Me, too. He was with me when I got my limp, stayed in close touch throughout my long convalescence. So I knew her socially long before Knight recruited her to Special Branch and promoted her to sergeant.

He rated her professionally; with good reason. She's an efficient, experienced operator, with real enthusiasm for the job; careful, thoughtful, loyal. Not once has she ever expressed the slightest reservation about working for Knight – or the secretive way he operated – and I've kept my dark thoughts about him secret from her.

I think – no, I'm sure – Knight didn't fancy her; not that way. He didn't play around any more than I do. Anyway, she has a long-standing love for a married super.

With both of us spoken for, we have settled into a relaxed relationship – no, more, a real friendship – so it's safe to say, 'OK, then. Debriefing time.'

You'd have barely driven on to the car ferry to start your hols across the Irish Sea, Hazel begins, when the balloon back here at base went up again.

Yet another call to Lincsline, the cattle boat company, with its main base on the Trent downriver towards the Humber and the

North Sea: 'Animal Salvation here. Fifty thousand pounds immediately or another boat goes down,' said the caller, a woman this time.

The cash was to be credited to an account with a High Street bank with a number the female caller gave. 'You should know from experience that we mean what we say,' she added menacingly.

Knight sanctioned two thousand out of police funds and turned Hazel out to the bank where the account had been opened. It was in that lovely town of Southwell close to the busy corner with the yellow sand box where the fake pay-out had been spirited away via the sewer.

The day before, she learned, a young man with a humped back deposited a thousand pounds across the counter. He claimed to be with a company which organised nationwide door-to-door deliveries of goods made by the handicapped. He sought no overdraft facilities, promised the account would be receiving a substantial top-up within forty-eight hours. He requested cash cards in the names of four travelling executives.

Hazel asked for a playback of the interior security video. 'A side-on view of him only, but you could see the bump on his back.'

'Richard Stone?' I ask, thinking of the clerk Lincsline sacked.

She nods very positively. 'No doubt about it.'

Inwardly I am purring like a cat about to lap up spilt cream. This job's going to be as big a doddle as Dale's rosters.

Knight, Hazel continues, finally took out search warrants on their houseboat, called the *Yorkshire Tyke* and moored at nearby Newark. Brother and sister had packed and gone, the place wiped clean. The green truck had not been seen for a couple of days.

Over the next twenty-four hours, there were maximum hundred-pound withdrawals from bank cash points at branches in towns just off the A1, M1, A43 and A34 as the trail headed south. 'A green truck was seen outside some banks,' she adds.

To stem the cash flow, Knight ordered the closure of the account. Lincsline got another phone call, same voice, very angry. 'There'll be reprisals,' she threatened. 'D-Day plus one. Remember that.'

'What did Silent make of that?' I ask.

'That there was about to be or perhaps already was a bomb planted in a Lincsline boat. All were searched. Nothing. Every mooring's been under observation since.'

'And?'

'Nothing.'

I nod her on.

'Same day,' Hazel continues, 'a card is fed into the machine outside the bank in Southwell where the account was opened. It flashed up the old "No can do" message and alerted bank staff. By the time they got outside, there was no one at the cash dispenser.'

She asked to view the video from the camera we'd installed at the junction to aid surveillance on the grit box and which the council had taken over to monitor traffic on busy race days at the track on the outskirts of town.

A youth in overalls and pumps had been captured on film walking towards a parked pick-up truck. His face wasn't visible. The truck's index plate was.

Driving it that day had been Alan Hicks, twenty-four, an assistant greenkeeper at the country club on Thorne's estate.

The suspected source of the explosives on the cold storage bombing last month, I remind myself, still purring privately.

Hicks was arrested, in overalls and pumps, gang-mowing one of the fairways.

Hazel and an inspector, a good interrogator, interviewed him. He claimed he'd watched a woman tap the number into the cash point's keyboard, then followed her to a pub and snatched her bag. His description vaguely matched Zoe Stone's; the old story. A cornered suspect will trot out the first description that comes into his head. There'd been no report on any snatched handbag in any pub. He flatly denied he knew the trio from the houseboat *Tyke* or that he'd set up the raid on the fertiliser store.

I smile cynically and dismissively. 'Have you charged him?'

'With theft of the card only.'

'Where's he on remand?'

'Knight bailed him.'

'What?' I can hardly believe it. 'What was he playing at?'

Eventually, Hazel goes on, Hicks demanded his right to a lawyer on legal aid and what little he had been saying dried up completely. He was kept in the cellblock overnight. Next morning Knight went to see him.

'Personally?' I query. Knight seldom strayed far from his desk, pulling strings, not letting the right-hand man know what the left-hand woman was doing.

Hazel nods briskly. 'And alone. Unusually, for him, he was beaming when he came back.'

He'd got the Stones' involvement confirmed and the name of the third man – Rex Lynch, thirty-eight, an ex-fireman with the Ministry of Defence who'd been fired – and served six months – for theft of government property.

A fireman, I'm thinking. And how was one of the men who moved the grit box over the sewer dressed – someone we'd not traced on inquiries round all brigades, public and private?

What's more, the green truck seen at the Stones' houseboat in Newark was identified as belonging to Lynch. Added to which he had attended courses on how to tackle bombs and the use of sewers to flush away toxic spillages in his fire-fighting days.

Meantime, Hazel had checked up on Zoe Stone with former fellow students. So anti-meat-eating was she that they'd dubbed her The Vegelante.

Superb, I'm thinking, the complete circle, neatly rounded off while I've been swanning around Ireland. All I'll have to do is make the pinches and earn promotion points. 'Did Silent strike some deal with Hicks?'

'Not half,' Hazel replies, rather disapprovingly.

According to what Knight told her, Hicks admitted off the record that he knew Richard Stone from college days where he'd studied greenkeeping and Stone took electronics. They still used the same pub. He'd confessed to telling Stone where to find the key to the fertiliser shed. And, yes, Richard Stone had given him a bank card and PIN number. 'Help yourself to a hundred for the info,' he was told. But Hicks categorically denied taking part in any bombings or phone call threats.

Knight told Hazel that he believed Hicks' story. 'Don't you see,' he reported himself as having said to Hicks, 'they set you up to use that card so we'd think they were still around here. You face the music while they go on holiday. You owe them nothing. Where have they gone?'

' "Well, he had some French francs on him," Hicks answered. He claimed he knew vaguely where they might be.'

Makes sound sense, I concur. All the withdrawals had been made heading for the south coast and Channel ports.

'So,' Hazel continues, 'Knight did a deal with Hicks: "Follow and find out where and when the reprisal is due to take place and we'll not only drop the charge, we'll reward you." ' She looks at me intently, head on one side. 'In fact, he sanctioned an advance.'

While she rummages in her thick file, I find myself privately approving of Knight's tactics. He was trading in the freedom of a minion for the big three before they strike again, putting lives at risk. Nothing wrong with that. Happens all the time.

Hazel has found what she is looking for and slips a receipt out of the informant's cash log. 'Operation: 6IW. Code name: K2. Sum: Three hundred pounds.' It was dated ten days ago. The initials and numbers against the first two entries mean nothing to me – or to Hazel.

'So,' I sum up, 'the three targets are in France with Hicks in hot pursuit.'

'He could have been there and got back by now.'

'Terrific,' I beam. This, it's obvious, is the imminent break-through the chief talked about on the phone yesterday. 'Whereabouts in France was he heading?'

Her little shrug sends a sudden burst of anxiety coursing through me. True to form Knight had not told her. 'When, how's Hicks going to get in touch?' I ask.

Another shrug. 'There's nothing in Knight's notebook, files or anything, that gives any clue.'

'You mean . . .' The cream has gone off and I am feeling sour. '. . . Silent was carrying it all in his head and now, with the gang running loose, he's . . .' I don't want to say it, even think it. Hazel nods solemnly.

'Maybe there's something in there,' she says, optimistically nodding at the brown paper bag on the desk.

Carefully, I begin to unpack what Dale gave me, holding each article up for examination.

Knight had dressed very off duty for his bird-watching at Red Gutter on a wet Saturday. Stout brown shoes, grey woollen socks, underpants, grey flannels and colourfully striped shirt, sports style, and green golfing jacket.

'I didn't even know he was into ornithology,' I remark absently, inspecting the shirt.

'Neither did I,' says Hazel.

I feel in the breast pocket noting a small brown stain, like an ironing scorch, just below it. The friction burn that occurred in his fall, I surmise.

There's nothing in the pocket, or in the trousers. I tip the bag. Out drops a cellophane packet. Inside are twenty pounds in notes, some small change and a plain postcard, slightly bent as though it's been carried in his back trouser pocket.

The stamp is red and French. The postmark says: 'Cherbourg – Mai 29' – a week ago today. It's addressed to: 'Andy Day, c/o The Fairways Hotel' – the police headquarters' local, right next door.

In block capitals it gives the road as The Fosseway, the nearest main town as Newark, Notts, then UK. Under that is written 'Zip Code'; and the usual two blocks of three letters and numbers.

'Odd that,' says Hazel, pointing to the words 'Zip Code'.

Odd, indeed. Almost every letter I get these days has the post-code on the envelope. None of my correspondents has ever written 'Postcode' in front of it, let alone used the American expression 'Zip Code'; – with a semi-colon after it, I now note. I'm no great shakes on punctuation, but, surely, it should be a colon, if anything at all?

The only explanation I can think of – and it's so thin I don't offer it – is that maybe the sender was being over-helpful to the French postal sorters.

The message on the reverse side is in cramped handwriting and the usual cryptic phraseology that overcomes holidaymakers:

K2. Monday

Dear Andy,

I've arrived safely. Very good trip. Wonderful weather. Terrific grub. Francs running low. Great coastline. Good digs. View superb. I'm in with a good crowd. Have been to D-Day beaches. Zoo soon. Get yourself over here. My lemon tea is getting cold. Let's talk Friday. Love to mum.

My best.

Hicksey

I slip the card back in the plastic cover and push it across the desk to Hazel who reads it several times with a blank face.

She offers to run it round to Forensics to check the fingerprints and handwriting against Hicks' custody records. 'What do you make of it?' she asks.

My answer is to pick up the phone, dial the Fairways Hotel and ask for the manager. He knows all about the card, he helpfully confirms.

Knight popped round on a rare visit. He hoped the manager wouldn't mind but he wanted to use the hotel as an accommodation address for a letter he was expecting, addressed to Andy Day. 'A communication I don't want to go through the mail room or to my home.' He tapped the side of his nose, making it seem as though he was lining up something on the side.

Knight asked for and made a note of the postcode. 'He phoned most mornings to see if there was anything for him,' the manager continues. 'On Thursday, I got a message to him via your switchboard to tell him to ring because it had arrived. He walked round and collected it.'

I put down the phone and get round to partially answering Hazel. Changing the name from Knight to Day and using the accommodation address I can understand. He wouldn't want Hicks writing to ACC Knight at police HQ with a trained MoD firefighter turned blackmailer at his shoulder.

His mole had penetrated the cell of saboteurs, I speculate. The reference to D-Day hinted that he had the gen on the reprisal raid and he wanted the balance of his bounty. He was fixing a rendezvous for Friday presumably at some zoo in Normandy. Either that or Zoo meant he was with Zoe Stone.

Hazel is shaking her head determinedly. 'Knight sat on his backside in his office all Friday.'

'Sure?'

'Absolutely.'

'No odd phone calls?' I am madly scratching around for something, anything. 'Did he ask the French police to keep the meet for him?'

'Not while I was around. The only call I heard him make was to Chief Super Dale to tell him something had turned up on Saturday and he'd have to stand in for him at some presentation of long service awards to Special Constables.'

'In that case, I'm buggered if I know what's going on,' I finally reply; a complete and honest answer.

'Maybe Mrs Knight will,' suggests Hazel, ever the optimist.

I ring the chief's office. His secretary, as helpful as a doctor's receptionist, can't fit me in until five. 'May as well start somewhere,' I tell Hazel.

4

The first roses of summer, deep red and plentiful to the left, white, bigger, more fragrant to the right, stand tall on each side of a flag-stoned path to a black front door; a lovely, early show. Clumps of daffodils planted beneath them have untidily died back; not so lovely.

Further to the right, Knight's car, a black Audi, is parked on a pea pebble drive in front of closed double garage doors. An older black Rover is blocking it in.

Behind a battered white Fiesta on a steep, narrow lane, where the weekend's rainwater has gathered in pot-holes, Hazel has parked her dirty, dark blue Peugeot.

I'm so bushed from last night's long drive, bleary-eyed and stiff, that she is taking the wheel on this short trip. To get in, I had to toss a map out of the passenger seat into the back on top of a pile of newspapers. The sweet wrappers were left were they were – in the foot well. Our car was cleaner after ten days on tour.

The lane, Hazel had told me on the way here, leads up to Red Gutter where Knight was found less than forty-eight hours ago. I declined her invitation to carry on up the lane for a look-see. 'Later,' I suggested, but privately I saw no point. I'll get all I need when I study the file.

An attractive, fair-haired woman, late twenties, in denims, opens the black front door before Hazel can ring the bell. Her pale, exhausted face summons up the briefest of smiles.

'I'm Anita Montgomery.' Knight's daughter, I'm already aware. 'You must be Sergeant Webster.' Her voice trails as her blue eyes, more tired than mine feel, switch from Hazel to me.

To disguise that she has forgotten my name, which Hazel gave her on the phone, she turns and says over her shoulder, 'Thank you for coming.'

On the way through a dim, cool hallway, into a low, modern kitchen, she apologises. 'Mother is still engaged with the funeral director, but she won't be long.'

She leads us outside again into a spacious garden; a surprise because the morning is sunless, not warm for June.

A man in his mid-thirties, in dark slacks and thickish grey sweater, is sitting in a red canvas chair, the sort film directors use. He is reading the *Daily Telegraph* at a pine table on a patio, edged with bedding plants, too immature to be very colourful yet.

'Rod,' she calls from the kitchen door.

Engrossed, he doesn't hear her.

'Rod,' she calls, firmer, in an accent that's been finished at an expensive school. Now he looks up. 'Two colleagues of daddy's.' Another short smile as she turns back inside, repeating, 'Won't be long.'

The man, dark, quite short, puts the newspaper on the table next to the separate Monday sports section and stands as we approach. 'Rodney Montgomery,' he says, holding out his hand in turn, Hazel first, as we introduce ourselves. His grip is firm, but without thumb-to-knuckle pressure. He has not followed his father-in-law into the Brotherhood.

He motions to cane chairs, politely drawing one back from the table for Hazel.

'Thank you,' she says, unused to such courtesy at HQ. He doesn't sit until we are both settled. The brown bag is leaning upright against my light grey trousers.

Condolences are expressed and acknowledged. He tells us that Mrs Knight's sister Stella is also inside the house. 'Everyone is rallying.'

'You taking a few days off?' asks Hazel.

'Only today and, of course, for the funeral . . .' He sighs. '. . . whenever that is.' Rodney looks a touch unhappy at being excluded from the family conference currently in progress, left out here in the cold. 'We're up to our eyes right now.'

'Business good, then?' asks Hazel, seizing gratefully on a change of topic.

'Reasonable.' His open face is suddenly closed. Odd that, I think. In his position I'd be delighted to be discussing something other than the sudden death of father-in-law, which must have been the sole topic of conversation in this household over a long, painful weekend.

'What line are you in?' asks Hazel engagingly.

'An airline, actually,' he replies guardedly.

To more prompting, he tells her rather reluctantly that he and a couple of chums run Ark Air (or maybe it's Arc Air. I don't ask for a spelling.).

'Just a small outfit,' he adds. All three had left the RAF at the end of twelve-year commissions and had bought a cargo plane. I amuse myself wondering if it might be an old Hercules transporter, taken out of the service with them, like a pensioned-off police dog handler taking his Alsatian into retirement. 'Short hauls mainly.'

While they chatter, Rodney in a clipped, officers' mess accent, I glance down at the table to see what was preoccupying him when we walked in. More than half the front page is filled with the Bosnia crisis over United Nations hostages – something neither Em nor I knew anything about, so out of touch have we been, until we tuned in to the news on the way home and back to the real world last night.

I look up again to catch Hazel asking, 'You're not, perchance . . .' She gives him her most mischievous look. '. . . blockade-busting, airlifting animals, are you?'

Oh, my God, I groan inwardly. My old mate is right about her. She does talk too much.

For some months major companies running ferries over the North Sea and the Channel to the Continent have been refusing to transport livestock. The ban followed horror stories of cattle, pigs and sheep being crammed into lorries for hours without food or water, some dying on the journey.

The companies claim the sight upsets their human cargo, but I suspect it has less to do with animal welfare than with fear of sabotage, heightened, no doubt, by the bombing at Lincsline.

Sensing a financial killing, a few air firms had plugged the gap. One cargo plane crashed, killing its five crew, on a fog-affected flight. One demonstrator was crushed to death under the wheels of a cattle truck outside the same airport.

Exports dribbled to a halt amid a welter of writs and started up again when the High Court came out on the side of the rule of law against the rule of the mobs. The demos started up again, too, fanned by anarchists, who latch on to any campaign, like ticks to sheep. The last thing we want here and now is a debate on the pros and cons of the veal trade and the rule of law.

Rodney goes into his shell to such an extent that he slides down in his chair.

I butt in, a bit annoyed. 'It's, well, very sensitive.'

'Oh, come,' Hazel chides me. 'No one blames the farmers. It's their livelihood.'

She launches into a quick tour of places in the South of France and Italy she's been where fresh meat, especially white veal, is part of the culture. 'If we don't supply their needs, other countries will and bang goes the balance of trade.'

Visibly encouraged by her moral support, Rodney opens up. 'Well, yes, as a matter of fact.' He hurries on. 'Not our main business, of course.' That includes contracts for freight like flat-pack furniture, components and so on, but, yes, they were taking part in the airlift.

'Anywhere exotic?' asks Hazel.

I deduce now that she has picked up the tip, perhaps from Knight himself, that Ark Air is in on the veal trade and she's cleverly grabbed this opportunity to check it. I'm going to leave it to her, just sit here, trying not to pull a face, wondering if the animals board Ark Air two by two. It seems an inappropriate name.

He is pulling a face too. 'Rotterdam and Normandy. Every day. My partners are over there now.' He looks up into the clouds as if expecting to see them.

I know I am frowning, can't help it, and Hazel's face has become solemn as she speaks. 'You didn't happen, at Mr Knight's request, to give a lift to a young man called Alan Hicks, did you?'

'No.' Rodney looks puzzled. 'Why?'

'It's just that Hicks is involved in a special operation that Mr Knight was running with a French end,' Hazel explains.

'Is he a police officer?' Hazel looks away, not replying. It's a question Rodney, presumably experienced in the secretive style of his father-in-law and being ex-armed service himself, realises he shouldn't have asked. 'No.' He shrugs. 'No. I mean, if there's a seat free, friends and relations, yes, but no one by that name.'

He's silent for an awkward moment. 'Andy . . .' At least, he was on first-name terms with Knight, more than me. '. . . never asked for a lift for himself or anyone.'

He smiles fondly to himself. 'He rather took the rise out of us.' 'Rise' is a quaint, old-fashioned word for someone so young, but then he's a quaint, old-fashioned young man.

'Brylcreem boys, he regarded us as. The army runs in his family, I'm afraid.'

I didn't know that, and say so.

'Oh, yes,' he confirms. 'His father was in intelligence in the war. Andy had some youthful ailment that precluded him.'

Safely back on family affairs, he tells us he and his wife Anita rent what he calls 'a biggish little cottage' not far away and have two small daughters he doesn't see enough of.

Suddenly, he pulls himself up and out of his chair, smiling cautiously beyond us.

I crick my neck round. Emerging out of the kitchen door is a heavy-set woman, mid-forties, brown raincoat unbuttoned over a mustard-coloured dress, dark hair in a severe fringe, and a facial expression to match.

Mrs Knight, I assume, and I stand. Hazel, who has met her briefly a couple of times, makes no move.

'Miles not here yet?' she asks querulously.

Standing, Rodney Montgomery replies with the obvious 'No', then introduces us to Mrs Thorne. Stella, I tell myself; sister of Mrs Knight, wife of Brian Thorne.

I'd had long sessions with her husband before and after his cold store melted in the explosion that followed our short-changing of the extortionists, but had never met her.

Close up, her belted cotton dress accentuates broad hips and high bosom, a fruity figure. Its colour is a bit bright for such a sombre duty call.

After nodded acknowledgements, she tells us that Mrs Knight is deciding on the finishing touches for the funeral service and tells Rodney it has been fixed for Wednesday at noon.

She looks back to me in vague recognition. 'You the superintendent dealing with our bomb business?'

I nod again.

Rodney sits. She doesn't. 'What a mess,' she sighs. 'We're still picking up the pieces.'

'Insurance going OK?' Hazel asks.

'Slowly.' Mrs Thorne hesitates. 'Any developments?' Neither of us answers. 'It's just that Andy mentioned a week or so ago that there's been a bit of a breakthrough.'

33

'There are a couple of hopeful leads,' I finally confirm.

She glances impatiently at a gold watch on her wrist. 'Where the devil is he?' Miles, whoever he is, she means, I assume. Rodney doesn't know, so she has to explain. 'He went off to Combined Counties first thing. Looking at their chill-down equipment.'

While I take in the wide, sloping garden, tree-lined, lovingly tended, they chat briefly about what Stella calls the gite near a place that sounds like 'The doll', the American friends who hold the key and some problem with a car. Only half listening, I gather the Montgomerys will be on holiday at the Doll's House soon and the trouble with the car has left Stella without transport of her own and unhappily dependent on lifts.

She looks down at the paper on the table – oddly, for a woman, at the sports section, not the news pages. 'What with everything, we're missing all of that.' She nods down at coloured photos and reports from the rugby World Cup. 'What's happening?'

Rod reports on England's thus far unbeaten progress and, though I'm no rugger man, I can tell her that Ireland pipped Wales, explaining that I have sort of adopted them since it was the sole topic of sporting conversations in the bars on my holiday.

'Unites them in a way politics and religion never will,' says Rod gravely.

We break off when Anita calls from the kitchen door, 'Ready when you are.'

The unoccupied front room where she leads and leaves us has a view through leaded windows of the red and white beds of roses.

Anita invited us to make ourselves at home because 'Mother has slipped upstairs', but I stroll on to the window.

A man in dark clothing, the undertaker, I guess, is backing the Rover out of the drive. By process of elimination, that means the battered Fiesta is Rodney Montgomery's.

The space the Rover vacated is almost immediately filled by a sporty, white car which scrunches on the gravel to a noisy stop just short of Knight's car.

There are footsteps in the hall. I turn, but no one enters, look out again.

Mrs Thorne flits by the window. A fair young man, mid-twenties, casually dressed, leans across from the driver's seat to open

34

the passenger door. He smiles, mouths something, and gets no audible acknowledgement as Mrs Thorne rather inelegantly climbs in.

I turn back into the room, which is small, intimate and book-lined with thick sage green carpeting and a patterned, mainly lime green, winged three-piece. Hazel has sat on the couch. I drop the brown bag at her side. Not sure which was Knight's favourite chair, I determine not to do domestically what Dale's done back at HQ and stay standing.

One small table, dark, antique-looking, has been taken from its nest in the corner and stands before a black empty fireplace. On it is an olive green book with 'The Works of Shakespeare' in gold letters above a scroll of gold and green flowers. There's a maroon Waterstone's bookmark poking out of the top.

The door opens.

Hazel stands.

Enter Mrs Knight.

'Sorry to have kept you waiting.' Mrs Knight is altogether quieter than her younger sister and that's not just her manner of speaking.

She is daintier, has allowed her hair to grey naturally. She wears a purpley paisley frock and carries a square maroon attaché case I recognise as her husband's in her left hand.

In turn, we shuffle forward to take her right hand. Her touch is soft and icy cold. Her smile is tired and forced, especially for Hazel, who does most of the respect-paying.

Mrs Knight how-kinds and thanks us automatically, tells us about the funeral arrangements as she lowers the case next to the brown bag on the couch. She gestures us to take the places on the couch either side of them and sits in a chair with its back to the window.

She nods at the attaché case. 'That, I presume, has to be returned. His red box, he called it.' Which, I assume, means work he brought home like government ministers do.

I elbow the brown bag. 'His things. There's only one item we have had to retain.'

From the inside pocket of my grey suit jacket, I slip a photocopy Forensics made of the plain postcard with the red French stamp addressed to 'Andy Day'. 'We found this.'

I hand it to her, explaining, while she reads, that we thought her husband had infiltrated a mole into the bombers' hide-out. 'We can't fully understand it.'

She studies it for some time, a small smile playing on her dry lips.

'Obviously,' I point out, 'the addressee is cod.'

'Perhaps it's all code,' she replies, leaving me thinking that she has misheard me.

I'll not correct her, frown, something troubling me, and manage to mumble, 'In which case, we're not sure that we've absolutely cracked it.'

Her chin drops over the card again. Her pale blue eyes glisten. Soon tears will fall, I fear.

A tense moment, this. Here is a widow who was a contented wife this time two days ago. The grief, the shock at such a sudden loss will have caused deepmost, indescribable pain. We're intruding into that grief, no doubt about it. There's no certain way of knowing what her reaction will be. She may want to nurse her agony within the bosom of her family, clamming up to outsiders. Or she may want to talk – therapeutically opening up.

If she clams, we'll leave, wait till after the funeral. A forty-eight-hour delay when I'm desperate to push on, get a quick result. It's the compassionate thing to do, I tell myself. I'm not sure I altogether believe myself. Talk, lady, talk, I privately plead.

Her eyes glisten into a fond smile. 'He often used codes handling informants in Ulster. Learned at his father's knee.'

'I gather that his father was in wartime intelligence.'

'MI9,' she says crisply.

I know of MIs 5 and 6, of course, but this is new to me and I say so.

'Escapes and evasions,' she explains knowledgeably. 'Disbanded after the war.'

Alarm bells ring in the distance from an undetectable direction. 'He didn't, by any chance, pass on the codes to you or his daughter . . .' This, I realise belatedly, is close to alleging leaking official secrets, so I add, '. . . you know, old, discarded codes, as a childhood game.' I nod at the copy. 'In case there's a hidden message in there.'

She shakes her head. 'Someone somewhere will still have them, I suppose.' She hands the copy back and says very positively, 'He didn't show me that.'

I go on. 'Did he mention Hicksey or an Alan Hicks?' She gives me a steely look which I have to hold. Sometimes, I've learned over the years, you have to give something of yourself in interviews to get something back. Now is such a time. I shrug guiltily. 'I bounce things off my wife, just thinking aloud, really. I know we shouldn't, but it can help.'

'Sometimes,' she concedes reluctantly.

Her husband's last case had caused him stress he could have done without in his state of health, she begins. He'd suffered pains across his chest – 'like bands of steel' – for weeks before he mentioned them to her.

She'd insisted he consulted the family doctor. Hospital tests were ordered. Angina was confirmed. A bypass would eventually become necessary. Meantime, he was to take it easy. He told the chief constable. The family knew. No one else.

He was never one for much physical exercise, but retained membership of an old-established golf course in the parklands that surround HQ, kept playing, only nine holes, no competitions.

'Never transferred to the in-laws' new country club then?' I ask.

She shakes her head. 'He declined. He was careful about accepting favours.'

I decide against asking her if he was still active in the Masons. Instead, I smile. 'Would that all MPs were the same.'

She laughs, just a tiny laugh, for the first time. 'He paid a green fee at Trentside once. "Bad greens and boring," he said.' She smiles rather slyly. 'You won't tell Miles that.'

I reveal that his name cropped up in the garden, but I'm unsure who he is. 'My sister's son.'

It was his idea, she said, to turn the bequeathed land that her father's cattle had grazed over to golf. Miles' degree was in business studies, not agriculture. His father's background was in butchering, not farming.

Gently Hazel moves her from family to police business.

Knight had been concerned about the first bombing of the boat in the Wash, Mrs Knight continues. Experience told him it could be the start of a campaign. His worries were compounded by the publicity Animal Salvation subsequently achieved.

The extortion demand on his brother-in-law Brian Thorne followed by the explosion compelled him to 'declare an interest' to the chief constable who suggested he take a back seat on the inquiry.

She looks at me again, steadily. 'He said he'd left it to you –' She smiles. ' "In good hands," he said.' I try not to pink. '– to avoid any clash between professional and personal interests, but, naturally, he monitored matters.'

'Did he . . .' I shrug. '. . . share any views, thoughts about the case?'

She looks down, in thought. 'He wondered out loud if there was any connection, wondered if it might be a copycat crime, the meat depot, I mean.' She looks up at me. 'Same sort of explosive, of course, but no claim of responsibility, no publicity-seeking.'

He'd briefed his wife better than me, I realise, alarm bells closer, louder. This is a theory he'd never shared with me. Nor Hazel, judging by her startled expression. When I'd pointed out to Knight that poisoning a bull was hardly good PR for animal lovers, he'd replied rather dismissively that half the many terrorists he'd come across just used a cause, any cause, to enrich themselves.

This is new, intriguing, sensational, and I must pursue it, but before I can slip in a question, Anita annoyingly knocks on the door and puts her head round it. 'Coffee?'

'Please.' Her mother answers for all of us.

Mercifully, Anita retreats.

Knight, his widow goes on immediately, worked long hours and spent a sleepless night when Animal Salvation targeted Lincsline again a week and a half ago with demands for a ransom to be paid into the bank.

Next night he came home, rather late for a family party to celebrate her birthday. 'A breakthrough,' he announced, relaxed and happy. 'At long last.' They had the names of all the gang, he told her, and had arrested one.

'That one is Alan Hicks,' Hazel points out.

'Didn't know his name. He never mentioned it. But I did know he worked as a greenkeeper at the country club and that was the source of some of the explosive material.'

The room goes silent apart from the bells that are now clamouring in my head. She's already told us that her husband believed there was something iffy about the middle job, the Thorne depot fire. What did he suspect? Something like an insurance scam? Involving someone in his own family?

So confused am I that my next question stumbles out. 'Did he . . .

here . . . at the party, I mean . . .' I almost say 'question' but change to, '. . . talk to Mr Thorne or his son Miles about their employee who we all now know to be Alan Hicks?'

'Miles wasn't here, busy as usual,' she replies immediately. Then, slower, 'But Andy took Brian to one side, I seem to recall.' She doesn't know what was said.

'Were your daughter and son-in-law present at the party?'

'Anita, naturally. And my grandchildren. Rod was flying.'

I nod her on. 'Next day he said he'd let a pigeon loose – a phrase from his tour in Belfast – and he'd have a message by the following weekend.'

He'd released Hicks to fly into the enemy's loft, he meant.

'He was unruffled all week, apart from Thursday morning before he set off for work. Someone phoned him. He just replaced the phone and said, "The pigeon has landed." '

She laughs, lightly again. 'Sounds silly, I know, but we got used to this sort of talk in Belfast. He wanted to share things with me, but never could; not fully. Wives had to be protected in case they were ever kidnapped and questioned. It became a sport, sort of a game, between us.'

It doesn't sound silly to me. It meant the manager of the Fairways had told Control the postcard had arrived and Control had phoned Knight.

'What happened on Friday?' I ask.

'Nothing much. Why?' she asks, puzzled.

I explain that the postcard from Hicks hints at a Friday rendez-vous at a zoo in Normandy.

She's even more puzzled. 'It was a normal day, quieter than normal.' She comes to Saturday. She'd been due to go with him to present awards at the Special Constables' parade. He told her it was off. 'Instead, he said he was going egg-collecting. He was quite, well, thrilled, like old times.'

Hazel interrupts. 'We never knew he was an ornithologist.'

Mrs Knight shakes her head. 'Bird-watching in Belfast meant surveillance. Egg-collecting meant taking delivery of information.'

Hazel persists. 'Yesterday's papers reported he'd been bird-watching.'

Another shake. 'That's what I told your Control when I asked if they'd seen him and it must have gone out to the press. He said he'd be an hour, back for lunch.'

'Did you know he was going to Red Gutter?'

'No.'

'Did he walk or go by car?'

'Car. A constable returned it yesterday. I know it's not far, but it is a steep climb. He was well overdue. I thought he might have taken his informant into the office.'

I nod back at the copied postcard, still in my hand. 'The clear impression from that message is that the meet with Hicks was at some zoo in Normandy on Friday.'

She shakes her head. 'No, it was Saturday and somewhere round here. Where and with whom I don't know, I'm afraid. He never, ever told me that much.' Pause. 'There must be some misunderstanding; a change of plan perhaps?'

'And then?' I ask, a silly question, too unspecific.

'Well . . .' She collects herself. 'Suddenly the lane outside was full of police cars. I didn't know for sure, because I didn't know exactly where he was, but . . . well . . . He was going to retire, you know. Once this business was out of the way.' Tears begin to well.

Anita comes in carrying a silver tray with cream pots of coffee and milk, a bowl of sugar, four cups and saucers with spoons. Four, I note. Blast. She's joining us.

She shoots her mother an anxious glance. Mrs Knight composes herself. She removes the book from the table and holds it in her lap. 'The Works of Shakespeare', it says on the spine, in gold on green. 'Vol. 4 – *Richard II* and *Richard III*'.

Anita rests the tray in its place.

'I've picked a nice little extract,' her mother tells her while looking at me.

Anita pours, hands out the cups and sits in the vacant chair. She gives me an accusing glance; blame, no doubt, for her mother's tears.

'So,' I resume, dropping all names in front of Anita, 'the assumption has to be that our man is back and the meeting was hereabouts a day later than we thought.'

Mrs Knight sips. 'It would appear so.'

'What's that, mummy?' asks Anita innocently.

'A small loose end on one of your father's cases,' she says flatly, giving nothing away. Abruptly, she changes the subject. 'We've been discussing our Belfast days.'

'Happy days,' sighs Anita pleasurably.

Hazel cocks her head, quizzically.

'Young love,' her mother explains. 'She met her husband when he was a pilot on the Aldergrove run.'

Explains Rod's philosophical little comment in the garden about Irish sport, religion and politics, I think.

To make it absolutely plain she will not return to the topic under discussion, she pats the book. 'Either of you Shakespeare devotees?'

'My wife,' I reply.

'I took *Richard III* for O level,' Hazel volunteers.

'Ah.' Mrs Knight's face lightens a little. 'Hide thee from this slaughterhouse.'

I'm too ashamed to confess that my only knowledge of *Richard III* comes from a late night Laurence Olivier film, refreshed by a half-hour animated version on 'Bard on the Box' I watched with Em. I remember 'Now is the winter of our discontent' and 'My kingdom for a horse' but nothing much in between.

Hazel has also forgotten it, looks mystified, recovers quickly. 'There's something I don't follow.'

Mrs Knight gives her a silencing 'not in front of the children' look which Hazel ignores, continuing, 'The papers said that the Stoke Field . . .' She flicks her head towards the window beyond which the lane leads up to a plain between here and the police headquarters. '. . . was the final battle in the Wars of the Roses.'

'So it was.' Mrs Knight smiles, seemingly relieved.

'Well,' Hazel goes on, 'I don't know whether this comes from my school history or English Lit – I wasn't too hot at either – but I always thought the last battle was at Bosworth where Richard was killed.'

I'm going to duck this debate. The Wars of the Roses to me are Yorkshire versus Lancashire over a holiday cricketing weekend.

'Most people do,' she says. 'But there was an uprising two years later, in 1487, when rebels installed a pretender to the throne in Ireland and invaded England. You know what it was like in medieval times. Royal family at war.'

I feel a quip coming on, but Mrs Knight beats me to it. 'Nothing changes.'

The women smile. I laugh very briefly.

'There was quite a celebration locally for the quincentenary,' Anita says. 'That's when mum planted the roses as our contribution.' She nods towards the window and the red and white flower beds in the front garden. 'Let your flowers speak to you, eh, mum?'

Mrs Knight blushes, rather shyly, touchingly.

'That's what her own mother used to say,' Anita explains with a deeply affectionate expression.

Hazel, who often speaks with devotion of her own mother, smiles fondly at them both.

'Er, anyway . . .' Still a trifle embarrassed, Mrs Knight gets back to the subject. 'Henry saw them off. Not personally. He watched the battle from the safety of a church tower, I believe. He didn't lead from the front.' She looks at me again, rather severely. 'Unlike some.'

It was a tribute to her husband or a dig at me and people like me who doubted his leadership qualities. I'm beginning to think I may have underestimated Knight.

'Why then . . .' Hazel won't shut up.

I pray that she doesn't push this to its conclusion, recalling from the Sunday papers that the battle ended in the massacre at Red Gutter, scene of Knight's death five hundred and some years later. This conversation could still end in a flood of tears.

'. . . isn't this village famous?'

'Perhaps . . .' Mrs Knight pats the book yet again. '. . . because no one famous wrote a play about it.'

'How did it all turn out?' Hazel wants to know.

'The imposter was removed and Henry continued to rule – or, rather, misrule.' Mrs Knight looks at me severely again. 'Beware imposters, Mr Todd.'

I sit back and say nothing. Well, she's talked all right, but in riddles; in code.

Questions crowd in on me. What's she telling me? That someone other than Hicks turned up for the meeting? Who? Someone in the family connected with the meat depot job? Isn't she happy . . . wrong word . . . convinced that her husband's death was natural?

Can't grill her here. Not in front of a member of the family who shows no sign of leaving us alone. Take her back with you to HQ, get a full statement.

No, brief yourself fully first. You've missed ten days of this inquiry. Read it thoroughly. See all the witnesses, the suspects, first. Then take her through it line by line.

'Would you mind if I popped back to see you, say, tomorrow?' I ask tentatively.

'Why?' asks Anita protectively.

'Not at all,' says Mrs Knight with a faint smile.

'Ring first,' says Anita with no smile at all.

5

The red box is sitting where the brown bag stood this morning – on my small desk back at HQ.

The first priority, we agreed on the short trip back, is to trace Alan Hicks – and fast – to find out precisely what he knows. What we need urgently is the inside info on the terrorist trio, their whereabouts and, above all, their next target. I have this awful feeling that somewhere the countdown has already begun.

It's academic whether Hicks met up with Knight or not or where. If he did and told all, Knight is in no position to repeat it.

'Was it possible', I'd asked, 'for Knight to have collapsed into Red Gutter while waiting, and Hicks to have turned up a bit late and not spotted his body?'

'It's in the middle of a wood, ideal for a clandestine meeting. It's a fair fall, old logs and undergrowth as well as rocks all the way down. You can stand on the top and see nothing much below you.'

Silent, I surmised, could have lain there undiscovered for weeks. Hazel seemed to have read this thought. 'We were just lucky that the historian scrambled down and found him so quickly.'

I told her my fear was that Hicks did show up and told all and that Knight gave him a thank-you and disappearing money. 'That would make him doubly difficult to find,' I added. 'Let's hope Knight died on the way to the rendezvous. If so, Hicks may get in touch again.'

Good thinking, that, even if I say so myself, so we dropped into the Fairways Hotel to tell the manager that if a second card arrived for Andy Day he should call us straight away.

We brought a couple of rolls each, tastier than the canteen's, back with us. We're chewing them and still chewing over our problems now.

Studying the photocopy of the card, I ask her, 'There's no point yet, is there, in trying to crack the code?' I am trying to convince myself. 'Even if we do, it's not going to lead us to Hicks. His date with Knight has been and gone.'

'Unless Hicks writes to the Fairways again,' she replies.

A deeply troubling answer, that, since we wouldn't be able to decipher his message. I pick up the phone, dial Intelligence and tell a constable who answers to get details of Mr Knight's father – rank, regiment and so on – from Personnel and ask the Ministry of Defence to dig out the wartime codes he used.

'Could take yonks,' says Hazel, filling me with gloom. Her face brightens. 'Still, find Hicks and he'll tell us the code and he won't have to send us a card.' Then, even more logically, she nods at the red box. 'Maybe all the answers are in there.'

On top is Hicks' bail form. Age: twenty-four. Address: a cottage in Southwell. Occupation: assistant greenkeeper. Charge: theft of cash card. Name of surety: Geoffrey Powers with an address in Newark. Amount: a hundred pounds. 'Who's he?' I ask.

Hazel picks up the phone to ask the custody sergeant.

I read on through Hicks' record. Lots of motoring offences, including an expired three-month ban after two yellow cards for speeding.

The next file in a pink wallet is totally new to me – accounts of the Trentside club, Arc Air (with a c, I note), Thorne Meat Depots and Combined Counties, a meat business.

A quick scan shows that the first two are losing money heavily, the last two making mints, largely due to European Union subsidies.

Hazel replaces the phone. 'Powers is the boss of Combined Counties.'

Where young Miles called on his way to pick up his mother this morning, I recall.

'Silent can't have been checking on Powers' financial status merely to stand a hundred-pound bail, can he?' she ventures.

'No,' I agree. 'So what are they doing in here?'

'Could be he just packed them away in the box and they've nothing to do with the bombings. Maybe he, or more likely his wife, has got shares in them,' Hazel speculates.

I turn the folder face down on top of Hicks' antecedents, wondering if I'm doing the right thing.

Knight's diary logs appointments only, no useful details.

There's a file of press clippings, all about Animal Salvation's boasts after the boat bombing, nothing new. The cock-up over the ransom at Thorne Meat Depots has not yet been made public; nor the cash point caper. The file will be a lot fatter when they break, I brood.

'Do you think Silent was right to regard the cold store explosion as a possible copycat?' asks Hazel.

I don't want to share unformed thoughts on this line yet. 'Why?'

'Unlike the boat bombing, the terrorists haven't yet blown it to the media, have they?'

I wince, privately pleading, Don't remind me. I see myself featured as a Keystone Cop, standing on the river bank, watching the drop whizz away, no help to my promotion prospects at all. 'Neither have they publicised your cash card wheeze,' I respond.

'Ah, yes, but –' her clever smile, irritating me – 'they haven't carried out their reprisal over that yet, unlike the meat depot,' she answers, giving me no comfort at all.

The last sheet of paper revives my spirits. It's a draft of a memo to the chief constable in which Knight argued that VIP protection could be spread among the branch now that the Irish problem no longer caused such a heavy workload. He recommended that Chief Superintendent Dale be transferred to 'other duties' – point-duty, I hope.

So, we decide, there's nothing in the red box that gets us closer to Hicks.

Hazel phones his legal aid solicitor, but he's not expecting to hear from him till a date is set for the court case over the stolen cash card. I phone Finance, but Knight has not ordered any additional payments out of the 6IW/K2 account, whatever that is.

I hold up the draft about Dale's future. 'What shall we do about this?'

Hazel grins gleefully and promises to dispatch it on to the chief by a circulatory route that doesn't cross Dale's borrowed desk.

That's my girl, I think, warming to her again.

On the trip over the river, crossing a narrow bridge alongside a Victorian hall that's all dark red turrets and towers, depression descends, a greyness to match the afternoon. Don't ask from where. Nothing that Hazel, driving again, has said. Most of the way we listen to Classic FM.

Maybe it was *Fingal's Cave* and thinking about Scotland, where I should be now, pottering through the Borders, with Em, carefree, instead of here, in the rat race, bucking for promotion.

Or maybe it was the closing chorus from *The Magic Flute* with its overtones of Freemasonry that sparked a private rant against on-the-square Knight and his top secret games of hide and seek, then dropping dead in his hide and leaving me to do the seeking with the clock and the next bomb already ticking.

Why did I spot that story on the front page? Why did I phone in? Why didn't the chief yank Dale off his arse to put him in charge?

The roadside sign says 'Southwell' and now I know with absolute certainty why I'm so down.

A lovely place, this, off the beaten track, streets of small stylish shops, nothing garish or modern. Soon Em and I will have to move to a bigger place and this is where I would have loved to live, close to the tree-dotted green, for preference.

Not any more. Imagine passing the Saracen's Head every day and not daring to go in. How can I ever go in again until we have caught the rats from the sewer who made such an utter fool of me?

Thirty-six hours I spent there, sheer luxury with its good grub, twelfth-century beams and flower-bedecked cobbled courtyard, soaking up its history of royal visits, including the last night of freedom for King Charles after the Civil War before he was carted off to be beheaded.

I was polishing off a seafood platter when Hazel's call came informing me that the *Lindum Arch*, twin sister of the safely defused *Lindum Castle*, had been blown up miles from the port my team was watching. Not only that, the fake money with which we'd baited the trap in the sand box across the road from the hotel had gone via the sewers; right from under my nose.

Never went back to the hotel for my Bramley apple crumble after I'd sloshed a hundred yards through the sewer to find out how they'd done it. Never been back since and don't plan to.

I visualise the regulars who, like the rest of the nation, will have seen Knight on TV trying to explain my failure away, elbowing each other when I walked in, sniggering.

And that trio from the *Tyke* are still out there somewhere, plotting to make public how they conned me a second time, from under my nose again, and got away with two thou before torching Thorne's cold store just down the river.

Lately, even on holiday, I've suffered early morning awakening – 5 a.m. sometimes – and the first thing that pops into my head is a vision of me on telly, trotting out lame excuses while the nation laughs, and I can't get to sleep again.

The road bends and into view comes the Saracen's Head, white-plastered, half-timbered, at its T-junction, the scene of the crime, my crime.

I avert my eyes, glancing left at the Minster with its semicircular, magnificently carved chapter house. The stone work is a pale sandy colour, restful, comforting somehow. Twin towers, slender pyramid roof. The huge tower at the centre has a clock with golden numerals which shows a quarter after two. I've only ever been inside once, not to pray: for a Beethoven concert.

I look ahead of me again, back to the Saracen's Head, and all comfort has gone. I feel like King Charles after his last night of freedom, waiting for the axe to fall.

Got to crack this, I vow; got to find them personally and only then will I walk in there with my head held high.

Facially, Melanie Dexter has beautiful bone structure, photogenic if you brush out the flaky complexion. Her dark hair is long, dull and lifeless, falling over scrawny shoulders. A skimpy white top is bound like a bandage across a flat chest. Her stained, black slacks are tight to wide hips. There's six inches of midriff visible. There'll be fluff in her navel if I bother to look.

She's early twenties. Two sons in hand-me-down clothes, close to rags, both under school age, run wild in a small, muddy front garden that's no advert for a member of the greens staff at Trent-side Golf and Country Club, the man about this house. The lawn, if that's what you can call it, is riddled with molehills, scores of reddish heaps. The boys are not by the same father, judging by the looks of them; one barrel-chested, the other as thin as his mother.

Hazel makes the introductions on the doorstep of a semi-detached cottage which took some finding. It ought to be declared unfit for human habitation. Through the opened door I can see floral wallpaper peeling away from damp patches that will never dry out and a plain brown carpet so worn there's more straw-coloured threads visible than dark pile.

Hazel is sweet-talking her. I can't be arsed.

47

In this sort of mood, people like Melanie Dexter piss me off.

Apologists will point to a deprived childhood – inadequate parents, penny-pinching education, no jobs at the end of it, even if she was capable of one.

Well, my father was so absent I still don't know or care who he is, much less where he is, and my mum dumped me on her folks to travel the world.

They brought me up well enough to qualify to study music – the clarinet – at college. Totally blew it, of course. Big city life offered too many distractions, girls with classy accents who introduced me to wine, conversation according to the current agenda set by the *Guardian*, and sex.

'You're seeing how the other half lives,' said my grandma, a touch uneasily.

Accepting that I hadn't the talent or application to play even in an end-of-the-pier band, I followed my grandad into the police service.

A shock, that first post-training beat after campus life – the inner city of a big city, nothing like grandad's pastoral patch. Knew such places existed, of course, but vaguely thought conditions in them had been exaggerated for political effect by the *Guardian*, required reading in my early twenties till I ditched it in training.

I'd been prepared as a cadet for drug-linked petty crime, booze-related violence, the litter, the broken glass, the beer cans, the total squalor. Birds in hedgerows are reared never to foul their own nests. People in high rises I've seen, actually seen, peeing on their own doorsteps.

You don't expect 'em to have pride of ownership, but peeing on a rented doorstep? And rent that Welfare pays for them, too.

Fuck me, I can swear with the best of workmates. But not at kids, cowed neighbours and veteran motorists who are driving too carefully. And the racket they made; louder than any disco. They have no concept, no idea, of good neighbourliness.

I worked harder on promotion exams than I ever did on a music degree to get out of it and into CID. They remained, these scum-bags, the greater part of my pinches, but in CID, away from community policing, I didn't have to listen to their gripes and taunts or offer unheeded advice for an eight-hour shift each day.

In Special Ops, the graduates from petty to major crime, the armed robbers and dope pedlars, the psychos, the jailbreakers were tracked down at the point of a .38. You get no respect from them still, but you get no lip either.

Even more distance has been put between them and me in my time on Special Branch. Our targets these days may be more dangerous, but at least some have beliefs, principles, intelligence, however warped.

Now I feel back in my first days on the beat. Inner cities, outer villages, minster towns, all the same, it seems to me, stepping over this dirty doorstep, watching out for pee. I'm glad I'm not her next-door neighbour.

'Alan about?' asks Hazel above the blare of pop music from a radio on a table stacked with dirty pots and clean washing that includes men's clothes. A headshake. 'Heard from him lately?' Another headshake, dumber still. 'Not even a postcard?'

'Or a birthday card.' She looks at me insolently. 'That your doing?'

'What?' I ask brusquely.

'Nicking him, then sending him off like that.'

'My boss's,' I say.

'Needs his head examining.'

If only we could examine Knight's head, I think longingly.

'So when did you last see him?' Hazel asks.

She turns to the table, thankfully switching off the transistor. 'A week last Friday.' The day he got bail, I remind myself. She doesn't ask us to sit, just as well by the looks of this rickety furniture.

She hadn't seen him the night before, she goes on, but that was not unusual. If he went drinking in some distant village with his mates, he'd doss anywhere.

'No transport?' asks Hazel.

A sullen headshake.

'His driving ban's up,' I point out.

'But insurance costs an arm and a leg after disqualification, so he sold his machine.'

'What did he say when he finally came home?' Hazel continues.

'That he'd been in custody again.'

'For what?'

'Don't you know?'

49

'We know,' I say, just about hanging on to what little patience remains. 'It's what he told you that counts.'

'Got a fag?'

I shake my head resolutely. Even if I smoked, I'd not give one to her. She gets hand-outs enough out of my taxes. 'Bad for you,' I say, lecturing a little.

'That's what Hicksey says,' she replies unoffended. 'Hates them.'

Hazel doesn't smoke either but she fishes a blue packet of Embassy Regals from her shoulder bag and hands them over, unopened. 'Help yourself,' she says. It's an on-the-road detective's gambit, an unspoken invitation to sing to satisfy her craving. Clam up and Hazel will ask for them back.

She'd been living – if that's what you want to call it – here for a couple of years since the second kid arrived and her parents in an outlying village insisted on her finding a place of her own.

The council, I suspect, was required to come up with this place for her, a young mother, under the Homeless Acts. Having sold the few council houses in her small, native village to its sitting tenants – another law – it would have forked out housing benefit for this turn-of-the-century two-up and two-down, and moved her in, several miles from her family and friends.

She'd met Alan Hicks on a girls' night out. God knows who babysat that night. I don't ask. Hicks had been mobile in those days, popped round a few times, then stayed over Christmas and became more or less a fixture.

'Do his parents live round here?' asks Hazel.

'Dead. Brought up by his grandparents. Dead, too.'

'So where was he living before he moved in?'

'A bedsit in Newark.'

As she notes the address, Hazel asks, 'Was he in a job before the Trentside club?'

'Labouring in Newark.' A smirk. 'For what it was worth. Two quid an hour. Mind, he's only on three now.'

'Better than the dole,' I snap.

She shrugs, not sure, annoying me even more. He stayed in some nights, when there was summat on the box, she goes on, but mostly he was out drinking with his mates.

Hazel doesn't ask if he gave her any housekeeping. To have acknowledged that officially would have cost her in benefits.

Last time but one she saw him he was collected in the morning by a workmate who drove him to the club as usual. He didn't come home that night.

'Next day, he popped in, only stayed a few minutes, just time to throw some underwear in a bag and collect his passport.'

'Passport? He'd been abroad before, then?' Hazel inquires. 'Holidays?'

'On his pay?' She raises her voice and plucked eyebrows – a you-must-be-joking expression. 'Grape-picking. Before I met him. Twice. In France. When he was in college. Musk-something.'

Muscadet, I think.

'What was he studying at college?'

'Er. Mmmm.' I can almost see her brain churning. 'Ag-something. Not agriculture.'

'Agronomy,' I prompt with a tired sigh.

She looks at me angrily. 'You taking the mick?'

'Just get on with it,' I command. 'We don't want to spend all day here.' I put on a disdainful expression and look around. Hazel matches it and directs it at me.

'But he couldn't get a job in it,' she goes on sullenly, 'not for months. So he laboured at Combined Counties.'

'The meat mart?' asks Hazel. She looks at me again, telling me what I am already recalling. Geoffrey Powers, the surety who stood bail for Hicks, is the boss at Combined Counties.

Melanie nods, but when the name of Powers is put to her, she shakes a don't-know.

'Did he tell you on that brief visit home what had happened to him?' Hazel continues.

'Some drinking mate had given him a cash card to help himself to money he was owed. Turned out to be a dud and he got himself pinched. He said he was going to get his money and more besides.'

'What about his job at the club?'

'He'd been fired, hadn't he?'

'Did he tell you that?'

'No. His boss did. Came round here looking for him and said so. Something to do with missing fertiliser.'

'When did his boss call here?'

'Same day as Hicksey left.'

51

'For France?' I ask, making sure I've got it right.

Melanie nods. 'He knew the place he was going – the district anyway – but never mentioned it by name. All he had to do was get some gen and he'd be off the hook, he said.'

I'm straining at the bit, ready to be off in pursuit of two good leads, but Hazel chats on a while. She writes her name, no rank, in a plain notebook, adds the number of her direct line, tears it off and asks that Alan get in touch when he turns up. 'We may drop by to see you again.'

Melanie flicks her head towards the wall that divides this place from the adjoining cottage. 'If I'm not in, just knock next door.'

'A friend?'

'The landlord . . .'

Hallo, I think. In lieu of rent.

'Poor old bugger. Nearly eighty. Dying. Won't go into a hospice. Not yet, he says. He's been good to me, babysits now and then, so . . .' She shrugs. 'He's got nobody, a widower, gets no visits. Least of all from you lot.'

Hazel and I exchange frowns.

'Village bobby,' Melanie explains. 'Retired before I was born.'

She takes us next door. 'Just for ten minutes,' she pleaded. 'It will do him good.'

His name is Larry Dove, retired twenty years from the force, and ten from his second job as a gamekeeper. He sits in an easy chair, a huge tartan blanket over his knees. What's visible of him is very thin.

On a stand next to his chair is a modern, mushroom-coloured phone that doesn't look as though it's seen a damp cloth since it was installed. The rest of the cottage is cluttered with old furniture, but quite clean.

He coughs as he recalls the old days, mentioning names we don't know.

When Melanie departs to sort out a squabble in the garden, he talks of Alan Hicks. 'Not violent or anything. Bright really. Speaks French better than me and I served two years there in the war. But I don't know . . .'

He tries to work something out, fails.

'And Mel?' asks Hazel.

'Absolute angel. She and her kids keep me going.'

Driving away, not having collected the Embassy Regals, Hazel remarks, 'You were quiet in there.'

'Thinking,' I say, but don't tell her what. I'm thinking how appalled my grandfolks would have been if they'd read those private thoughts about Melanie Dexter, the way I treated her, a kind-hearted girl doing for free what force Welfare gets paid to do and has failed to do.

Somehow, somewhere along the way through college and career I've lost touch with my roots. I'm middle class, know things like Muscadet is best when it's *sur lie* and Camembert should never be kept in the fridge.

I've a wife who's easy on the eye and ear, who reads Shakespeare while I listen to Beethoven over the CD headphones. We go on out-of-the-way holidays, touring in a trendy car, anywhere that's not infested by package operators. We have a lovely little cottage and I aspire to a home like Knight's in a place like, say, Southwell, that will come with his rank.

How the other half lives?

I am the other fucking half.

In this silent moment of guilt and self-disgust, I hate the fucking feeling.

6

The Trentside Golf and Country Club has the sort of skin-deep attraction of high-rise flats when they were new – superficially smart, economical use of land, a good idea at the time.

Lots of landowners have formed consortiums and constructed them over the last few years to cash in on EC subsidies for reduced food production and the golf boom at the same time. To recoup astronomical outlays, each invariably set their fees far too high at a time when the country suddenly started to suffer from under-employment and there was an over-production in golf clubs. But that's the Euro mixed market for you.

A collection of old barns and stables have been skilfully

converted, knitted together with matching, reconstituted bricks and extended into an H-shape surrounded by a spacious car-park.

The park, however, is pot-holed, awaiting a coating of Tarmac, and the trees around are staked and spindly, unhappy in the heavy clay soil.

It is so sparsely filled that it's easy to spot Miles Thorne's white sporty job in a line of spaces marked 'Reserved for officials' near to smoked glass double doors with a sign: 'Members' Entrance'. Further away, close to the professional's well-stocked window, is the red pick-up whose videoed index plate led to Hicks' arrest.

Down a low, carpeted corridor, its cream walls plastered with notices and posters, is a door with a plate that says 'Managing Director'. 'Come in' comes from behind it when I knock.

Miles Thorne is sitting in a bigger office than mine at a bigger desk than mine with more phones than me.

His long picture window has a view through white horizontal blinds of a narrow, multi-tiered tee and a horseshoe green surrounded by deep bunkers. Both are empty.

The trees that are visible alongside damp fairways don't seem to have made much better progress than those around the car-park. Rainwater has gathered in one saucer depression and not drained away. Moles have left fresh excavations dotted in heaped piles here and there.

Thorne junior is dressed for a game. A short-sleeved salmon pink shirt exposes strong, tanned forearms. Dark tartan slacks are tight to big thigh muscles. He looks as though he can hit the ball a long way.

He lacks the social graces of Rodney Montgomery and doesn't immediately get up for Hazel who follows me in. He's forced into a semi-standing position when I extend my hand. His uncle, ACC Andrew Knight, had not enrolled him into the Masons.

After the introductions, he sits and I begin. 'We're making inquiries about Alan Hicks.'

His reply is offhand. 'You won't find him here.'

'We gather he worked on your green staff.' A curt nod. 'We need to trace him.' I head off an understandable 'Why?' and move on. 'I have taken over Mr Knight's caseload and I want to reinterview him.'

'You had him in custody,' he says, somewhat reproachfully.

'But I didn't speak to him then. Now I need to.'

As with his mother this morning, my name seems to have rung a belated bell. 'Aren't you in charge of my dad's arson?'

Yes, I confirm, and I was his uncle's No. 2 on the much publicised boat bomb before that, but I missed the developments of the last fortnight. 'Away in Ulster,' I add, making it sound like duty. 'You see, Mr Knight was handling Hicks' case personally, part of a wider, much more serious inquiry, and there are a few loose ends.'

'I see.' Finally he motions us to sit in two armless chairs by a wall facing the window through which there are still no players in view.

Alan Hicks joined the staff late last autumn, he begins. He didn't do the specialist jobs like treating and cutting the greens. He was the apprentice – raking sand bunkers, controlling (by which he means exterminating) vermin and trimming weeds from around saplings. 'He is . . . was well qualified.'

Originally Miles had not suspected Hicks of any involvement in the raid on the fertiliser shed back in April when a lorry load of nitrogen in blue plastic bags vanished overnight. 'Did you?'

Hazel answers for me. 'He was alibied for the time of the break-in, but there could have been some careless talk in pubs, I suppose.'

The week before last, Miles continues, he missed out on Mrs Knight's birthday party because of a golf society function here at the club. His father phoned him from Knight's house.

'Did I know an Alan Hicks, he wanted to know. Yes, I said. Works for me. "Well," he says, "your Uncle Andy has just told us he has him under arrest. He's part of this extortion gang that did my cold store and the cattle boat on the Wash before that." It all made sense then.'

It doesn't to me so I ask, 'What did?'

'Well –' a tiny shrug – 'the fertiliser theft.' Miles looks at Hazel. 'Maybe he didn't take part but he could have tipped off the gang where to find it.'

'So what did the pair of you decide about him?' I ask.

'My decision.' He straightens his back in his comfortable chair. 'I run this place. Dad takes care of the rest.'

I put on my put-in-place face. 'So what was your decision?'

Miles looks undecided. 'I was going to listen to what Hicks had to say first, or for the outcome of the court case maybe, before deciding whether to fire him or not.'

'And did you?'

He shakes his head. 'Never had the chance. I went round to his place to see him, but his lady told me he'd packed and gone.'

'Did she say where?'

'France. Grape-picking or fruit-picking or something.'

'She says you told her he was fired.'

A resolute headshake. 'No. Suspended maybe. Not sacked. Not till I'd heard his side of things. Dismissing someone without a hearing can land you in the industrial court.'

He'd learned the lessons of his college business course better than Lincsline, I think admiringly, judging by their handling of Richard Stone's departure, the root of all this mayhem. 'Did you know the circumstances of his arrest?'

A brief nod. 'Dad told me what Uncle Andy told him. That was another matter I was going to take up with Hicks. At the time he was caught at the cash point, he was out and about in the club pick-up during working hours. He wasn't supposed to be doing private errands at banks.'

'What was he supposed to be doing?' Hazel asks.

'Collecting blood and bone.' A fertiliser, he explains, mainly for the benefit of a puzzled Hazel.

'And did you tackle him?'

'He turned up here while I was out there . . .' Miles nods towards the window. '. . . dropped off the pick-up, emptied his locker in the staff mess and told the head greenkeeper he'd collect any wages owing later.' A little headshake. 'So I never saw him.'

'And since?'

Another headshake, longer.

'Has he collected his wages?'

He flicks his head towards a steel filing cabinet in the corner. 'Still have them there. Two weeks. Nearly three hundred pounds.'

After tax, that's considerably more than the three pounds an hour Melanie Dexter told us he was on, I calculate.

I ask to see the head greenkeeper. Miles picks up a cream phone, fingers a button and tells someone to find him.

While we wait, he chats about Hicks. Not a particularly good timekeeper, he says, but a first-rate mole catcher.

'He worked for a while as a labourer at Combined Counties Meat Mart,' I say.

'So it said on his CV. They gave him a good reference.'

'Did you recruit him personally from there?' He is frowning, confused. 'I mean, did you meet up with him there?' Still puzzled. 'Do you have business ever at Combined Counties as a result of which you met up with Hicks, liked what you saw and hired him?'

An understanding expression. 'No. He came to us via the Job Centre.'

I persist. 'Do you have any dealings with Combined Counties?'

A cautious expression. 'I was there, matter of fact, this morning. Just dropping off some insurance docos for dad on my way through.' Thorne Meat Depots and Combined Counties Meat Mart, he explains, are in the same line of business and share each other's spare capacity. 'But I never saw Hicks there.' He repeats, 'The Job Centre sent him.'

Eventually, the head greenkeeper comes in, a stocky man in his forties, dressed for work in green overalls. Yes, he confirms with a Scots accent, Hicks was a good worker. 'Liked a drink but, if he was ever late, he made up lost time.' He names a couple of pubs Hicks uses and adds he's sorry to lose him. He looks at Miles. 'You found a replacement?'

An uncomfortable stir. 'Not yet.'

'We're taking lots of flak.'

A shrug, still uneasy. 'Just tell them the feeding programme's been delayed by the break-in. It's not officially solved yet, is it?' Miles looks at me, rather sheepishly.

I'm reading into this that members – what few they have – are grumbling about the state of the greens. Even Knight complained to his wife.

Miles' excuse is that the greens are not getting their growth-boosting shot of nitrogen because of the raid on the shed. He'll have been issued with a routine crime report number to verify the loss to his insurance company. He doesn't need arrests and court appearances. If insurance claims depended on crime clear-ups, they'd settle only a small percentage of all thefts.

Miles had banked the settlement, I'm guessing, and wasn't replacing Hicks. The accounts I saw in Knight's red box revealed financial problems. Something's wrong here, and I doubt that it's just cash flow.

The head greenkeeper sighs unhappily and returns to the topic of Hicks. Yes, sometimes he was allowed to take the club pick-up home if he had to make an early collection next morning. If not, he travelled to and from the club with a workmate.

And, yes, he saw him the day Knight released him from custody. 'He said sorry, like, for all the trouble. He was returning the pick-up and collecting his things. When I told him he . . .' He nods down at Miles. '. . . was out playing and wouldn't be passing the clubhouse for an hour or so, he said he'd be back in a week or two for his P45 and anything owing. He patted his pocket and said he was OK for readies in the meantime.'

He would be, I remind myself, because Knight had released him with three hundred pounds to go undercover in France. 'Did he say where he was going?'

'Only that he was away on a short trip.'

So, with the money Knight advanced in his pocket, he was off to France on his undercover assignment, I think, gazing through the blinds out of the window, something troubling me, miles away. Then it came to me.

Hicks had returned the club pick-up and had no transport of his own. 'How did he leave? I mean, was he going to catch a bus, train . . .' I yank my head in the direction of the railway line with its many stops at Trent Valley village stations.

'No. He said he had wheels waiting down the road.'

'Did you see the vehicle?'

'No,' says the greenkeeper in his soft burr. 'All he said was that he was departing in style.'

A big, black barge, broad-bowed, low in the water, is tied to the concrete wharf that serves the riverside commercial estate where Thorne's cold store used to stand on the western bank. It is stacked from stem to stern with metal girders.

Brian Thorne's manager is complaining to a hard-hatted young man in a check shirt, dirty, ill-fitting jeans and black boots with reinforced toe-caps. 'Where is the bloody thing then?'

Even the outer walls of the cold store, all that survived the blast, have gone. Only the foundations and floor remain, fifty yards by fifty, a lot of concrete, and the semicircular guttering and slatted drains down which I watched the thawed blood flow on the night of the explosion.

Around and about are huge, square stacks of bricks and breeze blocks, metal frames and, under blue tarpaulin sheeting, bags of cement. A fork lift stands idle.

Taking my cue from it, I gaze right, up the river, reflecting the fading grey of the afternoon, towards the out-of-sight weir and the field where Thorne's prize cattle (less one poisoned bull) graze. On the other bank the tree-coated Trent hills tumble down steeply, then gradually towards the wood with Red Gutter at its heart, and finally merge into the plains that lead into the flatlands of neighbouring Lincolnshire.

My eyes return to Thorne's manager, hoping to hurry him up. He's called John Bell; mid-thirties, gingery wavy hair that clashes with his blue boiler suit. He's short, all lean meat.

It was Bell, on his boss's orders, who collected the cash from the bank to pay off the ransom demand. He's a different breed to Thorne, much cooler. He took my side in the river-bank argument over how much we should put upfront in the blackmailers' pot. Such was Thorne's panic that, without Bell's backing, I suspect we would have lost the lot.

If I'm catching the drift of the heated conversation – and it's not hard – the cold store's rise from the ashes is being delayed by the non-arrival of a mobile crane.

To add to Bell's anger, the man he is berating has adopted a languid pose, elbows on a stack of bricks, leaning forward, the waist of his jeans riding low, exposing the chink of his arse – builder's cleavage, they call it.

Bell rounds off his rant with 'Well, bloody well hurry 'em up' and approaches us shaking his head heavily. Since he's not family, I dispense with the usual grave-faced exchange of grave words about Knight's sudden death. 'Mr Thorne not about?'

Without a reply, he fishes into a deep trouser pocket, takes out the black battery phone on which he got his instruction to go to the bank. He fingers down one button. It rings for some time before he switches off.

'No one's in,' he needlessly reports. He thinks. 'At the track, I think.'

Hazel expresses surprise at the absence of traffic we met on the way here.

'Not a race day,' he explains. 'He's going to see a couple of his nags gallop.' He smiles malevolently. 'Mind, they need it. Three runners over the sticks there on Saturday night. Three fallers.'

Hazel laughs happily. 'Sounds like three of mine.'

I express surprise now, telling him I wasn't aware his boss was into horses as well as cattle. Only for the past two or three years, he says. Since his wife came into money, I calculate.

I explain we're looking for Alan Hicks, but don't say why. His face registers nothing. Greenkeeper at Miles' club, I prompt. Still nothing. Used to work for Combined Counties before that, I prompt on.

'As what?' I confess we don't know. 'There's a score or more there.' He shakes his head again. 'Best ask the old man – or his missus. They deal with them.'

'Not Miles?' I ask.

'Not these days. Not since he opened his own club. We seldom see him now.' A disapproving countenance. 'Even when he was here, he never worked weekends. Always golfing.'

He'd turned a passion into a profession, often a financial mistake, I surmise.

'Seldom see his old man, either. Always racing.' He gives his head a single shake, put upon.

He tells us what vehicle Thorne is in – a green Range Rover with the depot's name on the doors.

For a non-race day, there's lots of vehicles parked beyond the 'Owners and Trainers Only' sign at the racetrack. At first glance, a Range Rover of any colour is not among them.

Then I take pleasure in pointing out to Hazel she has driven into the car-park for a golf club neither of us knew was there, tucked away in what looks like old stabling and a single-storey stand, altogether more modest than Trentside, but better patronised and cheaper, I guess.

She backs out, rather huffily, and drives across an adjoining, much bigger car-park so fast that loose flint plays a tinny tune on her exhaust pipe.

In front of a row of wire-enclosed wooden stables are two brown horse boxes, ramps down, and Thorne's Range Rover. We come to a skidding halt on the loose surface and get out. The sun has finally broken through, high and weak.

We walk beyond a brick admin block and the owners' and trainers' bar, cream clapboard, with flower baskets hanging from its single-storey eaves. There's a strange quiet about the place, like a seaside resort out of season.

Thorne is not hard to spot. He's the only person in view, apart from half a dozen workers walking in a line on the grass track, carefully treading back the divots of Saturday's meeting when the going must have been soft. They've already cleared up the crowd's debris – not a scrap of litter to be seen in the two smallish stepped stands and the lush lawns in front of them.

All we can see of Thorne is the back of his grey suit. He is on an odd-looking platform, like a saluting dais. His posture is far from upright. His back is straight enough, but his long legs slope back. His elbows are splayed out on a white rail forming a triangle, the apex of which is out of sight.

He doesn't hear our approach up a wooden ramp – I can see now it's a viewing platform for wheelchair-bound racegoers – or acknowledge us when we come to a standstill beside him. He is watching through binoculars two horses, denimed riders crouched in the saddles, heading towards us, leaving sprays of dark sand in their wake on the all-weather track, the nearest circuit to us; no fences or hurdles in place.

The horses, both chestnut, pass the winning post almost in front of us, one well ahead of the other, which is sweating and blowing harder than me in rehabilitation.

He drops his bins in front of his chest and turns towards us. The suit, black pin-head checks on the grey, could have done without a gaudily striped tie.

Hazel switches on her flirting smile. Thorne is smirking. 'One for the knackers' yard, I'm thinking.'

Hazel switches off her smile. She's a big city girl. When she settles down and gets a dog, she'll probably knit it a coat for the winter.

She doesn't understand us country folk. Years ago, my grandad organised a whipround in the village pub for a pig farmer who'd been wiped out and put into isolation by foot and mouth.

They sent him a signed 'get well soon' card which informed him they had bought him a piglet, so he wasn't entirely without stock; a nice neighbourly gesture that made the *Derbyshire Times*, the local weekly paper.

Once vets gave the all-clear, the farmer collected the piglet and lots more besides. Later, he was asked how the pub's present was getting on. 'Just gone to Walls',' he said, which meant it had become sausages and ice-cream.

Everyone understood that's what pigs are reared for. Hazel is the city sort who would have given it a name and a bow to wear round its neck.

Commiserations somehow seem out of place here, so I go straight in. 'We're on our way back from seeing Miles. Looking for Alan Hicks, we are. Know him?'

'Of him,' he says deliberately. 'Never met him.'

Never even heard of him, he goes on, until his sister-in-law's birthday. Laboriously, he yanks his head in the direction of the village where she lives.

'What did you hear?' asks Hazel, grim-faced.

'Isn't it on your files?'

Hazel, back in her acting mode, puts on a sad expression. 'Mr Knight didn't have time to complete it.'

Well, he begins in his bluff, rural accent, the party was going full swing despite the host's absence. When he did turn up, Knight told Thorne more or less what Miles had already reported to us.

Let me get this right, I caution myself. Thorne would know all about the cattle-boat bombing. The whole world did from the newspapers. Obviously he'd know all about the river ransom and the fire there as he'd witnessed both. 'Did Mr Knight outline the circumstances in which Alan Hicks was arrested?'

'Caught at a cash point, wasn't he? Linked to three other people who were still at large.'

'Did he say who or where they were?'

'No. Very close he was with info like that. I think he only mentioned it so it wouldn't come as a surprise to me or Miles when he appeared in court or whatever.'

'Why Miles?'

'Good Lord.' An annoyed look. 'He was his boss, wasn't he?'

'So you phoned Miles at the country club to break the news of the breakthrough?'

'Course. It tied up all the loose ends. The fertiliser theft there. The explosion at my place. All you had to do was catch the rest. Case closed.' Pause. 'Have you?'

I ignore his question and ask another. 'Did he mention how he planned to go about catching them?'

'Course not, no.' A determined headshake.

'Or tell you that there had been a third case of commercial blackmail the day before?'

A heavy shrug accompanies a baffled look. 'News to me, that.' As indeed it should be to anyone outside the target firm, Lincsline, the police and the terrorist trio from the houseboat *Tyke*, since news of it had not been released. 'He just said there'd been a development, that's all. Is that how he got on to the gang?'

I nod, but don't expand much on it. Instead: 'So how were you able to help him?'

'I don't think he was seeking or needed my help. He was just informing me as a matter of courtesy that he'd made some progress at long last. I am a victim of the crime after all. Don't you keep victims up to date with progress?'

Another nod. 'Did he say what was going to happen to Hicks?'

'No decision had been made then, as I understood it.'

'Did you know he was freed on bail?'

'Miles told me. A day or two later. A surprise, that, I must admit.'

Hazel explains yet again that Knight had charged Hicks with only a minor offence while his story was being checked. 'And you told Mr Knight that you didn't know Hicks?'

'Correct. Miles would, not me. Told him that, too. I seldom go to the club. That's my lad's province. 'Fraid I couldn't help him much.' Pause. 'Nor you.'

'Did you know that Alan Hicks worked at Combined Counties?' I ask.

A slightly startled look, no reply.

'Before he joined Miles' staff?' I continue.

'No,' he finally answers.

'You have business there, don't you?'

His expression now is more gruff than bluff. 'What are you driving at?'

I explain we're anxious to reinterview Hicks, but can't find him. 'Is it possible on your calls there you may have seen him without realising who he is? You may have seen him about.'

Thorne senior seems satisfied. 'What's he look like?' He studies the photo taken in custody which I slip from an inside pocket – a choirboy's smile, curly, shoulder-length blond hair.

'You can't see it on there, but he also has a gold ring in his left ear,' Hazel adds, tugging her own.

Thorne is already shaking his head. 'Never. No. Never seen him before in my life.' He hands the photo back.

Tucking it away again, I ask, 'Do you know Mr Geoffrey Powers?'

A curt nod. 'Top man at Combined Counties. Why?'

I tell him Powers stood surety for bail.

A deep frown. 'Best ask him then.'

He seems to be itching to go, looking urgently across me, to join his trainer who is leading the losing horse back towards its box. Hazel's eyes follow it. On a railed walkway from the track, it deposits a steaming pile, undoing the clearing up of the cleaning staff. 'Will you really shoot it?' she asks anxiously.

'No. No. No.' An energetic headshake. 'Why? Want to buy her?'

'Well . . .' She's silenced for once.

He laughs matily. 'A better bet than the three I had here on Saturday. Lost me five.' He holds up a hand, spreading fingers and thumb.

Hundred, I guess; not oncers. 'You'd have been better off watching the rugger on TV.'

He screws his face to tell me: Not interested.

I tell him we've dropped by his old depot. 'Good to see you're getting back to business. No hold-ups on insurance?'

'Not with the structure, no,' he replies, suddenly distracted. 'They're still messing about over the contents.'

'Why's that?' asks Hazel.

'Much of it was EC. From their meat mountain. Earmarked as relief for Bosnia or somewhere. You know what these bureaucrats in Brussels are like. Always dragging their feet.'

His expression now is impatient. 'Well . . .' To emphasise that he wants rid of us, he sticks out his right hand. I reach to shake it and also catch whisky on his breath. There'd been no time for formal introductions on previous chats, such was the panic over the anthrax threat and ransom demand. I feel that distinct grip. Thorne, like his brother-in-law and unlike his son, is in the Brotherhood.

As we shake, he peers at me intently, rather furtively, out of the corner of one eye. 'If there's anything I can ever do . . .' He just leaves it there, hanging.

64

Masonic code that; an invitation to join. Never sought or had one before.

Once I was more or less invited to join the Buffs, the Royal Antediluvian Society of Buffaloes, sort of working-class Freemasons.

In my CID days, there was a break-in at a city centre pub the local lodge used for meetings. The room assigned to them had framed photos of old Buffs on the walls, antique chairs with wooden spells as back rests and gavels on a polished table. I felt like a TV panellist as I sat at the table before a small frame which flicked over to display combinations of coded words – Strict Order, Dummy Lodge, Liberty Hall and Round Robin.

I asked the landlord what they meant. 'Confidential,' he said but he offered me sponsorship to join. 'Sort of chap we're looking for.' 'What's expected of me if I do?' I inquired. 'That's secret, too,' he replied. I laughed and left it there.

I've about as much understanding of Freemasonry as I do the Buffery. Heard the tales, of course, of *Boy's Own* initiation rites with rolled-up trouser legs and tongues that are pinned fifty fathoms deep if they wag.

My grandad loathed them, told lurid stories about favouritism and incompetent chiefs, blamed his lack of promotion – he never made it past sergeant – on his non-membership. My gran blamed it on lack of ambition. 'Never bellyache about bosses unless you're prepared to throw your hat into the ring to become one,' she said, more for my benefit than his; words, I suppose, that first sowed the seeds of ambition within me.

There must be some reason for grown men to join such a secret society, policemen notable among them. A private club that doesn't care to talk about its charity work? Or career advancement, making contacts, scratch my back and I'll scratch yours.

Some of my drinking pals are Masons. It's quite good fun taking the mickey out of them, knowing that they can't answer back because of their secrecy oaths, watching them squirm as they try to change the subject. But, in the canteen, among non-members, there's always speculation that there can be no other logical explanation for, for instance, Dale making chief superintendent.

A couple of years back – no, to be honest, a couple of days ago – I'd have laughed off Thorne's blatant attempt at recruitment.

Now I find myself wondering if the chief constable, about to replace Knight, is, as they claim in the canteen, a Mason. I am wearing a sincere face and saying a sincere 'Thanks'.

And, for the second time this afternoon, I fret about what my grandad would make of the changes that are taking place within me.

None of this, of course, I share with Hazel, but I do swap a thought as we drive down narrow lanes with grass verges running wild to get back to the main road. 'I wonder if his slow horses have anything to do with the bank releasing only ten grand instead of the fifty he wanted to meet the ransom.'

'Maybe his wife has put a limit on him,' Hazel speculates. 'It's her inheritance he's going through, after all. Fancy him coming racing on Saturday when his brother-in-law had just dropped dead. He should have been there, at his wife and sister-in-law's side.'

'I wonder if there's a fast woman somewhere in the background,' I ponder on.

'She'd have to be hard up.' Her shoulders shrug into a shudder over the steering wheel. 'Dreadful man.'

7

In the way that new motorways breed cars, bypasses woo industrial estates. The next and last call is on one just off the relief road that runs west round Newark.

From the communal car-park serving several warehouses, it looks like two buildings. One is a good forty yards long, but only about half as high. On the top are two buttercup yellow pyramids, added, I guess, for the cosmetic purpose of breaking the long, flat line of the roof.

Red bricks run half-way up, then grey metal cladding; no windows; just one door with 'Entrance' above. On it, in yellow that matches the roof feature, is the name: Combined Counties. The other building is oval-shaped, smaller and doorless.

Southwell Minster it isn't, but as modern industrial estate buildings go, it isn't bad, either.

Outside, it's low sixties, cool for the time of year. Inside is cooler still, a distinct nip in the air.

A young man in a white smock and wearing a stiff, white trilby looks up from a paper-strewn desk in a glass-enclosed office lit by a side window. 'You the new inspectors?'

'No,' says Hazel, smiling sexily. She motions to me. 'He's a superintendent and I'm a sergeant.' She adds our names, produces her warrant card from her shoulder bag and says: 'Police.'

'Sorry.' The young man's face is masked in embarrassment. He was expecting Ministry of Agriculture inspectors from the newly formed hygiene services. They had just taken over the job from the council of examining samples of meat, passing most, but condemning some as unfit for human consumption.

'Much rejected?' asks Hazel chattily.

'Gets tougher every year. Five years ago, when I first started here, there was hardly any wastage.'

'What happens to it?' Her clever smile, leading him on. 'Is it turned into blood and bone for golf course greens?'

He laughs, still shyly. 'Pet food, some of it.'

We ask for Geoffrey Powers, but are told he's out. 'Don't know when he'll be back.'

Hazel is no veggie, never watches her figure. (Men do, me included. The jacket of her suit is open now and the cream shirt fits just fine.) While we stand around, waiting, she talks of her favourite foods.

Behind him, through the window, a man dressed in a fur-lined anorak, hood up, emerges through a door, much bigger and thicker than a safe's.

A cloud of frosty fog follows him out. Through it I catch a glimpse of waxed brown crates stacked in numbered rows from floor to ceiling.

For a place with a staff of a score or more there's remarkably little activity to be seen.

Hazel is getting an enthusiastic tutorial on how the Ministry's inspectors examine cattle before and after slaughter, consigning anything suspect because of infections like, say, jaundice to something he calls the Detained Room, making it sound like a police cellblock.

I break in, nodding at the window. 'How long can you keep stuff in there?'

'At thirty under, vacuum-packed, years. You can buy in a glut when prices on the hoof are low and sell in a shortage, but most of it goes out fairly regularly to bulk buyers – supermarkets, school dinner services.'

'And the police canteen?' Hazel suggests.

Too fresh for that, I think acidly.

I disclose we're looking for Alan Hicks.

'Left here last autumn, works at the Trentside club now.'

Hazel tells him his knowledge is out of date and asks where we might find him. He names the same two pubs the head green-keeper gave us as his regular haunts.

'Seen him since he left?'

'Pops in now and then. His last visit was last month sometime,' he adds.

'What's he like – as a bloke I mean?' asks Hazel.

A short laugh, not affectionate. 'He was over-qualified for his job here. Just working his way through college, beer money till something better turned up.'

'But?' Hazel cocks her head pertly.

'A bit of a bullshitter.'

Worked in the right place then, I think.

He finally drags his eyes away from Hazel when the knob on the door rattles.

Geoffrey Powers is well named, I think, turning to view a dark man in his early forties, in a dark grey suit, white shirt, and dark blue tie, coming through the opened door.

He's handsome, I suppose, in a beaten-up kind of way, with one eyebrow ragged, his nose slightly bent. His back is unnaturally straight, his steps small.

The young man rises from the littered desk and introduces us to the gaffer. 'They're looking for Hicksey,' he adds.

'Thanks.' Powers scowls. 'Give us five, will you? And close the door.'

The young man smiles goodbye to Hazel, doesn't even look at me, as he walks round the desk and out of the office. Powers waits for the door to shut. Then, 'Well?'

I repeat what his clerk had told him.

'No problem, is there?'

'No,' replies Hazel with a coy smile. 'Should there be?'

'I mean, I'm not going to lose my hundred quid, am I?' – meaning the money he underwrote as surety to guarantee Hicks' reappearance when his bail expires.

'Hope not,' says Hazel. 'He's walked out on his job. He's not at home. And we want to talk to him again. We thought you might know where he is.'

A worried expression. 'He's not done a runner, has he?'

'Well,' says Hazel, smiling, 'help us trace him and we'll save your hundred quid.'

Finally he gestures us to sit on two wooden fold-up chairs and sits himself behind his desk. Across it wafts the fruity smell of good wine. He has clearly lunched later and in more style than us.

His daughter used to date Hicks during his college days, brought him home now and then, he explains. 'He was taking groundsmanship. She was doing computers.'

Powers found Hicks a job as a Saturday boy. The dating came to nothing. Not that he was sorry. She's seeing a teacher now, a more acceptable catch, I suppose. There was no animosity, though. When Hicks couldn't find a job to go with his qualifications, Powers fixed him up with labouring at Combined Counties to tide him over.

'We were all chuffed for him when he landed a job up his street at Trentside. Left with no hard feelings. I gave him a good reference. He was popular here.'

A week last Friday, Powers got a call from the police. They were holding Hicks on a theft charge and he'd put up Powers' name as surety for bail.

'Why you?' I ask.

'Well . . .' He shrugs, uncertain. 'Because I know him, I suppose. Naturally, I was a bit cautious. He's been up for motoring offences, as I suppose you know . . .' He looks from Hazel to me. '. . . but nothing criminal, like. I asked what it was all about. "Stealing by finding of a cash card," I was told. "Nothing was actually obtained and he denies it anyway." '

'I asked if he couldn't find anyone else, family or his employer, and was told his parents were dead – I'd forgotten that – and his current lady had no assets. He didn't want to trouble his boss in case it got him the sack.'

'But, despite your reservations, you still stood bail for him?'

'I was more or less talked into it.'

'Your sergeant. I drove to the police station. He was waiting in some office with the sergeant. I asked what was going on. He said it was all a mistake and he could prove it. Well, I didn't want the poor little sod locked up in a remand wing, did I? So I signed the form the sergeant gave me.

'He signed for his personal belongings. There was three hundred quid in an envelope. It took me a bit aback. "Nothing to do with the alleged crime," the sergeant assured me.'

The cash advance from Knight, I tell myself. 'Did you part in the station?'

A nod, then a quick shrug. 'Well, in the car-park outside. He got in a red pick-up, said he was returning it to the club. I drove back here.'

'Did he say anything?'

'About what?'

'Anything,' Hazel replies thoughtfully. 'Like, for instance, did he mention a college contemporary of his and, I assume, your daughter's – Richard Stone?'

'Never heard of him. Why?'

'We think he could be with him.'

'Can't help on that.' He pauses, thinks and seems to come up with nothing. 'Sorry. No. He just thanked me, repeated it was all a misunderstanding that could be sorted out, said he was going away for a few days to do just that and he'd keep in touch.'

'Has he?'

'No.' Then, rather glumly, 'Is this going to cost me?'

I should call at Hicks' two regular drinking haunts tonight, just sniffing around, but sod it, I tell Hazel, that's a job for foot soldiers like her. With her expensive taste in clothes, she needs the overtime.

Besides there's plenty on file on the background of the terrorist trio and how Hicks got to know them. So I return to HQ only to collect Knight's red box and Hazel's dossier and to see the chief constable.

I'm five minutes late for him. He keeps me waiting another ten.

'How goes it?' he inquires, sitting behind a desk big enough to play table tennis on.

Now he's lured me back, there's no first name, no mention of

70

acting rank, no rising from his high-backed swivel chair to shake my hand, no apology for a cut-short holiday, all typical.

He's a consummate politician and a man-manager of few wasted words, saving most for budget battles with local politicians and the Home Office. I admire him, but I'm not sure I like him.

I tell him of the trouble I'm having locating Mr Knight's informant. He clearly knows nothing of his ACC's operational tactics, but that's his style, too, hands off the tiller until the storm breaks.

All he knows is what Knight told him on Friday evening on the phone and he runs through the conversation for me, as well as he can remember it.

Knight: 'Should have a clearer picture on this sabotage by this time tomorrow, sir.'

CC: 'Excellent.'

'Might need to see you on Monday.'

CC: 'Not for more resources, I hope.'

'No. No. We're getting there.'

CC: 'Good.'

'It's just that the final outcome may affect my personal position *vis-à-vis* the force.'

CC: 'In what way?'

'That conflict of interest is cropping up again and, with Mr Todd away . . .'

'When's he back?'

'Wednesday, but I anticipate a breakthrough before then.'

'Where is he?'

'Touring Ireland. No contact address.'

'Well, we don't really want to turn out the Gardai and the RUC to locate him, do we, until we're sure? When will that be?'

'One aspect of it could be within twenty-four hours, the whole job lot by midweek.'

'Good. Excellent.'

'It looks like my last case, sir.'

'Surely not. Feeling ill, are you?'

'Sick, certainly. I won't be able to do the interviews.'

'That off colour?'

'It's not entirely that. All things considered – and I'll explain on Monday – I just feel it's time to go.'

The chief instructed Knight to take the load off himself by delegating any positive developments over the weekend, take it easy and see him at five today to discuss the whole situation in detail; the slot his secretary gave to me.

A macabre feeling overtakes me of wearing a dead man's shoes.

We don't chew over it long, me needing time to think, he running late for a council cocktail party. And what I'm thinking as I drive home is this: Was Knight planning to use retirement on health grounds as a cover for some sort of domestic involvement? Something to do with the middle case at Thorne's depot?

Twice now he'd talked of going – to his widow and to the chief. In the middle of a major inquiry? Why would he do that?

Because he knew – or, at least, feared – what the outcome was going to be. A family scandal?

I'm home reasonably early for boiled ham and buttered cabbage, a traditional Irish dish. Em, in red leggings and a white shirt that all but buries her, explains that she'd been too busy all day with almost a fortnight's washing and ironing to cook anything fancy. I tell her I'd have bought a box of prime steak had I known.

She asks about my day. Having heard me out, she sums it up brutally, but honestly. 'You've not got very far, have you?'

The black Bakelite phone, fifties, but still about the youngest item in the lounge, rings raucously. I pad bare-footed across the beige carpet in front of the empty fireplace with its Victorian flowered tiles.

'Hazel,' says Hazel before I can give the number.

'Getting very far?' I ask, mainly for the benefit of Em who's draped on the two-seater which she, in turn, has draped with material that looks like an Aztec rug.

'Well . . .' Hazel sounds undecided.

On her pub crawl, she came across a drinking mate of Hicks' who'd seen him last night, she recounts. It was soon after seven. Hicks was walking through the cobbled market square in Newark with a four-pack of strong lager under his arm.

Hazel begins to read from her notebook. 'His pal suggested they dropped into one of their regular haunts for a pint. "Keeping my head down," replied Hicks. "Trouble."

' "What sort?" asked his pal. "Big trouble," replied Hicks. "I'm getting out of it."

' "Where to?" asks his mate. "I'm fucking off to France as soon as I've got all my dough together," Hicks answered.

'His pal describes him as very jumpy. He kept looking around the square, couldn't get away fast enough. Acted like a fugitive, says his mate, as if someone was after him. Unusual for him. Normally he's Jack the Lad. Wouldn't say what the trouble was. There was no mention of him being on bail on the stolen credit card charge.' She pauses, done. 'What do you make of it?'

It's a question I often ask fellow detectives myself when I can't fathom something out. 'Do you believe him?'

'Absolutely.'

I don't know what to think so, cruelly, I turn her question back on her. 'What's your reading of it?'

'Well, it means he's around and about.' Hazel's voice drops. 'Or at least he was twenty-six hours ago.'

'Yes,' I agree, 'but has he already been to France, done the business for Silent, and is now going back again on a fresh mission or what?'

Unsurprisingly, Hazel doesn't know.

I tell her to check neighbours at his old bedsit and to drive out to Melanie Dexter's cottage to see if he's turned up there and, if so, to ring me again.

'Progress?' asks Em when I replace the phone.

I tell her I don't really know. No more calls; we go to bed, me reading long after Em has gone to sleep over her sonnets.

8

D-Day

Rain this morning, just a gentle drizzle, an Irish-style soft, not worth wearing a mac on the walk from the car-park to the office.

Hazel worked late last night but is still here ahead of me. As it should be in a public service with a bit of discipline and regard for rank. Keep this up and I'll reward you with a first-rate annual assessment, I'm predicting.

She looks bright-eyed, not hungover from her trawl round the pubs. She is wearing a suit, cornflower blue, high collar, short skirt, just above the top of the knee.

I'm in the same grey suit. I only have two; both grey, one light, one dark which I don't want to crease. I'll need it for Knight's funeral tomorrow when there'll be a big turn-out of top brass. It's already occurred to me that I really ought to extend my wardrobe by buying a new one for the promotion interviews.

Hazel follows me into my office, soundless in flat navy blue shoes. She is holding two messages in her hand. 'Forensics,' she announces. 'There's a clear thumb print on the postcard. Hicks'. His handwriting, too.'

So, I think, setting down the red box and Hazel's file on the desk and sitting down behind it, he did get to France, penetrated the saboteurs' cell, got his info, fixed a debriefing date with his handler and came back again.

'But . . .' She is still standing. '. . . they say the postcard was made in Britain.'

What a bloody case, I moan inwardly. Like lacing up your shoes as a kid. Pull one end out the shoe and the other disappears into it. 'Maybe Knight issued him with a pad of blank cards.'

Hazel pulls a face. 'You'd have thought that with a three hundred advance he'd have been able to afford to buy his own over there, and a picture one at that.' She stops for a second, another thought forming. 'And you would have thought he'd send his lady a card, too.'

I'm getting bad vibes about Hicks. He's used Melanie's place as cheap lodgings, I suspect. 'She's still not seen or heard from him?'

She shakes her head. They'd had another long chat last night. 'Neither sight nor sound nor postcard.' Nor had ex-neighbours at his old digs seen him since he'd moved out.

She stills her head as she studies the second message – a copy of the fax the Intelligence constable had dispatched to the Ministry of Defence with details of the wartime army service of Knight's father. She tuts. 'No reply yet.'

'So,' I recap, 'we know Hicks went because his dabs are on the card. We know he's back because of that Sunday sighting in Newark market square.'

'And we know he is talking of going back again,' says Hazel with a deadpan face. 'What we don't know is when or why.'

Why is easier to debate than when. 'Could it be that he met up with Silent Knight, gave him what he'd got and is being sent back again to get further gen?'

'In which case, he'd want a further payment.' She tries to look on the bright side with a smile to match. 'Maybe he'll come round to collect it.'

'There's only one thing to do.' I pull an A4 pad out of my top drawer and begin to list today's assignments.

'Find Hicks – Urgent,' I write, then look up at Hazel, still standing before me. 'Shall we put out a wanted for questioning on him?' she asks.

Not a bad idea, I concede, but I restrict it to sub-division only, not region-wide.

'Let's try Powers' daughter,' she volunteers. 'If they're still friendly . . .' She tails off, no need to say more.

I write down 'Powers' daughter' and put H. W. alongside it, her initials. Without consultation, I add: 'Confirm Powers' story with station sergeant' and initial that to myself.

As I do so, Hazel reports, 'Nothing from surveillance on Lincs-line and its vessels. Want 'em maintained?'

I nod. They've been on dockside guard now for almost two weeks, but there's no way I'm going to call off a watch ordered by an assistant chief constable. The minute I lift observations the bombers will blow up something and, with it, my promotion chances. If they don't strike, I can always blame Knight when the ACC in charge of finance starts screaming about the overtime being run up.

I look up. 'Know what I can't follow?' Several things, to tell a private truth. One will do for now.

I lean back in my solid armchair, not swivel. 'Hicks gets bail and drives the pick-up back to the Trentside club. He's had no trans-port since he was banned. He has a lift – "departing in style" he says – waiting down the road. Knight wouldn't chauffeur a mole to the bus station, railway terminal or ferry port or wherever Hicks was going.'

'No,' Hazel agrees, smiling slyly. 'That would be a job for a sergeant or below.' Her smiles fades. 'Check his diary against the time.'

I open the red box, find his diary and the day Hicks was bailed. At the time of his release, Knight had scheduled a meeting with

Chief Superintendent Dale. 'Check with Prof' goes on the list against me. So does 'Reinterview Mrs Knight'.

'Put me down against Mel,' says Hazel. 'Hicks' lift picked him up at the club, then drove him to Mel's to collect his things. Maybe she saw his transport.'

I do as I'm told, then fiddle further into the red box and extract the accounts of Arc Air, Trentside Golf and Country Club, Thorne Meat Depots and Combined Counties.

'Something else is bugging me from last night's reading,' I resume, letting her know I was working, too, proffering the file towards her. 'We can't assume these are private papers, nothing to do with the case. There's no family connection with Combined Counties. The rest, yes. But not Combined Counties.'

'Mmmmm,' says Hazel pensively, but she can only come up with a non-explanation she offered yesterday. 'Knight won't have been checking on Powers' financial status for a piddling hundred-pound surety.'

She's not accepting the file, wanting nothing to do with financial matters.

'We need company profiles.' I drop the file on the desk, pick up my pen and write, 'Claude.' No one ever uses the real first name of the inspector from the Fraud Squad. Few even know it and I doubt if he'd answer to it if they did. Everyone calls him Claude from Fraud.

Relieved at being off the hook, Hazel finally picks up her returned case file, musing for a moment. 'Hicks will have spent his three hundred advance – or a good part of it – on his first trip.'

She's talking as she thumbs. 'Yet Knight didn't withdraw any more dosh on Saturday from the informants' fund against the coded account . . .' She pauses till she finds what she's looking for. '. . . K2 or 6IW. Odd that?'

I don't ask why, just think: Maybe he dropped dead before he could.

She'd called at the Fairways on her way in. There was nothing in the mail. 'I mean, if I was Hicks, having completed my assignment, I'd be hammering on the door now demanding the balance before I undertook a second mission.'

I nod. 'Perhaps that's what he meant when he told his mate on Sunday that he was off to France when he'd collected up all his dough.'

I add another note. 'Check with Miles if Hicks has collected his back pay.' I can think of nothing left to do.

Hazel can. 'We need to know for sure what that postcard says.' She glances down at the photocopy. 'We can't have decoded it, can we? Otherwise, the meet would have been a day earlier at some bloody French zoo.'

'No,' I concur, writing down 'Chase MoD re codes'.

I look up. 'We also need to know what the file references mean.' At the bottom of a lengthening list I write down 'K2/6IW'.

Hazel gives a tiny mousy squeal, as though she'd just been mildly molested and can't make up her mind whether she enjoyed it or not. Her wide mouth hangs wide open, gaping. 'Look.'

Now she is pointing with a crooked index finger down at my pad. I look and see nothing I don't already know. 'Turn it upside down,' she urges.

I turn it upside down. K2 upside down looks like K2 upside down. 6IW reads MI9.

Ring, telephone, ring, I plead. It stays silent.

Most of the morning I've been on the phone. Four times I was rerouted through the Ministry of Defence switchboard, chasing yesterday's fax that no one will admit to seeing, each time telling the story in full, never once being stopped in mid-flow, before the buck was passed on.

Finally I finished up in Archives where, at least, I was asked a question: 'Have you the details of your late Mr Knight's father?'

Yes, as a matter of fact, from records Personnel gave the constable who originated the query. 'Major Cyril Knight, Intelligence Corps,' I read from the fax. I offered to arrange hand-collection of any sensitive material.

'Let's see if it's classified first,' Archives replied in a surprisingly youthful voice. He said he'd ring back. He hasn't.

I phoned Knight's home. Sister-in-law Stella answered. 'She's not up to seeing anyone today, I'm afraid.'

Chief Superintendent Dale was obstructive, wanting to know why I wanted to know about his meeting with Mr Knight. I told him it was a query over an informant's payment, adding: 'Chief constable's request.' Straight away he confirmed the time, which means Knight can't have collected Hicks after he'd returned the pick-up to the golf club. He asked how the inquiry was going. 'Fine,' I lied. He sounded disappointed. It was the only fun I've had all morning.

The station sergeant was more forthcoming. Sure, he remembered it. It wasn't every day an assistant chief turned up at his station.

'Hicks was put in a cell after his taped interview produced a confession to stealing the credit card, but nothing else. After his legal aid solicitor left, he was kept in the cell overnight. Mr Knight arrived next morning and asked for the cell to be opened.

'They were in there nearly three hours. Never known anything like it before; not from top brass. I looked through the spyhole now and then. Didn't want an ACC croaked in my cell, did I? Mr Knight was sitting next to him on the bunk, heads together over a pad of paper.'

Coaching him in codes, I surmise.

'Finally he came out and told me to arrange bail. Not in Hicks' own recognisance, he insisted. There had to be a modest surety. He suggested trying his boss at the Trentside club first –'

'Miles Thorne,' I interjected, cross-checking.

'Yes, but the steward told me he was out playing. So I was told to contact Hicks' former boss –'

'Geoff Powers, of Combined Counties.' I complete the sentence for him, then inquire, 'What's his background?'

There's the clucking sound of a tongue sucking a palate, disapproval at my ignorance. 'Around here he's Mr Rugger.'

Powers, I'm informed, sponsors Combined Counties rugby club. The sergeant isn't sure if the team was named after the meat business or vice versa. They were a sort of regional Barbarians, nicknamed the Yellow-Bellies, because of their buttercup-coloured strip.

He'd been a high-class player himself, county junior, Combined Services in his army days and then a B international until a back injury ended his amateur career. 'A great after-dinner speaker,' says the sergeant.

'And what did he have to say about being a bail bondsman?' I ask.

'He was a bit chary over the phone. Most sureties are when they're told their names have been put forward. They see hard-earned cash disappearing down the plughole. But eventually he came round and sprung him.'

'Powers claims you more or less sweet-talked him into it.'

I was expecting hot denials, but his reply is quiet and composed. 'You could say that, sir, I suppose.'

'Why?'

'Mr Knight's orders. He wanted Hicks out, but with a surety.'

'Why?'

'I didn't ask, sir.'

Well, a wise old bird of a station sergeant wouldn't question an assistant chief, now would he? 'Was Mr Knight still about the station when Hicks was eventually freed?'

'No. Said he had a meeting at HQ.'

I thank him, put down the receiver in such deep thought that I fumble its return to its cradle.

Knight couldn't have made a bigger show of freeing Hicks if he'd taken out a display advert in the *Newark Advertiser*. He'd told Brian Thorne at his wife's birthday party. He'd originally tried to get Miles to stand bail. When he couldn't contact him, he went to some lengths to arrange for Powers to stand surety.

And yet a hundred-pound bond on a minor steal-by-finding charge was totally unnecessary. He could have let Hicks go unconditionally on his own recognisance. What the devil was he playing at?

Hazel has been just as busy. No, Miles told her from his office at the golf club, Hicks had not yet turned up to collect his wages.

She circulated his 'wanted' photo and description to Newark and Southwell police stations. She dropped off the financial file with Fraud. She tracked down Powers' daughter who claimed she hadn't been in touch with Hicks, her steady from their student days, for months. She'd heard of, but never met, Richard Stone.

She raised Melanie again on her next-door neighbour's phone, but all Hicks had told her was that he had a lift waiting up the road to take him to the railway station. 'It's as though he and the driver didn't want to be seen together.'

The bad vibes about Hicks return, redoubled. I glance sideways at my receiver. Ring, telephone, ring. It still stays silent.

Nothing better to do, I go through the dossier I speed read last night, Em sleeping at my side in bed. This time Hazel is sitting across the desk. The trouble with speed reading, I found in my college days, is that you don't take in every detail. To achieve that, I need debate and occasional note-taking to plant the detail in my mind.

'Let me see if I've got this spot on,' I tell Hazel.

Hicks met Richard Stone at college and remained a chum, drinking together now and then at two regular haunts just a short walk away from the houseboat's mooring close to the ruined castle at Newark.

The *Yorkshire Tyke* belonged to sister Zoe who'd lived there since she dropped out of university. Her brother moved in after he lost his job at Lincsline shipping company further up the Trent and left his digs.

Hazel stops nodding. 'He was bitter and twisted.' Not the most politically correct of descriptions in view of his Richard III-type back, I think, smiling to myself. 'Zoe was furious about his treatment, spitting blood. I've seen her letters to Lincsline.'

'Were they right to sack him?' I ask.

'According to workmates, he made a few admin cock-ups, but no more than . . .' Hazel looks up to the ceiling in the general direction of Dale's temporary abode. 'Whether it was right or wrong, it's a motive, isn't it?'

There's no disputing that, so I ask about sister Zoe, looking down on a criminal records photo of a pale, pinched face, hard for someone so young.

'Younger than her brother, but she's the brains,' she replies. 'Both parents dead, but they left their children reasonably well provided for.'

The *Tyke*, for instance, cost fifteen thou paid for in cash when Zoe had to leave her student quarters.

'Why did she drop out?'

'Funked her first-year exams. Spent too much time on animal sabbing and not enough on studying.'

The third picture is shuffled to the top of my papers – Rex Lynch, dark and thin-faced, in the MoD fire brigade uniform he disgraced by helping himself to government property. Had a good record till then. Blamed domestic difficulties for his downfall. 'Young wife having a bit on the side,' Hazel explains.

'How did he meet Zoe?'

'His wife cleared off while he was inside. They split the proceeds of the house. He rented a caravan, bought his old green truck and set up as a dilly man.'

A dilly man, I shudder. Emptying cesspits and septic tanks on caravan parks and boating marinas that aren't connected to main sewers.

'We think he called at the houseboat touting for business,' she goes on.

So there they were – the three of them. Lynch literally in the shit, Richard embittered by his sacking, Zoe enraged by man's inhumanity to animals. An explosive combination.

I can imagine them now, burning the midnight oil, huddled over maps, each feeding off the others' hate, plotting to get even.

I remember what Knight told me, recalling his Ulster days, in one of the few chats we had. 'Only a small percentage of terrorists are freedom fighters. They're not in it for flag, green or red, white and blue. Those that aren't psychos want the buzz, the status and the money.'

Two decades ago, Zoe Stone, I conjecture, would have been in the Baader-Meinhof group or the Red Brigade. She'd missed out on a generation of anarchy, was too young for the great street industrial battles of the seventies and early eighties, so animal lib would have to do; anything to cause a bit of chaos, get talked about and have a go at the establishment and the state police.

And it becomes a way of life, a weekly jolly. They hijack peaceful protests and turn them into riots, lots of flowing blood and cracked bone, much of it belonging to police officers.

They know the publicity business. Peaceful protests don't get a line in the papers or a single shot on TV. There has to be violence, blood, before the media will stir their arses.

Next year they'll be shedding blood – our blood – on behalf of the Front Against Flower-Pressing because it's cruel to plant life; any excuse for a get-together, a demo or a picket or a bombing.

Her brother's sacking was a heaven-sent excuse, a real motive. And Lynch? He was probably going along with it for the sex.

They target Lincsline. Richard has the inside info, Zoe some chemical expertise from her student days, Lynch a fireman's knowledge of bomb-making and of sewers for the money drop.

I sum it up. 'They ran rings round us and when we screwed them over the ransom they made sure the whole world knew. Now they are somewhere in France planning an encore and we haven't a clue when or where.' Anxiety claws at my gut.

'But that', Hazel points out, 'is jumping from case one to case three, leap-frogging case two.'

'Have any of them any connection at all, the slightest link, with the Thornes?' Hazel is already shaking her head. 'I mean, did Richard ever work there? Was Lynch ever turned down for a contract there?'

She cuts me short. 'They're on mains sewers. Silent had us check and double check. Nothing.'

I sit back, facing up to it. 'Thorne Meat Depots doesn't fit the pattern, does it?' She shakes again. 'They keep meat, not livestock, if you ignore the herd of prize cattle, a sideline. No claim of responsibility, was there? No threats of reprisals?'

'No,' she agrees. 'Unlike both hits on Lincsline.'

'Which means, if the Stones and Lynch didn't do it, who did?'

She keeps her head still.

'Someone in his family?' My heart is sinking. Just as Knight's must have done when he covered this ground all alone, the way he always operated. 'Why? For insurance? Subject to what Claude says, the business looks good.'

Hazel's head is still; not helping me any more.

'Let's put ourselves in Knight's place.' Suddenly the seat I covet is not at all comfortable; hot, in fact. 'OK.' It is taking time to settle into the role.

'Right. I'm Silent Knight. I'm leading a hunt for a gang of saboteurs who have made a public monkey out of me and my force after bombing a cattle boat. Next month the attack is on my own family. I do the right thing and delegate that inquiry to a subordinate. While he's away on holiday, there's a third case, same target as the first.

'I take charge again, treating them as a series, a campaign. But the middle case begins to stick out like a sore thumb. It doesn't fit the pattern. I suspect someone in my family has pulled a carbon copy crime. Why? For financial gain. Who? Brother-in-law, nephew? Let's not speculate who or why now.

'Enter Hicks, snapped by that street camera in the act of trying to make a withdrawal from the ransom fund.

'He is socially associated with Richard, who my able aides, Todd and Webster . . .' Hazel smiles with forced coyness. '. . . have already drawn my attention to as a possible suspect – a lead I've neglected.

'Hicks tells me all. I'm convinced he's just a minion, left behind with a cash card to create confusion. The big three have fled, taking with them knowledge of where the next reprisal will take place.'

Hazel interrupts the flow. 'If you ignore Zoe's last phone call to Lincsline. "D-Day plus one," she said.'

I am so deep into the role that I do ignore it. 'My priority is to find them. Must be. Stop the next explosion and the danger to innocent life that may entail. Whether there's a fraudster in my family takes second place to that, surely?'

Hazel breaks in again. 'Find the bombers and you'll find out the answer anyway.'

I nod vigorously. 'Hicks thinks he knows where they could be. Somewhere in France – a country known to him from grape-picking, where he speaks the lingo. I offer him a deal. Locate them and report back. There's cash and indemnity in it for you. I give him an advance and teach him codes so he can report back from the hide-out without fear of blowing his cover.'

More meditation. 'I don't altogether trust Hicks.' No cop does any paid informant, I tell myself, no need to tell Hazel. 'So, to keep him on a long lead, I charge him with a minor theft and grant conditional bail which means he must return to this country.'

'Why not,' Hazel is speaking slowly, in thought, 'on the basis of Hicks' statement implicating them, issue warrants for the arrest of the trio?'

There's no quick answer from me, so she continues. 'Knight could have co-opted the French police in the hunt for them. Catch them and let Hicks turn Queen's Evidence and appear for the prosecution at the trio's trial.'

'Because . . .' My answer comes just as slowly. 'Maybe . . . Well, I have to catch them first. I don't know how long that's going to take. Meantime, they are going to blow up something else.'

I am warming up again. 'Maybe Hicks' evidence against them is thin, nearly all hearsay. There's no Forensics to tie them to any arson?' She shakes her head. 'Maybe his testimony, as it stands, wouldn't pass the test of an extradition proceedings.'

Hazel looks down and away. 'Would you, in Knight's place, tell the gendarmerie what you were up to?'

'Why? Hicks is a private citizen. It's not as if he was a policeman undercover on their patch, is it?'

'No. But he is a police agent. And Knight was, by his very nature ... well ...' She takes the plunge, head up again. '... more cautious than you.'

I can't decide, and don't answer.

'Bearing in mind what Zoe said on the phone to Lincsline. "D-Day plus one." '

I'm not sure what she's driving at and still stay silent.

'Today's June 6th.'

D-Day. Christ. After last year's massive commemoration, this year's anniversary is passing me by amid last month's VE Day celebrations. D-Day plus one, the day my own grandad hit the beach. Are they planning something tomorrow? In Normandy perhaps?

'Put like that, well, yes, I just might ring the gendarmerie,' I finally concede, chilled by the thought.

Hazel has been on the phone for five minutes to a number Interpol gave her, talking French fairly well – or so it sounds to my schoolboy's grasp on the language which collapsed on the hurdles of auxiliary and irregular verbs.

She seems to be getting the usual runaround from various departments. Suddenly her face breaks into a smile and her voice back into a language I can understand.

She hands the receiver on to me. 'Chief Inspector Dubal,' she says. 'Speaks better English than you.'

I introduce myself. I explain I've taken over the running of a case from my chief who has died suddenly, leaving me in the dark about certain lines of inquiry. He clucks sympathetically.

'He had a lead in France,' I go on. 'He dispatched an agent, a civilian, in pursuit of it to –'

He butts in. 'We must exchange certain formalities, must we not?'

'Why, yes,' I agree, holding back a sigh of frustration. From his point of view I could be a journalist fishing for info. Or a saboteur trying to find out how close we are behind.

I give my phone number, he his fax number. We hang up.

Hazel has gone upstairs to get the chief's office to fax Dubal with proof of identity on headed notepaper. On the way back she'll pick up sandwiches and coffee from the canteen. She'd forecast a long wait. 'You know how these French love their lunches.'

So I sit here alone by the phone which still doesn't ring. Bell me you bugger, I beg. Somebody. Anybody.

9

The bell rings when I have a mouthful of cheese and pickle. I manage 'Hallo', sounding like Quasimodo. I have humped backs on the brain.

'MoD Archives here.' The same youthful voice introduces himself as a colonel, making me think that I'm in the wrong public service for rapid promotion.

'No need to scramble or anything.' A light laugh. 'Nothing sensitive. Your chief's widow is right. MI9 was disbanded after the war. A Major Cyril Knight did serve in it.'

I have swallowed. 'As?'

'Lecturer and decoder.'

MI9 handled prisoners-of-war, he explains. They trained troops in how to avoid or escape from capture. They taught high-risk outfits like, say, bomber crews how to communicate from behind the lines if they were shot down and taken.

PoW camps became valued sources of intelligence, he continues. Their inmates got about the countryside in working parties and could report home on enemy troop movements or pin-point bombing targets. To get the information past Nazi censors, many were taught the techniques of coding letters home. They were sent to fictitious relatives at UK addresses – MI9 letter-boxes.

All this is new to me, fascinating, and I say so.

'There's nothing secret about it,' the colonel replies. 'You'll find books on the subject in any public library. Some actually give examples of various codes.'

'Various?' I query, slightly unsettled.

'Major Knight was an expert in most.' My sigh must be audible to him. 'Want to send me a sample?'

'Sure,' I reply disconsolately, 'but I was hoping for a speedy breakthrough.'

He pauses. Then: 'Tell me, has the dateline got any lines underneath?'

'No. Just K2, Monday.'

'Pity.'

'Why?'

'Underscoring sometimes gives the key to what code is being used.'

I remember a query I raised with him in my earlier call. 'Did this K2 mean anything to you, by the way?'

'Sorry, no. It wasn't the major's department, on his files or anything like that.'

'Well . . .' I'm about to take up his offer, send him the photocopy.

He breaks in. 'Tell me about Mr Knight's contact. Bright, is he?'

'A qualified sportsground worker.'

He laughs again. 'Pioneer Corps material.' Fit for digging trenches, he means, and not much else. A bit cruel about someone who'd mastered French where I failed.

I recall what the custody sergeant told me. 'Mr Knight only had three hours to coach him.'

'Lot of short sentences in the message, are there?'

'Lots.'

'In that case –' his tone lightens – 'try the reverse alphabet. The least sophisticated of them. Discarded because it was too simple.'

'How's it work?'

'Take a piece of paper. Write out the alphabet across it, then directly underneath reverse the order – Z to A. Take the first letter in the first word of every sentence. Sentence, mind you. There must be a full stop. Go to the start of that sentence. The first letter. Substitute for it the corresponding letter in the reversed alphabet. Simple.'

'Mmmmm,' I hum unenthusiastically.

'If it doesn't work, whack it down to me. OK?'

'OK,' I say.

'Good man.'

Across the top of my pad is:

A B C D E F G H I J K L M N O P Q R S T U V W X Y Z
Z Y X W V U T S R Q P O N M L K J I H G F E D C B A

'Dear Andy,' I read.

'W,' says and writes Hazel.

'I've arrived safely.'

'R.'

'Very good trip.'

'E. Makes WRE. Keep going,' Hazel urges.

'Wonderful weather,' I read.

'D.'

'WRED?' I query. 'Shit.'

She studies my pad. 'But . . .' Slowly. 'Knock off the greeting and it becomes RED.'

I look at the photocopy. 'Sorry. The greeting has a comma, not a full stop.' I explain again what the Archives colonel told me.

She looks at me, irritated. 'Go back, missing it out.'

I go back.

'I've arrived safely.'	R
'Very good trip.'	E
'Wonderful weather.'	D

I look at her. Her head is down. 'Go on.'

I go on.

'Terrific grub.'	G
'Francs running low.'	U
'Great coastline.'	T
'Good digs.'	T
'View superb.'	E
'I'm in with a good crowd.'	R

I was expecting that mousy squeak of hers, but she makes no sound. 'Jesus,' I sigh tremulously.

She looks at me. 'That can't be it.'

I shake my head.

'Well, go on then,' she says impatiently.

I go on.

'Have been to D-Day beaches.'	S
'Zoo soon.'	A
'Get yourself over here.'	T
'My lemon tea is getting cold.'	N
'Let's talk Friday.'	O
'Love to mum.'	O
'My best.'	N

I throw myself back in the chair, repeat, 'Jesus.'

'Red Gutter. Sat noon.' Hazel reads it out loud again, as if she can't believe it. 'Hicks was setting up the meeting.'

An appointment with death, as far as Knight was concerned, I brood.

We both fall silent, eyeing each other. 'You don't think . . . I mean, Hicks was talking about big trouble. Could it be . . .' She goes no further, doesn't have to. The same ghastly thought is stirring in me.

Knight had turned Hicks. When he got to the saboteurs' cell in France, had they U-turned him and ordered him back here to kill?

'I'll talk to the pathologist.'

The phone rings again. Marvellous, isn't it? When you want time to think, it never bloody well stops.

I snatch it up. 'Yes,' I snap.

'Dubal, Cherbourg.' A fruity voice.

'Chief Inspector.' My greeting is hearty, trying to make immediate amends.

'You give the appearance of being very busy.' He's not letting me get away with my initial rudeness.

I sigh. '*Oui.*' I can't remember the word for 'Sorry' so: '*Mon regrets.*' I do remember my Maigret and add, '*Patron.*'

He laughs delightedly. I discovered on a weekend with Em in Paris that the French will forgive you almost anything if you have a bash at their lingo, no matter how badly it comes out.

'I have been anticipating hearing from Mr Knight,' Dubal continues. 'I am sorry to learn the news of his death.'

So surprised am I that I'm rather rude again and fail to thank him. 'You have heard from him before?'

'Yes. On Friday, May 26th. He phoned to say that he was in command of a search for saboteurs connected with animal liberation and responsible for two or three outrages.'

Two or three, I'm thinking. So Knight hadn't made up his mind, either.

'In the most recent case, their full demands having not been met, they had made a threat which they had not yet carried out. In that case, he had arrested someone on the outskirts of the case . . .'

He means 'periphery' but I'm not going to correct him.

' . . . someone he was intending to use as an *agent provocateur*. He had reason to believe his three main targets were in hiding somewhere near here. He wanted us to know, out of courtesy, that he had dispatched his agent. I have heard no more since. Is there a problem?'

Well, yes, there is. For starters, how much do I tell this guy? Well, he's being honest with me. And I need him. I'll give him the lot, I decide.

Most of the operational secrets died with Knight, I explain. His informant appears to have returned safely home from Normandy, but has disappeared again, so we can't find out yet what he knows.

'What we know – or at least think we know – is that the terrorists have pledged reprisals tomorrow.' I explain Zoe's 'D-Day plus one' threat.

'In your country or mine?'

'Not sure. All I can say with certainty is that both previous attacks were here, both connected with the meat trade. One a cattle boat. One a frozen meat store. The next target, we think, will be another cattle boat from the same shipping company as the first.'

'Do their boats come here?'

To beat the blockade, they must land somewhere in France, it occurs to him faster than me. I promise to find out where and when.

'Do you wish me to seek the suspects?'

'Well . . .' I hesitate. 'The evidence against them is very thin, incomplete. I doubt if we have enough to issue warrants yet.'

'Yes, but if we catch them in the act . . .' he suggests and I can almost see him shrugging.

Yes, indeed. Does it matter where they serve their time as long as we prevent that next attack? 'I'll send you photos and descriptions.'

Dubal makes his counter offer. 'And I will make discreet inquiries to see if we can establish their whereabouts here. If so, we will observe. If not, we will shadow any cattle boat you name to us. Agreed?'

'*D'accord*,' I agree.

I put down the phone, wishing I'd asked one more question. I nearly snatch it up again.

But Hazel, who has had her head down over the photocopied card throughout, not taking the slightest interest, is looking at me excitedly, hurrying me up.

'What?' I ask rather harshly, more annoyed with myself than her.

Hazel tells me what.

'Jesus.' I reach for the phone, dial MoD Archives, but am told the colonel is away from his desk, and he'll phone back. Down goes the receiver. 'Hell.'

Things are moving so fast now, after yesterday's slow start, that I have to keep the momentum going.

I pick it up and call the pathologist. I have to wait till someone drags him from his lab. It gives me time to slow my thoughts down, thinking through what I'm about to ask, getting it about right.

'Yes, Sweeney.' The doctor knows me well.

'Mr Knight,' I begin. 'I know that there's no question other than that he died from heart trouble. How could that fatal attack have been, well, brought on?' I have hit the wrong words.

'Over-exertion. Stress. He'd been warned. His family doctor told me so.'

'Yes, but . . .'

He won't let me finish, find the word I need. 'A pleasant stroll on the flat is one thing. Scrambling up and down rough terrain like Red Gutter watching for birds is another. Madness.'

I'm not going to explain that Knight wasn't bird-watching, just keeping a secret rendezvous, or that he had driven his car most of the way. 'Could it have been –' finally I find it – 'provoked?'

'How?'

'Someone tricking him into giving chase, for instance? Or giving him a scare?'

'How?'

I don't know, so, clutching, 'That scorch mark on his shirt.'

'Friction on the fabric in the fall.'

'Could it have been – oh, I don't know – someone pushing him in the chest, someone with a cigarette in his hand?'

He snorts. 'Think about it. You push with the palm of your hand. The cigarette would be between the fingers facing away from the palm. A hot pipe I might buy, but not a cigarette.'

'No.' I am beginning to feel foolish. 'I see.'

'You're not suggesting, are you, that we order a delay in the funeral and conduct another post-mortem because . . .'

'No.'

' . . . if so, it won't alter the cause of death.'

'I'm not doubting that.'

'Should think not.' Moodily.

I have questioned his professional competence, upset him. 'Sorry.'

'Tell you what.' He's friendly again. It's amazing what a simple 'sorry' buys you. 'Get a pipe-smoker to admit pushing him in the chest and down the gulley and you still haven't got murder. Manslaughter, maybe, but only if the pipe-smoker knew how ill he was.'

'OK,' I say miserably, deciding I'm more diplomatic when I'm ad-libbing.

'Any time.'

Only when I've put down the receiver and relayed the conversation does Hazel point out that Alan Hicks doesn't smoke anything, hates it, according to Mel Dexter. And how would he know of Knight's heart condition anyway?

'Trouble?' asks the colonel from Archives, returning my call.

'The reverse,' I assure him. 'Wonderful, in fact.' I tell him what's been achieved between us, adding, 'Just one small query.'

'Fire away.'

'If a phrase, rather than a sentence, ends with a semi-colon that's grammatically out of place, does that signify anything?'

'Let me see.' I hear him up to something, can't tell what. Soon: 'A full stop means the first letter of the sentence, as you know, a colon the first two, semi-colon, the first three.'

I return the phone to its cradle after fulsome thanks, look at Hazel, smilingly shaking my head in admiration.

The ZIP in 'Zip code'; in the address on the front of the card means ARK.

OK, Hicks spelt it wrong. But, as Hazel points out yet again, how would he know? I didn't myself when I was talking to Rodney Montgomery in Knight's garden only yesterday.

Alan Hicks had fingered Arc Air.

10

The registered office of Arc Air is Rodney and Anita Montgomery's biggish little cottage across the county border.

The village stands almost beneath the flight path to the regional airport. There are blue breaks among fast-moving clouds and an uninterrupted sight of an airliner so low overhead that I can just about make out faces of passengers staring out of the line of windows in the wide, white fuselage.

I'm solo this trip. Hazel has stayed behind, summarising her case file for urgent transmission to Cherbourg, and pin-pointing the movements of Lincsline cattle boats.

What we've decided is that we'll make no immediate decisions. We can't trust anyone in Knight's family. There's a chance that there could be a fraudster among them, acting on inside info to pull off a copycat crime – an insurance swindle perhaps. We'll have a better idea when we get breakdowns of their business affairs.

OK, Hicks has named Montgomery's air firm in his coded card to Knight. But do we really believe Rodney blew up that boat on the Wash to get the cattle trade switched from sea to air, and then blew up Thorne's cold stores to cover his tracks?

We can't trust Hicks, either, let alone find him. In security service terms, he could be a double agent. Tipping Knight off about Arc, albeit misspelt, hinting at more info to come when they met at Red Gutter, could be laying a false trail, luring him into a trap.

On every front we must proceed with caution and not go around getting heavy. The fact that the collars to be felt would have included the family of a police chief on the very eve of his being laid to rest was a consideration in that decision, admittedly. Imagine being wrong; doesn't bear thinking about.

'Play it by ear,' Hazel had advised. 'I'm a college-trained classical musician who must follow a score,' I protested. 'Slum it and busk it,' she insisted.

The front of the cottage is small, one of a pair with an entrance between them, joined at first-floor level in dark red brick. An unkempt garden, the hallmark of rented accommodation, is fenced off from the road. Clumps of herbaceous flowers stand in weed-clogged borders. The small lawn, mostly flowering clover, hasn't been cut or the edges trimmed.

Nothing in it suggests that Anita is doing what her mother and grandmother did – let flowers speak for her. Unless, of course, the deep green patches of clover remind her of young love in Ireland when Rod was on the Aldergrove run.

The white paint on the picket gate has peeled away here and there, exposing wood rot. Not a lot of cash flowing into this household, I'm deducing.

It's just a few steps to a green front door on which, in the absence of a bell, I tap. No response. Knock. Still none. Hammer.

Finally Anita opens it. 'Sorry.' A breathless smile becomes a worried frown when she recognises me. 'Nothing wrong, is there?'

'No,' I reply easily.

'With mum, I mean.'

'Mrs Thorne asked me not to bother her today.'

'Oh.' A frown is followed by a tiny smile.

Unable to tell whether she's relieved or puzzled, I ask for Rodney and am told he's not in, but I'm invited in anyway. She leads me through a small, shaded front room with old-fashioned furniture, two walls lined with books, and beyond the foot of the stairs. She apologises for keeping me waiting, explaining she was on the phone.

We pass through a light, tiled kitchen, sparkling clean, with modern appliances and fitted cupboards. Now she is telling me she had visited mum this morning, but, well, she worries about her, because it's a worrying time, isn't it? I nod at the back of her blue cotton shirt.

We enter a long, airy office as neat and up-to-date as the kitchen. The size of the cottage comes from its length, not from what little is seen from the front.

Head down, tidying up papers on an overflowing desk, she tells me the ferry passage to Brittany is booked and they will leave with mum mid-afternoon tomorrow. She talks as if in the mistaken belief that I was already privy to their plans. Her two children will miss playschool for a couple of weeks and accompany them, she goes on. 'They will take mum's mind off things, don't you think?'

I say, 'I'm sure they will,' thinking: So they are spiriting Mrs Knight away. She hasn't told me all yet. I'm sure she hasn't. But I can't grill her tomorrow – not on the day of the funeral.

She motions to a small, grey, swivel chair and perches her blue-denimed bottom on the cleared desk, giving me a serious smile. 'You've all been so kind.' I try to wave her thanks away, but she expresses them anyway.

I look down. 'Your mother said something . . .' I was going to say 'odd' but change to 'puzzling yesterday. You were there. "Beware of imposters, Mr Todd," she said.'

Anita nods, then sighs. 'She talks in riddles sometimes. Both of them. Comes with the job, I suppose.'

Not with my job, I vow. 'Any idea what she meant?'

She shakes her head absently. 'She's under a lot of stress.'

'Yes, but . . .'

'Both were being counselled, you know.'

Both? I think, startled. I knew Knight was, by his family doctor. The pathologist told me, but I'd assumed that was for his heart condition.

Saying nothing compels her to go on, rather lamely. 'You know. His heart problem, how to tackle it. Pressure of the job. All this security and secrecy got to him a bit and, through him, to her.'

Now she's making it sound more like a mental problem than a medical one, affecting them both. What's she suggesting? That her mum is suffering from some form of paranoia and for me to take no notice of what she says?

She switches off the subject. 'Now how can we help?'

Well, it was Rodney I came to see, I explain. She says nothing, forcing me on this time. 'I mentioned to him yesterday that we were seeking an informant of your father's. Name of Alan Hicks.' Her face registers nothing. 'I just wanted another chat about him.'

Finally she says, 'Never heard of him.'

I shrug, smiling. 'Your father was a, well, as you say yourself, a secretive operator . . .'

'You can say that again.' A sad smile.

'He was working on these three cases of commercial extortion.'

'Three?' She seems genuinely surprised.

I finger them off, thumb to little finger. 'The boat bomb down on the Wash.' A brief nod. Thumb to ring finger. 'Your Uncle Brian's place.' Another nod. Thumb to middle finger. 'And there's a third currently running.'

'News to me, that last one.' She sighs, almost a low whistle. 'No wonder he was under pressure.' She goes silent, in thought.

'At your mother's birthday party . . .' I'm ad-libbing slowly. '. . . which Rodney missed . . .' I wait a second. '. . . working . . .' She nods again. '. . . Mr Knight mentioned a breakthrough to your Uncle Brian.'

'Odd.' She frowns, pale blue eyes narrowed, interested. 'Why?'

'Like we've already said, he was very secretive.'

'Yes, but the middle case does involve Brian's property.'

The frown lifts; explanation accepted.

'Did he mention a breakthrough in the case to you?'

'No.'

'Did he, in your presence . . . mention . . .' I am struggling again. '. . . without giving a name that he'd arrested an employee at your cousin Miles' club?'

'Gosh. No. Not to me. Certainly not.'

So Knight hadn't broadcast the news about Hicks to the Montgomerys, I tell myself. If you believe her, that is. 'The lead, we think, came to him from Hicks who was working undercover for him, communicating in code.'

A touching expression, part poignant, part fond. 'Sounds like dad.'

'Trouble is we have the communication.' I deliberately hold back on her. 'But we can't crack the code. Passed down by your grandfather, apparently. He didn't, Mr Knight, in your childhood, pass them on to you, did he?'

Smiling, she shakes her head. 'Had he had a son, perhaps . . .'

'Pity.' I try to look downcast. 'We think our blackmailing bombers may be in Normandy and Hicks could be with them. It's just that Rod seems to go regularly to Cherbourg . . .'

'Every weekday, twice on Wednesdays, for the past two months since the High Court gave the all-clear.'

So Rod had underestimated the financial value of the cattle trade to Arc Air when we spoke to him yesterday, I note.

'They're returning from Holland now,' she goes on. 'Takes off again for France normally around five.'

I express surprise that they have kept the animal airlifts secret from demonstrators who had picketed – indeed invaded – other air cargo firms as well as barricaded air and sea ports.

She is flicking her head at a road map on the wall with a large black pin in it. Between here and the airport, she informs me, is a farm being used as a collecting point where calves are loaded into containers, then on to covered trucks which take the back lanes, avoiding the main terminal. 'The main contractor has managed to keep our connection with him very quiet, thankfully.'

A brilliant busk is welling. I must hit the right opening note. 'We were wondering if he would act as courier for some documents we have to get urgently to the police in Cherbourg . . .'

She is looking eagerly at me. 'I'm sure he will. Shall I phone?'

'Will he be there?'

She looks at several clocks on the cream wall which also has navigation charts held in place by white tape. 'Perhaps not. Pop round.' She gives me precise directions where I'll find him within the hour. Oddly, they will take me, not to the airport close by, but to another forty-five minutes away down two motorways.

Now she is dismissing my attempt at expressing thanks. 'The headquarters of the gendarmerie is right next to the airport, by the way, so –'

Over-eagerly I break in. 'You've been, then?'

'Just on a jolly. They take friends and relations if there's a seat free. A half-day trip. I only had time to nip to the supermarket.'

'Duty frees.' I try to appear envious. 'Recently?'

'End of April.'

Before Hicks was dispatched, I realise, but I need more on the travels of her family. 'Lucky you,' I enthuse. 'Mr Knight or your mother ever had a trip?'

'No. They like . . .' She pulls a pained face. '. . . liked to travel a bit more leisurely. We could have flown tomorrow, but mum prefers the boat and, besides, we need a car when we get to St Malo.'

'Some good golf courses round there, I gather,' I say, by-the-way fashion. 'Does Miles ever go?'

'Too busy at his own club, but Uncle Brian's flown a couple of times. It's their place in Brittany we're using.'

Casually as I can, I ask when, but Brian got his trip even earlier than she did.

'Nothing much to do, I don't suppose, until they rebuild his cold store.' She cocks her head, quizzically. 'Why these questions?'

Blast. I've overdone them, alerted her. 'I was wondering if any of them might have seen Hicks on their travels.'

It's a duff line and she seizes on it. 'Can't you ask them?'

I nod. 'I will.' If she finds out I've asked them already, I'm in a spot.

She doesn't pursue it. 'Do you think you'll ever solve it?'

'Oh yes.' I flash her my most confident smile. 'And when we do, it will be thanks in no small measure to your father.'

'Yes,' she says with a deeply affectionate sigh, 'he was a bit special, wasn't he?'

It's just a short detour off the M1 from the route Anita gave me to the spot on the wall map that was marked with a black pin.

A clay track up to the long, red-brick farmhouse is a bumpy ride which becomes squelchy in the pat-strewn crewyard behind dilapidated outbuildings.

A long, mud-splattered double-decked transporter, eight-wheeled, with closed blue sides, is parked ahead of me. From its opened back doors comes a cacophony of moos.

Next to the transporter is a much older, smaller lorry, wooden tail-gate down. Each side of the ramp chestnut paling has been erected funnelling towards an arched aluminium cage.

Two hefty young men, wellington-booted, roughly dressed, rougher looking, are at the top of the tail-gate. They are so busy, the upper bodies bent inside the back of the lorry, that they don't hear my engine above the farmyard noises. I switch off and watch, winding the window down. The smell of hot dung and fear floats into the car on sound-waves of sweaty panic.

No wonder this place is marked on the wall map with a black spot, I think.

A tan-coloured calf, so young it looks as though it should still be suckling its mother, emerges from the back of the lorry, running wildly, almost tumbling, down the ramp and into the fenced corridor.

Suddenly, it skids to a halt, like Sylvester, the cartoon cat, confronted by his bulldog enemy. It won't budge, refuses to take another step towards the cage.

Another follows, bewildered, running too fast, so that it canons into the lead calf which turns, trying to get back to the lorry. It falls on to its front knees, wedging itself side-on, blocking the gangway.

One by one, more calves poke their heads out, then stagger, weak-legged, into the heaving jam, getting nowhere.

One of the men shouts. He jumps from the tail-gate. In his hand is what looks like a thin black torch.

He runs to the lead calf and, with an opened hand, smacks its backside, but fails to dislodge it from the jam.

Now the man prods its rear with the long torch. The calf squeals and leaps on all fours into the air, like Sylvester on hot bricks.

A battery-operated cattle prod, I recognise. The boys in Special Ops once used one on a bullock that escaped from market, to corner and lasso it. They used one attached to a pole like a fishing rod, to avoid being kicked. With a fence to protect him, this stockman had dispensed with the attachment.

The calf makes a weaving dash into the cage. Ten or a dozen follow it in, some after the encouragement of the power prod. The door is swung shut and fastened. They seem to be gazing at me, with watery calves' eyes.

I'm a country boy who acknowledges that human existence has always depended on exploiting animals for meat and for milk and I'm not going to get sentimental about it; don't like to see it, though, I must confess.

Right now, more important matters worry me. Like can I find the saboteurs and stop them from blowing up something – or, next time, somebody – else?

Only now does the man see me, shouting above the crazed chorus to his mate who jumps off the lorry. Grim-faced, he strides purposefully towards me, carrying his prod, this one on a rod, like a rifle over his shoulder, at the ready.

'Police,' I call when he's still several paces away. Hurriedly, I fish for and flash my warrant card. 'Looking for the boss of Arc Air, Mr Montgomery.'

'Not here, mate.' He slows to a walk. His face dissolves in a relieved grin. 'Try the airport.' He, too, tells me how to get there.

I say thanks, start up and drive out through the brown, watery pats, thinking about the effects of a prod on a man with a dicky heart and wondering if it would leave a scorch mark.

Had I been an animal libber on a recce, I've a feeling I would have found out by now.

In the next village, by a brook with the water too low to babble, I stop at a red phone box and transfer the charges to my own direct line. 'How are we doing?'

Claude from Fraud has virtually done the business and wants to see me around six, Hazel updates me.

She'd established that Lincsline's boat, the *Lindum Castle*, the one with the bomb the army sergeant defused, is due in at Cherbourg tomorrow evening with a shipment of sheep.

'It's a likely target, isn't it?' she adds.

Yes, I agree privately. They started their campaign by planting a primed bomb in its hold, but sportingly gave us a warning with enough time to defuse it. When we screwed them over the ransom, they blew up its twin sister while we were watching the wrong bloody boat. Now they were going to sink their original target. Just think of the outcry, the outrage unless we stop them. On second thoughts, don't.

She'd faxed Chief Inspector Dubal full details, including the time of arrival, along with the case summary, pictures and the number and description of the green truck.

She'd added Hicks to the trio from the *Tyke* in case he'd doubled back there. She'd spoken to Dubal to confirm that the documents had arrived. 'What a sexy accent,' she adds dreamily. 'I wouldn't mind working for him.'

'What did he say, sergeant?' I inquire formally, feeling a rising tension within that has nothing to do with her.

'He's calling a council of war and did you want to attend? I said I thought you'd think it a good idea and would if you could.'

It is, I have to agree, and I will. I ask her to run off a second copy of the Cherbourg stuff and get Forensics to seal the envelope with a special tape that's easy for a snooper to open. It's just as easy to tell when it's been tampered with.

I ask her to bring it to a service station where the two motorways meet. 'Phone Dubal and inform him precisely what we're up to.'

'And what shall I tell Claude?'

I'm working out my timetable. I don't fancy the long trip back to HQ, an hour or more in conference and another half-hour driving home. Here I'm closer to home than the office. And that's where I want to be this evening – home with and close to Em.

I'm not, I vow, going to be one of those insecure senior officers who hang around the flight deck, pretending to be working, until the chief constable has gone home. Dale, for instance, is reputed to hang a spare jacket over the back of his chair and leave his office door ajar, so anyone passing will think he's just slipped away from the grindstone for a leak when he's long gone.

'To bring the stuff round to my home, between six and seven.' A bit bossy that, for an old mate. 'And tell him there's a bottle of Paddy's whiskey to be opened. Come, too, if you fancy it.'

'For Irish whiskey? No, thank you.'

'Dry white from the slopes of Connemara then.'

'Sold,' she enthuses.

The perimeter fence to the airport has been festooned with grimy white sheets with crudely scrawled slogans in black paint – 'Don't eat cruelty' and 'Meat is murder'.

On the grass verge, around the obligatory fire in an old oil drum, stand half a dozen pickets. All are as roughly dressed as the cattle handlers back at the crewyard. You can tell the men from the women by the beards – just.

Hazel, who has abandoned her car at the service station, gives them a cheery wave from the passenger seat. They'll get no recognition from me to raise their spirits.

Between us, I suppose, we sum up the great divide in this debate. Hazel, the townie who never queries how the meat on her plate gets there; me, the country boy, who knows and knows, too, that a vast and legal industry depends on supply and demand.

I don't doubt the sincerity of most of the campaigners. The only thing wrong with the Greenham Common women, for instance, in their long vigil against Cruise missiles, was that they were wrong. Had they won, the cold war would still be on.

The trouble with public demos is that they can't, by their very nature, be ticket only and so become open invitations to the malcontents and misfits and plain nutters who, in a perfect world, would send letter bombs and razor-blade packages to each other.

Eyes firmly to the front, I drive beyond them following the route

Anita gave which eventually leads to the main building – long, single-storey, all glass and darkly stained wood.

Behind it tower three grey hangars. Beside and in front of it are irregular lines of wooden huts and white, flat-roofed Portakabins.

On the half-glass door of the smallest is written 'ARC AIR' in colourful capitals; all the colours of the rainbow; strikingly different from all the other signwriting. Someone with schoolboy humour has hung a chip shop advert with a tubby man in a chef's hat and a bubble coming out of his mouth saying: 'Frying Tonight'. The hands of a clock on the black and white sign show five fifteen.

Smiling, I tap on the frosted glass. 'Come in' is called from behind it.

The crew room of Arc Air isn't much bigger than Knight's office which Dale has requisitioned. Most of the limited space is taken up by a large square table with four plain chairs around it.

In one, tilted back, sits a fair-haired, lanky man. He puts a green phone down to his white-shirted chest. 'Won't be a tick.' He resumes his conversation. 'This is all very well, sir, but . . .'

There's an assortment of clothes on pegs on the wall to the left. Clipboards hang in a line to the right. Straight ahead is a long window with a restricted view of the airfield through a wire fence with diamond-shaped linking. A silvery-grey plane is so close that not all of it is visible, just the rear end which has 'Arc Air' painted on the tail below a curved rainbow.

'So what the devil did happen then?' the man on the phone wants to know.

Through an open transom comes the heavy, sickly smell of aviation fuel and the sicker sound from somewhere unseen of calves calling for their mothers.

No wonder Arc Air is based in a cargo-only airfield. No holiday-maker about to depart in a kiss-me-quick hat would want to see what we're about to witness – calves jetting off to the slaughter.

'You'll put it in writing, I take it.' The man ends his conversation with an icy 'Goodbye'.

We introduce ourselves. He stands. His trousers are almost black, neatly pressed. 'Anita's been on. Yes, Rod says that's fine. Got it?'

Hazel pats her shoulder bag. 'He'll be along in a minute,' says the man. 'Just nipped to Maintenance.'

He throws out one hand languidly in an invitation to sit and

101

wait where we please and sits himself. 'Business good, I hear,' I say, unable to think of anything better.

'Now,' he replies with a quietly satisfied smile. 'First year was a bit slow.' He flicks his head towards the plane. 'Those brutes cost an arm and a leg.'

I nod out of the window. 'I like your colourful livery.'

'Snazzy, isn't it?' He smiles, delighted at what must be his idea. They use it on everything, letterheads, accounts. *Arc-en*-something is French for rainbow, he explains. He stirs in his seat. 'Charlie Disney, by the way. One of Rod's partners.'

'RAF together?'

'Yes.' We small-talk for a minute or two, me saying what occurred as I arrived at the airport, i.e. that its thrown-together feeling would make an ideal set for a 'Battle of Britain' film; he laughingly agreeing that it isn't Heathrow.

The thin, pathetic moos are drowned by the noise of an approaching motor bike. 'Ah,' he says, 'Rod and Betsy.' Betsy, I gather, is a two-stroke machine they use for local runabouts.

Soon afterwards, into the room walks Rod, in trousers and shirt that match Charlie's. He wears a peaked cap and black tie and tunic, too, with wings above the breast pocket and four golden rings at each cuff. As many as a group captain, I note, so he's given himself rapid promotion in civvie street.

'Hallo.' He seems pleased to see us again, Hazel anyway, and removes his cap immediately.

She produces the specially sealed envelope out of her shoulder bag, explaining she has made arrangements for it to be collected at the other end.

'Want a signature?' He takes it, but doesn't study the address as he drops it on the desk. Hazel says no.

He moves behind his partner. 'No problems?'

'No.' Charlie cranes his neck. 'But you'll never guess what!'

Rodney doesn't hazard a guess as he walks on to the window and gives the thumbs up. A yellow mobile lift on four chubby wheels chugs into view, a tin-hatted man at the controls. Rodney turns, small of his back against the sill, preparing to listen.

'Just had the MAFF on,' Charlie relates. All services, the police included, talk in initials. This, I surmise, is the Ministry of Agriculture, Food and Fisheries whose cabinet minister, a gentleman farmer, an old-fashioned Tory, has borne the brunt (and some letter bombs) of the protesters' rage with bemused resignation. 'Full of apologies.'

'Not before time,' Rod grumbles. He looks at us hard, but only to exclude us from more information.

He gets nothing out of me, either. We decided over tea at the service station to drop my probe into what members of the family were in France at the time Hicks was released. If Rodney goes home to Anita tonight and tells her, the whole family will soon know I've been asking questions about their movements.

I'll do it formally, in the presence of solicitors, if they want them, once the funeral is out of the way.

Hazel tells Rodney that the search for Hicks is still on. 'The gen on him is in there.' She nods at the brown envelope.

Behind Rod the yellow truck is making a return trip. On it is an aluminium cage, crammed with calves, eyes wide with confusion and fright. Even as it moves, its scissors lift is rising to a height, I presume, that will reach the out-of-view hold to the plane.

Hazel is praising the French police for their co-operation, building up to our request. 'There's a case conference in Cherbourg tomorrow which he . . .' She thumbs towards me. '. . . has to get to.'

On cue, I come in. 'Any chance of a lift?'

Rodney defers to Charlie, who says, 'Sure. There's room.'

Then Rodney explains he's off from tonight for the funeral and to get the family away.

'Same time tomorrow then,' Charlie breaks in. 'Pack your passport.'

I'll not ask him if I should pack a gun too.

11

The white front door to our place opens before the key is fitted. Em pulls it back, smiling. 'There's a very strange man waiting for you two.' From the lounge I can already hear Claude guffawing melodiously.

She kisses my lips lightly, draws her head back to speak again. 'Says he's investigating your expenses account for last week.' She has not dressed for company – khaki shorts with turn-ups well below the knees and a baggy cream T-shirt.

I slide in front of her, no mean feat in this narrow hallway. She welcomes Hazel with a kiss to her cheek. I walk on, talking ahead of me. 'But I wasn't working last week.'

'Then why were you claiming exes, I'd like to know?' says Claude, still out of sight.

It's an old routine he uses when he drops in to your office. Sometimes, when you know you have gilded the lily a trifle, it can be a mite unnerving.

I reach the lounge where Claude is on the three-seater. He has a number of thick files, all different colours, on the Aztec cushion at his left hand. His right is holding a tumbler with a stiff Paddy's which he raises towards me, grey eyes twinkling behind spectacles.

He doesn't get up. It would not be an easy manoeuvre. He's eighteen stone. With port and a cigar, he'd look like Orson Welles in that Sandeman advert. His suits – tonight's is dark blue pin-striped – always fit him immaculately. He's past fifty, could retire on full pension, but still loves his job, ploughing through cooked books day after day, discovering who's swindled what.

His technique is to painstakingly sort seized papers in files with coloured covers. Long hours of close reading have given him dark horn-rims that don't match his short, thinning silver hair.

Talking holidays, the girls head towards the kitchen from which the rich smell of bolognese comes. I'm glad it's not veal milanese.

Toe to heel, I remove my black slip-on shoes, then excuse myself to take the stairs that lead from the hall to two smallish bedrooms and an even smaller bathroom. Soon the whole place will be too small.

When I come down again, jacket and tie off, face swilled in cold water, Em and Hazel are sitting at a scrubbed pine table behind the door from the hall. Each has a glass of red wine in front of her. A tumbler of whiskey with a matching amount of water waits for me on the table.

I take a sip. The taste is strong and clean. I amble over the beige carpet to the three-seater, Claude making room by lifting the files on to his thick thighs.

We gossip a while, Hazel droning on about Chief Inspector Dubal and his sexy accent, Em smiling, too wistfully for my complete liking. She often mimics my accent from the next county, making it much broader than I think (hope) it is. She finally gets us down to business. 'Claude can't stay.'

'French lessons,' he claims, leering at Hazel.

'Neither can I,' Hazel says, turning down an invitation I assume was offered in the kitchen. 'Heavy date.' She nods at Claude. 'Not with him.'

'*Zut alors*,' sighs Claude, making us laugh.

'Right then.' I turn to him.

'What order?' he asks, businesslike.

Since I've spent the afternoon with them, I opt first for Arc Air. Claude shuffles a striped, multicoloured file to the top of the pile on his knees and slips out some accounts.

Founded two and half years ago, he begins. He gives the name of the third partner we haven't met. All sank their RAF pay-offs into it. The plane, a Merchantman, with a thousand flying hours on the clock for each of its thirty-five years, was bought from America at the cost of two and a half million dollars. Hazel whistles.

'Peanuts in that business,' says Claude. Mrs Knight was an investor – a quarter of a million pounds, which, he guesses, came from her late father's estate. 'The dates fit.'

I interrupt. 'Are Brian Thorne, his wife or son shareholders?'

'Not a penny in between them.' The bulk, he goes on, was put up by an American finance house. 'The second biggest investor, half a million, is the parent company of Lincsline, a multinational, Europe-wide in transport.'

He stops to let me think. Nothing's coming yet, apart from: 'Wasn't that a high risk?'

He shakes his head. 'The plane itself is substantial collateral. If Arc Air goes bust as a company, the creditors can sell it on and recoup.'

'Are they going bust?'

'First year was touch and go, massive overheads, but now, well, veal exports, that's big business.'

'How big?' I ask.

'Seven grand gross a trip and they're making two trips most days to either Rotterdam or Cherbourg. They'll be netting thirty to forty thou a month. The next accounts should put them well into clover.' Hazel whistles again.

'Thorne Meat Depots,' I request.

Claude feels inside a pale green file. 'Brian Thorne, his wife and son are sole owners. Solid as a rock. Never been in Queer Street.'

'Miles?' I query.

'An active director till a couple of years ago, drawing a substantial salary. Then his workload at the club must have got too heavy for day-to-day duties, but he remains on the board, unpaid except for a small annual fee.

'Black all the way in the balance sheets. Biggest single customer is the European Community. They've given them lucrative contracts for some years to store meat surplus. The insurance will cover the building replacement. The Thornes have nothing to worry about.'

'Not even with the Trentside club?'

Claude dips into a blue file now. 'Not in the long term, no. Major cash flow troubles at present, certainly. Miles is MD. He's pumped in more than he's so far taken out. Terrific outlay, meagre incomings in comparison.'

'Why no worries then?'

'Mrs Thorne owns the land. Miles' company running the club rents it from her. Even if that went through the hoop, another leisure company would move in. It won't close. The older golf courses get, the better. It's a long-term investment with the usual short-term problems.'

'And Combined Counties?'

A yellow folder is opened. 'Sound as a pound now. Dicey time five years back. Over-expanded into slaughtering as well as storing.'

'What's that mean?'

'They buy in at cattle markets or direct from farms, slaughter –'

I break in. 'Slaughter?'

'Now.' A single nod. 'They built their own on-site abattoir, state of the art. The costs got a bit out of control for a while. Why?'

I am thinking of the Shakespearian quote from Mrs Knight about hiding from the slaughterhouse, but don't say so. 'Any connection with Thorne?'

'Not in terms of stake-holdings, no. They rent each other's spare capacity. It's all invoiced. Nothing appears to have been creamed off.'

Claude awaits my views. I look at Hazel. On the mantelpiece, among framed photos of Em's stable family and my scattered one, is a Victorian clock, black slate and marble, so delicate that it tinkles rather than chimes. It's tinkling out seven. Her expression is anxious and I guess she is late for her date. 'Does this rule out Rodney?' I ask her.

She looks back at me. 'Why?'

'Well . . .' I shrug. 'Hicks names Arc in his coded card to Knight. It crossed my mind that his business was going badly. To corner the cattle trade, he gets someone to blow the opposition's boat out of the water.'

'Couldn't his RAF service in Belfast have given him the know-how to do it himself?' Hazel ponders out loud.

I don't know but I take her point. 'He blows up Thorne, too, to cover his too obvious tracks, create a diversion.' I stop for a second. 'But Lincsline are part owners of Arc Air. He'd hardly bite the hand that feeds him.'

'Means nothing,' Claude replies for Hazel. 'You find institutions and multinationals investing in the same companies, companies which will then cut each others' throats. As long as someone in their portfolio is making money, fine. They'll just jettison the loss-maker.'

All this high finance is a bit beyond me and I go quiet.

'What about Miles?' Hazel asks. 'He's so short of ready money that maybe he wanted to get his hands on the insurance and divert it to his club.' A weak theory is accompanied by a weak smile.

I'm stumped for ideas. 'We have to work out whether Thorne's association with Combined Counties is more than routine business. There must be something, otherwise Knight wouldn't have had their accounts in his red box.'

I have only one question left. 'Find anything in any account that sheds light on K2?'

'Not a mention,' Claude says flatly.

It's disappointingly inconclusive and the debate that follows is meandering, taking us no further.

Claude banters a bit as he finishes his drink, declining a top-up. Both he and Hazel depart soon afterwards. I see them off and watch them walking arm-in-arm down the front path towards their cars, Claude whispering pidgin French into her ear, Hazel laughing happily.

I wonder if they have as much fun as this on the force flight deck; guess not.

Em kept quiet through most of our discussion. She's like that. If she's not *au fait* (where do these bloody French phrases keep coming from?) with a subject, she stays silent.

Now we're alone in the kitchen, she stirring the sauce, me draining the spaghetti, she asks for and gets a fuller report.

Back at the table, the meal is interrupted by the Bakelite phone jangling away on an antique chest it shares with an overflowing bowl of colourful fruit and a fern that's trailing out of its earthenware pot.

'Jacko,' says the caller.

Jacko Jackson is the retired inspector who was with Hazel when Knight saved them from that bomber four years ago. He was at my side when I was wounded in the leg on the railway line two years back, his last assignment before retiring. All three of us – and Em, too – have remained in touch, a happy little crowd, lots of loyalty amid the mickey-taking.

His wife doesn't fancy Knight's funeral ('Nothing suitable in her wardrobe,' he says), making it sound like an optional social engagement. He naturally feels he must be there. He can't raise Hazel so what are my plans, he wants to know.

I cross-check with Em who backs out, claiming not to have anything dark to wear.

Jacko suggests meeting at the Fairways at eleven thirty. He doesn't want to call at HQ to collect us, chunters that he hates going back, having to sign in, wear an ID badge, feeling like an unwanted outsider in a place where he worked for ten years.

Suits me, I think, because I'll need to nip into the Fairways to see if there's anything in the post. I tell him the first thought, not the second, not chatting long, pleading that my meal is going cold.

After we've washed and dried the pots we sit, legs outstretched, side by side on the couch.

'Let me pick your female brain.' I do this often, have to, no real idea how a woman's mind works.

I begin slowly. 'You're fiftyish, married, one grown daughter, a

108

sister to whom you're close who's also married with a grown son. Right?' She is paying close attention. 'Someone kills your policeman husband.'

'Chance would be a fine thing,' she beams pleasurably.

This is her style and I know her flippancy will soon fade, so I press straight on. 'If someone in the family did it – and you knew it – would you report that someone to the police?'

'Of course.' A positive tone and suddenly serious face. 'You can't protect the murderer of your husband and father of your child whoever he or she is. That's obscene. You'd want justice for him.'

'Sure?'

'Certain. Why?'

'Because I think Mrs Knight has a shrewd suspicion . . .'

Em is back-pedalling. 'You didn't say think.'

'. . . that all is not well either with her husband's death or one of the cases he was working on . . .'

'You never said that,' she protests. 'You said, "If you knew." Not merely suspected or thought; knew the truth.'

'. . . and she's sort of flashing me hints, sending me code.'

She is shaking her head severely. 'Entirely different.'

'In what way?'

'Brief me properly first.'

I do, ending, 'I think Knight told more to his missus than she's letting on. Not the whole story. He didn't know the whole story any more than I do. But I think he suspected the Thorne arson could be a con. I feel that, too. I don't think it's connected with the Lincsline cases either side of it. If that's so, it's someone in the family. Knight could have confided that much to her.'

'Like you're telling me?'

'He gets a breakthrough when he catches Hicks. First he puts up Miles as surety for his bail. He gets the custody sergeant to phone his club. When he can't be reached, Knight suggests Powers, Hicks' old boss. Not only that, he breaks the habit of his secretive lifetime, to blab about Hicks to old man Thorne at a family party. It's as though he wanted someone in that family to know that he was getting close, that the cat was coming out of the bag.'

'Why?'

I have to look at this not entirely from a policeman's point of view. 'Say, I discovered your little brother was up to something naughty. First thing I'd do was to make sure I personally wasn't on the case.

'Then, because of my deputy's holidays or whatever, the file bounces back into my in-tray. Maybe – I don't know – I'd try to let him know the game was about up, pressure him into making a clean breast of it, turn up at the police station and confess. With a good enough story that could halve his sentence.

'Or, maybe . . .' I'm thinking of Thorne senior. '. . . it was the bonds of the Brotherhood, telling him without breaking any confidences to get himself a good story and a good lawyer.'

'Was Silent Knight a Mason?'

'Yes, and so is his brother-in-law.'

'Mmmmmm,' she hums, face disapproving.

'If it's just, well . . . a dark thought – absolutely no proof – but in Mrs Knight's place, you'd have to think of the consequences, surely?'

'Yes.' Em is silent for some time. 'Put yourself in her position. A widow at fifty. All those bleak, empty years ahead. You'd be confused, left in disbelief, by the suddenness of it. If his life had been deliberately taken away, and you were certain of it, you'd be angry and want justice.'

'And if you weren't quite sure?'

'Yes,' she repeats pensively. 'What if she officially reported someone in her family who was completely and utterly innocent? Say she shopped her brother-in-law or his son. Her sister would never speak to her ever again. Even worse, say she wrongly accused her son-in-law. Her own daughter might never bring the grandchildren round again, cut her completely. It would be a dreadful dilemma.'

'So, in those circumstances, what would you do?'

Several seconds' thought. 'What Mrs Knight's doing, I suppose.'

'Which is?'

'Throw out the odd hint and hope the detective succeeding my husband in charge of the inquiry is sharp enough to catch it.'

Her hand feels for and catches mine. Fingers entwined, they rest on the cushion between us. She likes feeling my fingers – sensitive, yet strong, she calls them. Actually, they are very long from all that clarinet practice from the age of ten. Now they only play on her. I disengage them, blow on the tips, warming up for a rhapsody. She laughs.

Among the fruit and fern, the Bakelite rings again. 'Control, sir,' says a young male voice. He's just had someone on claiming to be a police pensioner called Larry Dove with some urgent info for me.

I dial Larry's number. 'Hallo.' A weak wavering voice. I give my name and rank. 'Oh.' There's relief there now.

'Just had a strange phone call,' he says, almost out of breath.

'Who from?'

'Alan Hicks.'

I get him to go through it very slowly two or three times.

'Hicksey,' said the caller on a line so clear he sounded as though he was in the next room. 'Mel about?'

'Where the devil are you?' Larry demanded.

Hicks ignored it. 'Mel about?'

'Out. I've got the kids.'

'Where?'

Larry's turn to ignore it. 'What are you playing at?'

'Wotyarmean?'

'She's had the police round – a superintendent once and a sergeant twice.'

A slight pause. 'Wot they want?'

'You. They're after you.'

'What did Mel tell 'em?'

'Don't know. I wasn't there. She's enough worries on her plate. Come home and sort it out.'

A longer pause. 'Can't. Not right now.'

'Why?'

'I'm away for a few days.' Pause. 'In France. On business.'

'What bloody business?'

'Police business.'

'Then why have they been round here and keep on phoning?'

'Tell 'em nothing.'

'They pay my pension.'

'Tell 'em nothing. Nothing about anything, see.'

'What shall I tell Mel?'

'Nothing. Nothing to nobody. It's none of your business. Remember that.' The phone went dead.

111

Suppose I should have pottered out there. Had Hazel been free, I'd have assigned her. Instead I get the night car to run out from Newark, take a formal statement and keep an eye on the place.

Then I return to the couch and pick up Em's hand again, but the music has gone. I know I shouldn't be here.

12

D-Day plus one

To set a good example, as the branch's prospective leader, I get to HQ early, the day I'm officially due to return to work, no excuse any more for short shifts. My overnight grip is packed, passport in a pocket of my dark grey suit.

Action day today – if we've read Zoe Stone's coded message to Lincsline correctly. I'm more than hyped up and apprehensive. To be honest, I'm scared. Not that I feel in any kind of personal danger. But somewhere someone is. And I'm scared that I might miss a clue, a tip, a sign that could save them.

Grandad, who, with grandma, raised me when my unmarried mum dumped me, landed on the beaches where I'm bound fifty-one years ago.

He collapsed and died when I was still at school, just into his retirement, so I never talked about war experiences with him. Even now, when I'm troubled, I hold imaginary conversations with him. Like the time I lay in hospital with my shot-up leg a couple of years ago.

On Special Ops, you drew guns a dozen or so times a year, but I'd never fired one, not in action, still haven't and never want to have to. Sometimes I think that's why the killer with the shotgun, holding Jacko, got me. Because I was too slow, lacked the killer instinct.

What troubled me every bit as much as self-doubt and pain and worry over the future as I lay in hospital was the fact that in the terror of that foggy day on the railway line I'd wet myself. I could feel it warm at the groin, spreading through my Y-fronts.

Me, Sweeney Todd, leader of the X-Team, best in the force, bound for the very top, peed myself in fright. Such is my shame that I've never mentioned that before, not even to Em, only to grandad.

'Don't worry, son,' I imagined him comforting me. 'On D-Day plus one, I emptied both tanks.'

'But I was scared, paralysed with fear.'

'So is everyone with half a brain.'

'What did you do?' I asked.

'Looked around for an old sweat I rated and did exactly what he did, copied him when he took cover, moved when he did.'

I hope Hazel's feeling for Chief Inspector Dubal is right. I might need him today.

Hazel has beaten me here. For someone who had a heavy date last night she looks remarkably well rested – clear skin and eyes. She is dressed in a navy blue suit with matching court shoes, again very low.

Before I can sit down she relays from Surveillance that all is quiet on the waterfront. Lincsline's cattle boat, the *Lindum Castle*, has set sail with a crew of twelve for Cherbourg, a twenty-four-hour voyage, laden to its maximum seven hundred tons with sheep. 'It was searched from stem to stern,' she adds. 'Nothing.'

Chief Inspector Dubal – 'Monsieur Sang-Froid' and she rolls her eyes – has been told the estimated time of the boat's and my airlift's arrivals; he will meet me and take me straight to his council *de guerre*.

Her face clouds. 'He also reports that the sealed dossier we air-freighted last night via Rod arrived intact.'

Finally sitting down, I feel like a mole catcher whose baited trap hasn't sprung. I start to tell her about the phone call that frightened Larry Dove last night.

She stops me, pecking her head at my in-tray where there's a full statement the night car crew had taken. It doesn't add much, but they'd checked every two hours; no sightings of Hicks. Their relief had knocked on the door at eight. Larry had answered. A calming sensation is flowing through me to the tips of my fingers.

Hazel has already checked with the Fairways Hotel. 'Nothing in the morning mail.' She pauses. 'So how are we going to fill in time?'

Good question. Burials usually make a hole in your day as well as the graveyard. Knight's, though, couldn't have been better timed if Agatha Christie had arranged it.

Now and then, in reporting a funeral of a mystery death victim, the press trots out the line 'Detectives mingled with family mourners'. It's libel-free code for 'Detectives think the killer is a relative'.

I plan to listen intently to the reading Mrs Knight has picked for the service, trying to catch her Shakespearian straws in the wind. At the wake, I'll get alongside Rodney, Thornes senior and junior and their wives, just dropping the odd stone into the pool of polite conversation, see how far the ripples reach out. I hadn't really thought beyond that, and, since she had done all the routine, the honest answer is 'Dunno'.

I nod her to a chair opposite, an invitation to yarn till something occurs. 'Nice night?' I tease.

Her face lights up. 'Played Scrabble of a sort.' I cock my head, to encourage more. She and her fella had played word games with the MI9 code, she explains.

'Find any rude words?' I kid.

Ole transcribes as lov, she says, but sex was a very disappointing hvc. We laugh out loud.

Her face grows serious again. 'I can see spelling out "zip" points to Arc. Equally, signing off with a couple of Xs for kisses would have implicated Combined Counties.'

New to me, that. I hadn't puzzled it through that far.

'What we couldn't work out is how Hicks would have indicated to Knight had Thorne Meat Depots been involved, or Miles at the Trentside club.'

I give this some silent thought, then hazard, 'Extend the message by a few sentences to spell out one or other name in the first letters?'

She sighs dramatically. 'We're just going to have to find the little bastard. What happened at Red Gutter to turn him into a fugitive?'

What's still nagging at me, I tell her, is K2. It's a place name, she opines. I'm inclined to agree. The way 'Monday' immediately follows K2 makes it look like datelines you see in the papers – 'Moscow, Monday.'

Spelling out 2 turns it into a four-letter word with no vowel which didn't show up in her gazetteer. 'There's a bloody big mountain in Pakistan called K2, but there's no post office at the top of it dispensing red stamps.'

I smile but Hazel's face remains troubled. 'We know from Forensics, don't we, that Hicks wrote the card, so he must have been to France.' A tantalising pause. 'But is it possible he wrote it at someone's dictation?'

She had obviously taken more work home with her last night than I did. 'Who, for example?' I ask.

'Well . . .' She hesitates. 'Lynch. As an ex-firefighter, he'd know it would have to pass all laboratory tests.'

Her eyes sadden. 'Is it possible that Hicks conned Knight into letting him go on bail? And once he rejoined the *Tyke* trio in France, he blew the complete gaffe and threw his hand in with them. Lynch told him what to write, just to set us running down a wrong trail.'

'Or', I suggest, 'Lynch, not Hicks, kept the date at Red Gutter and silenced poor old Silent.' I can't get Mrs Knight's injunction to 'Beware of imposters' out of my head.

She nods solemnly.

I go on slowly. 'But how would Lynch or Hicks know that Arc Air is part owned by Knight's son-in-law?' I also remember what the pathologist pointed out. 'Neither would be aware of his heart condition. For all they knew he could have been fighting fit, fit enough anyway to make an arrest.'

Her face has that 'clever theory out of the window' expression – a forlornness that every thinking detective experiences from time to time.

There's no point in telling her that speculation is pointless. Every thinking detective speculates, if only to him or herself. Instead, I tilt my head towards the phone. 'Let's hope Dubal can find them, so we can ask them.'

Our task at the funeral, I instruct her, is to work, not mourn. Even as I say so, it's occurring to me that there's no reason for one name from Knight's red box to be there. 'Come on,' I say, rising, finally thinking of somewhere to go, something to do.

'Where?'

'To fill in time.'

'Where?' she repeats.

I blow her two kisses across the desk and let her work it out for herself.

The chatty assistant at Combined Counties doesn't tip his starched white trilby when we enter the office, but he flashes a welcoming smile in Hazel's direction. 'Mr Powers about?' she asks.

'Next door.' He flicks his head sideways. 'The abattoir.'

We were wondering, Hazel begins, if he's heard from Hicks again. Not that he knows of, he replies. Hazel again: 'You?'

He shakes his head. 'They might have done, I suppose, in the slaughterhouse. He worked there.'

'Thought he was a labourer here.'

'Here and there. Depending where they were short. Lairage, normally.' That, he explains for Hazel's benefit, is the point where cattle are collected in pens; a comforting name that gives the impression of the safety of their den before they are driven into the slaughterhouse.

So, I am venturing, Hicks might have used the sort of cattle prods I saw in action down on the farm yesterday on the way to Arc Air.

He motions us to sit. 'Not in trouble, is he?'

'Just a minor matter. It'll be sorted out when we find him, I suppose,' she says cagily. 'A witness, more or less.' She pauses. 'When did you last see him?'

He replies as he thinks. 'Three, say . . . yes, three weeks ago. He dropped off some stuff for Mr Powers. In a blue Co-op bag. Belonged to his daughter, he said. She and Hicksey knocked about a bit together, you know.'

Hazel says she'd already gathered that. 'What was in it?'

He looks quite shocked. He didn't peek inside the bag, he protests, just dumped it on his boss's desk.

Hazel lets it drop. 'Will Mr Powers be long?'

'All morning. He bought a hundred head yesterday.'

'We'd better stroll round to see him then,' I say.

Not a pleasant sight or smell at the end of our short stroll round the back to the smaller building next door.

Outside, in strong metal pens, are ten or a dozen mud-caked

116

black and white cattle. In the centre aisle, three dirt-stained men are shouting and slapping one beast hard on its rump with sticks, driving it towards a wide, low entrance in the breeze block building, like racecourse workers trying to force a reluctant horse into the starting stalls.

We walk beyond them, me careful where I step in my highly polished black shoes, through a smaller door. As we get closer that distinct smell from butchers' shops wafts towards us – raw, meaty, bloody. Inside is a hive of activity, impossible to take in with one look as we stand under a sign that says: 'Protective clothing beyond this point'.

There's six or seven men, all in gumboots and dressed in white boiler suits, some with their heads covered with tight white gauze masks, only their eyes showing. They look like white knights after a battle. Many are splattered with blood, its sickly, sweet smell hanging heavy in the cool indoor air.

The beast has made it inside into a narrow pen. Its head is poking out through a gap at the far end.

One man steps forward, pulling back the bolt on a grey hand-gun, a humane killer. He places it at the beast's forehead and fires. A bony crack. It drops to its knees, as if pole-axed. Its back legs twitch grotesquely.

Hazel gasps loudly beside me, irritating me, a country boy who's knocked wriggling fish on the head and gutted them, plucked and dressed overhung gamebirds, salted sides of porkers I've seen grown from piglets, necked chickens and strangled de-formed lambs at birth. What do these bloody townies expect? That the minced meat in their bolognese comes out of the same pasta-making machine as their spaghetti? Let 'em eat sodding soya bean then.

Another man steps up. There's a rod in his hand, not a stiff one. He slips it into the round, bleeding hole the bolt has made in the beast's forehead and wiggles it. What little reflex movements the bullock was making cease now.

In half a minute, less perhaps, it is hooked by its now still rear legs and yanked, upside down, on to a rail that hangs from the ceiling. With a hum, the rail starts to move. The bullock is carried towards hanging strips of plastic curtaining which blocks the view. From behind the curtains comes the sound of gushing liquid.

Out of the curtaining emerges another beast, slit open from

117

throat to beyond its stomach, dripping blood into a deep gutter that runs directly below this state-of-the-art production line of death.

The rail bends again into an S. Alongside it, at spaced intervals, are benches where more men work in teams of two. Above one, cattle heads hang in a row, hooked by their tongues. From somewhere comes the drone of sawing and the hiss of a high-pressure hose.

Even my hardened eyes have had enough and take a short cut to the end of the line where carcasses hang, beheaded, skinned, gutted.

The rail finally moves out of sight into a gap above which is the sign: 'Cutting Plant'. There's a branch line into a tiled alcove that's marked: 'Detained Room'.

One man signals to me, can't make out who he is, dressed all in white. I motion him outside. Only when I turn do I realise that Hazel has left my side.

'Heard from Hicks yet?' I ask as the now recognisable Powers follows me outside into the fresh air.

'No. You neither?'

I shake my head. 'If he's not around here . . . ' Powers is watching me intently. '. . . we think he could be in France.'

A blank look. 'I had no idea; otherwise I'd never . . .' The sentence dribbles away before he can say 'have stood bail'.

Hazel nods at me. 'He's off there this afternoon.'

He smiles quite broadly, carefree. 'Hope you salvage my hundred quid then.'

'He may be with a Richard Stone,' I go on, 'a drinking chum from college days –'

He interrupts me, looking brightly at Hazel. 'So she's already mentioned.'

'And . . .' I add what we never mentioned on our first call here. '. . . a suspected fire-bomber.'

'Lord!' He gasps it, square jaw dropping.

'Sure you don't know him?' I describe Stone, not difficult. Powers starts to shake his head. 'Did he ever call here while Hicks worked for you?' The headshake continues.

'Is it possible your daughter might know him?' I press on. 'All three were at college together.'

'Possible,' he concurs distractedly. 'Ask her.'

Hazel is not letting on that she already has.

'Good luck then.' Like Thorne yesterday, he appears rather eager to wrap up this chat.

I continue, 'You were a bit unlucky getting involved in this in the first place.'

Hazel comes in again. 'Hicks tried to get hold of his boss to stand bail, Miles Thorne . . .' She pauses, eyebrow arched: 'Know him?'

'Runs the Trentside club?' Powers waits for Hazel's nod. 'Reasonably well. Know his dad better.'

'Brian?'

'Right.'

'Hicks put up Miles' name as surety, but he wasn't available when the custody sergeant phoned. You got the short straw, I'm afraid.'

'Should have stayed out of it. Do someone a good turn, then . . .' He shrugs, put upon.

'Apart from the day you bailed him, when was the last time you saw him?' she asks.

He gives this some thought and we give him no help. He replies hesitantly. 'I think . . . well . . . He dropped off some stuff for our Dawn a couple of weeks back. Old college clobber. His new lady was spring cleaning and told him to get rid, apparently. Books and things. I wasn't in. I think . . .' Powers seems to remember. 'Must be three weeks ago. He calls round for a drink with his old workmates sometimes but I don't normally go.'

Hazel's cross-checking has got nowhere, so she widens her net. 'Have any of them heard from Hicks lately?'

'Ask around,' he says invitingly. 'No one's mentioned it to me.'

Something else niggles at me, something I never mentioned back at the office to Hazel; a vital loose end: Who gave the transportless Hicks that lift from the golf club to Melanie Dexter's cottage after he'd returned the pick-up?

I approach it with caution. 'After you bailed him, he took off in the club truck. Right?' A confirmatory nod. 'Did you see what direction he went?'

'Back to work, I expect. Well overdue, he said, expecting trouble.'

'And you?'

'Came back here.' A thin smile. 'As I've already told you.'

I decide not to push it further. Not yet, anyway, targeting another topic. 'We'll be seeing Brian and Miles later at the funeral of Andrew Knight, our assistant chief constable.'

'Read about it. No age, was he?'

'The Thornes are related to him – brother-in-law and nephew.'

'So I gather.'

How? I ask myself. 'You know Brian well then?'

'Do a bit of business with him, yes. Drives a hard bargain.'

'Really?' No response. 'You know about his arson?'

His face screws ahead of his question. 'A firebug? That's confirmed, is it?'

'How do you mean?' asks Hazel.

A small shrug. 'It said in the papers it might be electrical.'

So it did, I remind myself, because that's what I told the press. 'So what made you think of a firebug?'

'Well . . .' He looks away, eyes narrowing. 'Brian mentioned it was a bit of a mystery and the police were still investigating. I got the impression there might be more to it than was in the papers, that's all.'

'When did you speak to him about it?'

'When he came round to check the paperwork. I had some stuff stored there. He's claiming for it from his insurance. Still not settled, though.' He's relaxed now. 'Red tape. Miles told me it was still dragging on when he called on Monday.'

'Is he still in the cold store side of the family business?' I ask.

'Just a long-distance eye. His dad's not, well, on top of modern developments in freezing. More interested in his horses. Miles just wants to make sure the new equipment they get is spot-on.' He flicks his head back towards the main building. 'He's had a look at ours.'

I get him back to the delay on the insurance pay-out and ask, 'Much involved?'

'Of my stock? Oh. About fifty grand's worth,' he replies airily. His face goes suddenly solemn. 'Do you think Thorne's fire was arson, not electrical?' He gives me a flustered look and continues haltingly. 'I mean, neither Brian nor Miles – and obviously we've talked about the cause – have ever even hinted at it.'

I reply cautiously. 'Until we find Richard Stone and ask him, we can't rule it out.'

'Which is why we need to find Hicks, you see,' adds Hazel.

Powers doesn't appear to see, so she adds patiently, 'He may know Stone's whereabouts.'

'Oh.' Now whatever he is seeing seems to be concerning him deeply. He makes a barely passable attempt at a smile of encouragement. 'Good hunting then.'

13

A routine inquiry now, covering old ground; nowhere near important enough for a soon-to-be acting ACC, but, well, I tell Hazel, white-faced and unusually quiet, there's time to spare, so we'll drop in on Melanie Dexter and Larry Dove while we're this way.

A stiff westerly has scattered most of the clouds, exposing widening patches of blue sky. Across them have flown three planes heading north, leaving white vapour trails behind. A nice day for a flight. Or a funeral.

With Hazel silent, I let my mind drift. Had I been on my own, I think I'd have taken a bunch of flowers for Mel, so unnecessarily cruel were my put-downs on Monday; still feel a touch guilty about it.

I sometimes wonder where this hard streak in me came from. Not from my gentle grandfolks, that's certain. Or my scatter-brained mum who lives in Australia with her third husband. My never-seen father, I suspect. A bastard who begot a bastard with blond hair that doesn't come from my maternal side. Must be. Blame him.

I turn on Classic FM and, to a clarinet obbligato, give Hazel a burst of 'Speak for me to my lady', testing my tonsils for church.

At least I've made her smile again and feel better for it.

There's no reply at Mel's, so I knock next door. 'Come in,' calls Larry, the police pensioner.

Mel and the kids are out shopping, he informs us. Back soon, he adds, inviting us to sit down in two old oak chairs with spells at the back, rests for arms and flowered cushions.

If she's heard from Hicks, he says, she hasn't mentioned it.

'How about you?' I nod at his phone. 'Any more calls?'

'No,' he says. 'I didn't mention it to Mel, by the way. Was that right?'

'Yes.' God, do I feel ashamed. Twice my age and he's still thinking more like a policeman than me. 'OK if we put a trace on your line?'

'All right.'

'And we'll keep that between us three, too, OK?'

'If you say so.'

He's been through his account of the phone call twice, without changing his story, so I'm not going to put him through it again. I trust the old boy. 'What's he like, this Hicks character?' Deliberately I introduce an old police term, to make him feel part of the team. 'What's your feeling about him?'

'Not good enough for her.' He yanks his head towards Mel's adjoining cottage. 'Treats the place like a dosshouse. Comes and goes as he pleases.'

He asks if we knew about his driving ban and Hazel says, 'Yes.' He looks disgusted at the very idea of breaking even the most minor of laws, a copper of a bygone age. 'She could do much better than him,' he adds.

'What's his trouble?'

'Booze – that's what. Keeps her short of money.'

That, I'd already worked out. He told Mel he was on about fifty pounds a week less than Miles claimed to be paying him. The balance goes on drink, I guess.

I try the name of his drinking mate Richard Stone on him, but he doesn't recognise it.

Hazel probes to find out if he saw the vehicle that picked up Hicks from the cottage when he called to collect his travelling bag. No, he answers and he didn't even know he'd got into trouble over the bank card, walked out of his job and gone abroad until Mel confided in him.

'Bone idle, too. Infested, we are, with moles. Seen that yourself when you came in, no doubt. I asked him to get rid of them. Said I'd pay. He even had the stuff to do it. Promised he would. Never did. He's unreliable. Wouldn't trust him.'

Like Hazel, I am beginning to wonder if Knight was right to trust him. Still, if Hicks was the only way into the saboteurs' cell and their next target, what choice did he have? Better to try and fail than not try at all. Imagine a boat going down with all hands and you'd had a lead which you hadn't exploited.

Frowning, Hazel takes over. 'What stuff are we talking about?'

'Pestine.'

'What's that?'

'Controls vermin, strychnine-based.'

And what killed that bull? I ask myself, so startled I gulp. 'How do you know its name?'

'Saw the label on the tin. Used the stuff myself in my gamekeeping days.'

'And he had some here?'

He glances towards the small kitchen. 'Stored it overnight on the shelf. Didn't want it next door. Not with two young kids running around.'

'What did he want it for?'

'For a mate, he said.'

'And he wouldn't use any of it on your moles?'

'None to spare, he said. Another time.'

'Where did he get it from?'

'From the golf course, I suppose. Helped himself, I don't doubt. He's a real spiv' – a nice word from the war years, Larry's years, you don't hear much any more, but it accurately describes Hicks, I'm coming to believe.

We try to pin him down to the day the tin stayed overnight on his kitchen shelf but, with one being much like another, all he can manage is within the past month. 'He took it away next day.' Pause. 'In a carrier bag.'

'Not a small tin then?' says Hazel.

' "Enough to kill an elephant," he said.'

And certainly a bull, I'm thinking, with a touch of molasses added for taste.

Melanie Dexter, wearing Monday's clothes, smiles openly for Hazel, blanks me when she walks in, without knocking, ordering her two toddlers to stay and play in the molehill-dotted garden.

She dumps a well-filled Co-op shopping bag on the table, tells

Larry first what she couldn't get from his list before asking Hazel, 'Found him yet?'

'No,' says Hazel. 'Heard from him?'

She slowly rotates her head.

Hazel knows that Melanie will chat more to her than me, so she takes control, relegating me to second fiddle. 'We think he may be with someone called Richard Stone. Know him?'

A glum nod and, judging from her fierce expression, she didn't like him. Sometimes Stone popped round in a borrowed green truck, she says, to pick up Hicks to go drinking. 'He never comes in. Just pips his horn. When Hicksey climbs into the cab they giggle like schoolgirls. Bloody men.' The last two words are to herself, lips tight.

Hazel looks across at her neighbour. 'Larry tells us Alan stored a tin of Pestine here recently.'

She looks nonplussed, asks what it is and replies that she's never heard of it or seen it.

Larry nods at the table. 'In a bag like that.'

Mel shakes her head again.

Hazel looks at me hard, then softly at Mel. 'Tell me – within the last month or so, have you told Alan to get rid of some old college gear that was cluttering up your place, books and things?'

'No,' says Mel, firmly. 'Never. Whoever told you that?'

Hazel doesn't answer. She is looking at me again, harder still.

'What's your feeling?' asks Hazel, driving back.

'The carrier bag ties up,' I begin cautiously.

'So does the timing,' Hazel adds.

A moment's muse. 'Why should Powers want to poison a bull and blow up a business associate's freezer?'

'Insurance?' Hazel speculates. 'Fifty grand's worth of meat?'

'But he's no longer hard up, according to Claude.'

'Odd though.' Hazel is not letting go. 'After all, when Knight couldn't raise a member of his family to stand bail for Hicks, he roped in Powers. Is he involved with someone in the family and Knight rumbled it?'

'Was Silent putting them under pressure, you mean? Hoping someone would crack and make a clean breast of it?'

Hazel doesn't answer, so I go on as devil's advocate. 'Motive?'

She's still got none other than insurance.

'The Thorne business is sound, never in financial trouble,' I protest. 'You don't burn down a money-making concern.'

'Then why did Mrs Knight come out with that slaughterhouse business on Monday,' asks Hazel testily, 'if not to point us in Powers' direction?'

I'll ask her later, I decide, at the wake.

'Powers is in on it,' she adds, rather doubtfully. 'There he was asking us if Thorne's fire was arson, yet not questioning us about a possible motive. Wouldn't you, if you'd lost a load of meat in the blaze? Wouldn't you at least query if arson was the reason for the delay in settling the insurance?'

Eyes left on the floodlight pylons of a small, smart rugby stadium, I have an uncomfortable vision of Powers, in his all-yellow strip, sneaking past me on the blind side.

I think this through and have to accept that he displayed a curious lack of curiosity. 'He's in the same line of business as Thorne – a business that's been fire-bombed – but he expressed no concern about his own security, didn't pick our brains on crime prevention.'

She repeats, more positively now, 'He's in on it.'

'An arse-about-face case this,' I groan gloomily. 'We've finally got a suspect, but we haven't got a motive.'

'Yes, but Knight might have discovered one,' she points out.

The traffic ahead slows on the approach to a roundabout on Newark's ring road. 'Want to drive on into the town centre and take a look at the *Yorkshire Tyke*?' she asks. 'Just to complete the picture for you.'

'I thought Forensics turned it over.'

Inside out, she assures me, at its moorings just upriver from the old castle. 'Found nothing that helps. But then an ex-fireman like Lynch who'd watched scene-of-crime specialists operate on arson cases would know how to wipe a place clean.'

No point then, I decide. I look at my wrist-watch: nearly eleven. 'No time,' I say.

She takes the roundabout carefully, then picks up speed and, with it, the train of a former thought. 'We've always assumed, haven't we, that the nitrogen stolen by Stone with Hicks' help from the golf club was used on Thorne's cold store? But there's no proof, is there?'

'All the evidence went up in flames,' I remind her. 'Come on. What are you getting at?'

Well, she recalls, the source of the fertiliser packed in the defused bomb on the *Lindum Castle* was never traced. Yes, I agree, but anyone can order as much nitrogen as they like. It isn't a controlled substance, like dynamite and poisons.

'Exactly,' she says brightly. 'If the trio from the *Tyke* had a source of supply, they didn't need to raid the Trentside club.'

'Then who did?'

She doesn't answer for a moment or two and then turns it into a question by gradually lightening her words. 'An inside job?'

Someone in the family, she means, Brian Thorne or son Miles. But, pressed again, she still can't come up with a motive. Hicks, I recall, told Knight that he virtually drew a map for Stone to the fertiliser shed.

'Oh, yes,' says Hazel, darkly, 'but what if that stolen haul wasn't the explosive used at the cold store?' In other words, she's asking: Where is that lethal load now?

I look ahead, into space. Another vision occurs, far, far more alarming. A green truck, three or four passengers in the cab, watching, waiting. The *Lindum Castle*, packed with livestock, is chugging into the port of Cherbourg with its crew of twelve leaning on the rails.

A gendarme runs towards the vessel, shouting, screaming. The crew can't understand, look at each other, puzzled.

A fireball hits the docks. Carcasses everywhere. Humans as well as cattle.

I can feel the heat. My blood seems to boil. I have to screw my eyes shut to blink the vision away.

14

Jacko Jackson is sitting hunched on a bar stool in the quiet back lounge of the Fairways, a half-consumed pint of lager in front of him, a bad sign this early.

Hazel gives his creased cheek a quick peck. He orders Perrier waters for both of us and asks for another half.

He goes through the 'What a shock' routine that all mourners get out of the way first. 'You never know.' He shakes his head sadly, disturbing thinning brown hair that's been recently showered and won't settle.

I suspect he's going to make a day of it, turn it into an Irish-type wake. When he goes on a bender there's blood on the moon – and I've seen enough blood for one day. A wide berth is called for. It will do my promotion chances no good having the chief constable seeing me propping up an ageing drunk.

He is dressed in an oldish mid-grey suit he used to keep for appearances in the witness box. Must be ten years old, I josh.

The only time it comes out these days is for funerals, he sighs mournfully. 'When you get to my age all you're ever invited to are retirement parties and wakes.'

He's already two years older than Knight was, he complains, with a worried expression. 'Never knew he was ill. Should have kept in touch.'

He's going through the angst bit that seems to affect everyone when they hear of the death of a former colleague. Mine in Ireland, to my shame, lasted all of ten minutes. His is understandably lasting longer because Knight saved his life.

'Fancy dropping dead in a place called Red Gutter.' A macabre smile. 'Great title, that.'

Jacko has spent most of his time in retirement churning out detective novels fictionalising some of the cases and characters he'd come across in his time on CID. They're quite entertaining little romps, nothing likely to make James' and Rendell's bank managers blanch with fear.

His next is due out soon, he tells us, and he's working on one about the inquiry which ended with Knight's sharp reactions saving Hazel and him from the mad bomber. 'Always regarded him as a bit of a public school poof, to be honest, but he turned out to be a good governor.'

Hazel nods gravely. He and she are bound to remember Knight with great gratitude, I agree, but saving such a boring old fart from certain death counted against him in most right-thinking people's minds.

Jacko laughs, unoffended. 'My missus's view, too.'

I ask after his long-suffering wife. He complains that his retirement has changed her. 'She used to ask me: "When are you coming home?" Now she asks: "When are you going out, for christsake?" '

He asks about Em and our holiday and thanks me for my picture postcard from Westport. Then: 'What are you two up to?'

'That bombing and blackmail business,' I say.

'Mmmmmm.' He lights a cigarette and looks musingly through metal-framed bifocals into his glass. 'Interesting, that. Has possibilities. With peace in Ireland and the Middle East, there's bugger all terrorism left for us thriller writers, apart from animal lib militants.' Now he is looking appealing. 'Give me a fill-in, will you, if you get a good result?'

I answer acidly that I spent seven to eight hours dictating tapes about an undercover job I did for CID when I was on sick leave for him to turn into a book. 'Nothing's appeared.'

'Haven't got round to it yet. I'm in the middle of my first series. Then my current main character will be jaded, played out. You're his replacement, heavily disguised, of course. Are we on?'

'No, thank you,' I say, waving a dismissive hand.

'Bastard,' he says, not at all maliciously. I have a sinking feeling he is hatching up some blackmail of his own, fret about what he'll say to all the flight deck brass who'll be at the wake when the booze runs free. To limit the impending damage, I urge him to drink up, stub out, and get up and off to the church.

Ten minutes early, we hang around outside the village church, the way mourners do. Most are here to see and be seen. Like you, I remind myself, an uncomfortable admission.

There are handshakes from people I saw only yesterday, including a Masonic one from Chief Superintendent Dale who's had his uniform cleaned and pressed.

The conversations are stilted to the point of inanities and punctuated with smiling silences. The real crack, the where-are-they nows, the trips down memory lane, will come at the wake. Post-funeral pleasantries are much happier than pre. I quite enjoy a good funeral when the formalities are out of the way.

The church, an amalgam of styles, all complementary, is on the edge of a hill at the end of a wall, grey stones at the bottom, bricks in different reds above, that runs for half a mile, all the way from the centre of the tiny village of East Stoke.

The tower is very old, broad, not too tall, and the nave looks Georgian. It's a steepish walk up a newly Tarmacked path from the road below where I parked my car and changed pink tie for black.

I gaze over the gravestones, the older ones topped with mosses, to the already dug spot where Knight will be laid to rest. Beyond a wooden fence, on which a grey squirrel is perched eyeing us, is a glorious view of the Trent Valley, deep green pastureland where white sheep and black rooks eat lunch side by side; no cattle to remind me of this morning. It is a pleasant day, breezy but bright.

Our little knot is joined by Carole Malloy, late forties, with close-cropped red hair, quite small, a fine police officer, the chief superintendent in charge of CID.

She makes a big fuss of Jacko, an old friend. He is kidding her about seeing her in a frock for the first time. Actually, it's stylish black linen, collarless, with a matching jacket.

Dale sidles up to them. 'Hear you're writing crime novels.'

'Yes,' says Jacko, always happy to talk (sometimes to the point of tedium) about his new career. Not in paperback yet, he adds forlornly.

'I'm a Morse fan myself, so I can't say I've read yours,' says Dale rather incautiously.

'Well . . .' says Jacko, drawing deeply on yet another cigarette, '. . . there aren't enough pictures in 'em for you.' Everyone smiles tightly, Dale tightest of all.

Unwisely he tries to recover. 'Which one's the best? I'll get it out of the library.'

'That', says Jacko, grandly, 'is rather like asking Mozart which of his symphonies he preferred.'

Everyone laughs again and I wonder if we should be this happy at a funeral, but then again: Why not?

To get himself off the hook, Dale decides to display some local knowledge, pointing to smooth stones near the arched porch, its black iron gates opened. Legend has it, he says, that the King's men sharpened their swords there before the battle of Stoke Field. Then he points out a plaque alongside the church wall to commemorate the seven thousand who died here on another June day in 1487.

Someone asks about the monument of an elaborately cast angel, the most noticeable in the churchyard, and is informed it's to

Baron Pauncefote, the first ambassador to the United States, a local boy made good.

I suspect Dale has been mugging up to impress the chief constable in case he asks on the way to the graveside.

Carole Malloy, less cynical, observes that the village pub, a long white building on the main road opposite the winding turn-off into the village, is called the Pauncefote Arms and wonders how many of us will have a boozer named after us when we're gone.

None, I fear. Funerals never fail to remind everyone of their own mortality. All will go away with private pledges to be better, kinder, more caring which will be forgotten like New Year resolutions on January 2nd.

Soon Jacko appears behind me, whispering. 'Carole's in for the job.'

'What job?' I ask across my shoulder with as much innocence as I can muster.

He just winks and drifts away again across the grass, which is decorated by daisies, disfigured by mole hills, to annoy another group.

I'm quite relieved when Dale announces, 'They're on their way. Better get in.' He steps aside, to let Carole and Hazel and the rest of us take two or three stone steps into the porch and the same again into the nave, already well filled.

Inside it is cool and light with the sun shining through tinted lead-framed windows on to cream walls. From one wall hangs the Union Jack, half furled. We sit in a line in a short, wooden pew near the back of the central block, but Dale has hung behind.

A silver-piped organ in the timbered chancellery is already playing a Bach air and the police choir (all male, not enough sopranos and contraltos even in these days of sexual equality) is in its place.

The scent of early summer flowers beautifully arranged in a stone urn near the door fills the church. Ahead of me is a line of triple candle-holders marring my view so I gaze each side at the wall plaques. Several are to the titled and the gentry and one to the officer and five local men who didn't return from the Great War.

For such a small place – around a hundred, I guess – scattered either side of the main A46 road, it's had more than its share of deaths in battle.

The chief constable, in uniform, leads a stately procession of top brass and wives to near the front, shepherded by Dale, who takes a seat immediately behind him. He drops to his knees, lowers his head and clasps his hands in what looks like earnest prayer.

It's some time before the coffin arrives with the family following – time I don't spend in prayer, but asking myself: Can you believe that? Politicking at a funeral.

In slow, exceedingly short steps, six policemen, physically the force's finest, shoulder in the pale pine coffin on which sits a single, simple bouquet of red and white roses.

Mrs Knight and Anita follow, arm in arm, heads held high. The widow wears a small black straw hat, black suit and white blouse with a gold brooch at the neck; a special present, I guess. Anita is in a chocolate brown silky outfit – jacket Chinese style, high collar buttoned at the throat, ending just above the knees and just short of the hem of her skirt.

Behind comes Rod, grey-suited, alongside Stella, also grey-suited with a tiger-striped scarf knotted at the neck, the ends of which cover her ample bosom.

Miles and his father are side by side. Miles is in a dark blazer with grey sharply pressed flannels. Thorne wears his pin-head check suit, newly pressed, with a black tie that sets it off. Behind are another half-dozen family I don't know. When they are all seated, the church is full.

'Abide with me' fills it even further. It's the Cup Final anthem so I don't have to look at the printed order of service for the words. It's, what, twenty years since music gave me up, but I can still hit the right note on the right occasion.

After prayers, which I don't follow, head half up, observing, Miles moves to a lectern with a carved wooden eagle's head and rather nervously reads words that begin, 'Death is nothing at all.' These words, written by a canon, I do follow until, 'What is death but a negligible accident?' and I become professional again, trying to picture what happened at Red Gutter.

The rector, a tall, dark man, replaces him. His sincere tribute in a measured delivery dwells as long on Knight's good neighbour-liness as his public service.

Surprised, moved really, I wonder uneasily when, if ever, Em and I will put down real roots and belong, make a contribution to a community we can call our own.

More prayers are followed by Rod at the lectern carrying 'The Works of Shakespeare' in its olive green covers. He opens it at a pre-marked page and begins an assured reading:

> 'Ere you were queen or your husband king,
> I was a pack-horse in his great affairs;
> A weeder-out of his proud adversaries,
> A liberal rewarder of his friends . . .
> Let me put in your minds, if you forget,
> What you have been, ere now, and what you are;
> Withal, what I have been, and what I am . . .'

I follow the words on the printed order which adds: '*Richard III*, Act 1, scene 3'.

A longish prayer follows, everyone kneeling, me nipping my nose at the bridge between finger and thumb, hoping to force out a positive thought.

It's a message to me, all right, that bit about being the pack-horse weeding out adversaries, but which adversary? And the bit about 'What you have been and what you are'? Who's that aimed at? Can't be me. He didn't train me, teach me much at all. So who? Daughter Anita? Son-in-law Rodney for the financial backing his in-laws have given his business?

I can't make head nor tail of it and feel like a pack-horse whose load is too heavy.

The final hymn is 'The day thou gavest, Lord, is ended'. Know these words, too, without a printed prompt.

Whenever I hear them I see myself back in my untroubled childhood with my mates at Sunday school in the tiny village hall and outside at the gates will stand gran, ever smiling, never flustered, to take me home.

Not today. Today I see myself in a bigger church overlooked by cranes. Inside it is packed. The *Lindum Castle*'s twelve widows are in the front pew; so many orphaned children behind them that I can't count them all.

I stop singing and don't hear the words around me. Instead, another hymn 'For those in peril on the sea' swims around my head.

132

Now I do pray – for the first time in years. Let me get there in time, dear Lord. Help me put a stop to it.

We don't go, Hazel and I, to the interment. For family and much closer friends than me, I decide guiltily. We drive back alongside the long wall into the village and turn right at the Women's Institute, half dark wood, half brick.

Beyond Knight's house, the lane becomes an earth track with grass at its centre. It's a slow, bumpy uphill drive of more than half a mile.

We don't talk, Hazel wrapped up in her own thoughts which must go back four years to when Knight saved her and Jacko and gave her each day since and all the days to come.

A grass footpath from the gap in which we park takes us alongside the hawthorn hedge that borders a barley field. Ahead of us birds in the hedgerow call warnings of our approach.

At the end of the path, a five-hundred-yard walk, Hazel moodily gestures left. 'There's another commemorative stone down there. Want to see it?'

I shake my head. She unlatches a metal gate. We continue across a meadow where sheep graze on long, rich grass, dried by the wind. They baa occasional accompaniment to the incessant bird song and crow calls. We climb a locked wooden gate and enter shaded woodland.

A single-file path has been tramped through waist-high nettles, white cow parsley and thistles – by that amateur historian, I conjecture, and the emergency services he summoned, and, before them, Knight and Hicks.

Oddly, there's a wooden seat almost lost in dense undergrowth; a relic from the five hundredth anniversary, I guess.

The weeds stop. The path becomes mossy grass and rises between mature trees, mostly native and deciduous, but some darker pines among them. A cloud of black flies which joined us at the gate don't follow us in. Dried twigs snap beneath our feet.

It's a tough walk for a man with a stiff leg, tougher still for an older man with heart trouble, I decide.

The narrow, soft path peaks in dappled shade. At either edge it falls away, more steeply to our left, into a huge gully sixty or seventy feet deep, not a sheer drop, but almost.

All the way down on all sides are saplings, some evergreen, wild bushes, weeds, flowering elder, foxgloves, dark green creeping ivy, exposed roots of big beeches and birches in holed, pinkish clay, rocks, fallen and rotting trunks.

'Red Gutter,' says Hazel grimly.

So this, then, is the last sight Knight saw. Nature running wild. Someone else was running wild here last Saturday at noon. Something sinister, I'm sure of it, happened here. Something his widow knows more about than she's telling – yet anyway. Some adversary in the family.

15

The wake is slow to warm up; the chief constable's fault. He brought three senior members of the regional police authority with him (all, no doubt, claiming meal and attendance allowances) so everyone is on their best behaviour.

Knight didn't come through the ranks in this force, and there's no one here who started out with him – an old constable, for example, who remained happy on the beat while his fellow rookie went to the top with the salary and stress that come with it. No one is on the way to being plastered and telling indiscreet tales from their early days to enliven proceedings; sad, really. I will be at Jacko's wake, I can promise him that; a real celebration.

Hazel is the only cop below inspector and she's very sober. The rest are officer class; all sober, too. The flight deck must be denuded. In a normal lunchtime, provided the chief wasn't around, several sizeable tabs would have been run up in the senior officers' mess by now.

The conversations are no more sparkling than outside the church. Only civvies – neighbours, distant relatives, Jacko, of course, and, I'm happy to note, Brian Thorne – are helping themselves to drink from a trestle table inside a canvas marquee, a sensible precaution against rain that is holding off.

So many people have shown up that it would have been overcrowded indoors, even in a house that looks like three cottages knocked into one, plaster cladding and climbing pink clematis to cover the joins.

The marquee, roped to four tall poles, only the rear flap down, covers a fair amount of ground space, but still leaves a lot of lawn that slopes away from the patio where we sat on Monday to a semicircular terrace of broken slabs set round half a dozen silver birches and a copper beech.

Hazel and I have nibbled at the well-filled table of food. Hazel selected veggie quiche. I joined her, that slaughterhouse sight lingering. Now we are standing beneath the beech, leaves thick but still green, awaiting summer to bronze them.

Doing the rounds, the chief and his party, Dale in tow, are one chattering circle away from us when Jacko reappears from the tent, pint glass in hand. My heart goes to the bloodstained soles of my black shoes.

'Now then,' he begins. 'About this inquiry of ours.'

'Piss off,' I hiss.

'Either I get it or I'll drop into the conversation that little job we did together in Wolds College.'

I can feel myself flinch at a memory six or seven years old, long before I met Em. There'd been complaints of indecent assaults by a masked prowler at a women-only teachers' training college. One student, a witness, not a victim, was a very mature student indeed and, after a long interview and then a few drinks in the local, it was, well, you know, well . . .

All visitors had to be off the campus by eleven. Next night I didn't finish duty till midnight, and, well, there was an invitation and she did show me where I could climb in through a corridor window.

We'd reached the petting stage when in burst Jacko. Someone had dialled 999, reporting the sighting of the prowler climbing through a window. He'd been on surveillance and knew it was me.

Control had radioed him and were dispatching back-up. When they arrived, we had our story worked out. I'd popped back to see Jacko with a message, couldn't find him. While looking, I'd spotted someone climbing through a window. In pursuit I'd dropped and smashed my radio, so I couldn't call it in. Jacko had seen and heard me. Both of us had carried out a search, found nothing.

'A few days later Jacko caught him red-handed, flashing. He admitted six assaults and four break-ins with intent to assault, including the one on the night of the rudely disturbed date. I never queried it.

'You wouldn't,' I say. But I know that he would; not all of it, but enough to make me cringe. In booze he is about as smooth as workhouse custard. There's just time to whisper 'OK' when the chief joins us.

He greets Jacko with a smile and a handshake, nods to the rest of us. 'We were just recalling the time . . .' and Jacko launches into the tale of my shooting on the railway line, all but crediting me with saving his life.

The chief smiles at me, asks about my wife and our holiday and says publicly what he should have said privately on Monday. 'Good of you to return to take over this from Mr Knight.' Dale glowers at his shoulder. 'Going well, I hope?'

'Very,' I say with a confidence I don't feel.

He wanders off to round off his tour by chatting to Mrs Knight, holds both of her hands, kisses both of her cheeks, turns and retreats back into the house. I doubt that he'll ever return here to visit her in her long widowhood.

Within five minutes, the police presence is reduced by more than a half as a convoy follows him in hot pursuit back to HQ, Dale in the lead.

Time for work now, I think, eyes back on the marquee.

Clutching a small glass of pale sherry, Stella Thorne shakes her head disapprovingly as her husband turns his back on her at the drinks table.

She puts on a brave, over made-up face when Hazel and I, Perrier waters in hand, stop before her. She says, 'Hallo again.'

Brian says 'Oh' over his shoulder and returns to a conversation with a man at the bar about horses.

Hazel and she small-talk about the impressive size of the turn-out at the church. Soon Thorne turns round to face us with a topped-up tumbler of whisky. His face is purple-ish around his narrow nose. The grey waistcoat, not worn at the racetrack on Monday, is tight to his paunch. A man with a booze problem, I start to suspect.

'Just seen a business associate of yours at work,' I begin, dispensing with all formalities. 'Geoff Powers.'

'Oh,' he repeats.

I 'Mmmmm', giving him time to ask why. He doesn't. So I go on, 'He stood bail for Alan Hicks.'

He squints, shortsightedly, at his wife.

'You know, greenkeeper from Miles' club,' Stella reminds him, 'Andy mentioned him at the birthday do.' She inclines her head towards the house, 'Involved in our arson.'

His turn to 'Mmmmm'.

'Mr Powers stood bail for him,' I repeat.

'More fool him then.' Brian takes a short sip. 'Wants locking away.'

'Bit of luck for Miles, though,' I add. 'He was first choice for surety. They couldn't raise him.'

'Why?'

'Well, Hicks did work for him.'

'And repaid him by stealing the nitrogen to blow us up.' I don't confirm it. 'Didn't he?' Perplexed by my silence, he looks at Stella who nods encouragement. 'Stands to reason. The club's fertiliser store gets raided. We get blown up. Why did Andy ever grant him bail?'

'I don't know,' I answer.

'Didn't he say?'

I stay silent again and Stella answers for me. 'All he ever said was that he couldn't hold him, had further inquiries to make or something. I thought this chap was a – what do they call it?'

'An eyewitness,' Brian suggests.

'No. No.' Stella's face is filled with the frustration of a crossword buff with the answer on the tip of her tongue.

I think they mean hostile witness, but I'm not going to prompt. 'Didn't Mr Knight tell you?'

'Why should he?' Brian comes back sharply.

'Why not?' I stand my ground. 'There was no secret about it, was there? It was your cold store, after all.'

'All I know is what Andy told us here at the party. Why all this interest all of a sudden?' There's more than a hint of belligerence in his tone.

'Because', says Hazel, smiling, gesturing to me, 'he has taken over the inquiry and, as you know, we can't find Hicks.'

'Still missing, is he? Mmmmm. Jumped bail?' He looks rather gleeful.

'That's what we'd like to know,' I say.

An awkward silence indicates that I'm not going to get the answer here.

Miles, his blazer well cut, hand-stitched at the lapels, joins us carrying a gin and tonic in which ice tinkles. He talks to his mother for a minute about some distant relative he's just seen. He turns to us. 'Nice of you to come.'

'We're just discussing this Hicks chap,' I tell him. 'Remember telling us he worked for Combined Counties before joining –'

Brian butts in, grumbling into his glass. 'Can't say I know anything about him at all.'

'Saturday boy,' Stella remembers. 'He used to drop off Combined's surplus.'

Brian still looks vague.

'Mr Powers . . .' I look at Miles. To make sure he's following I add, ' . . . of Combined Counties . . .' Miles gives a slightly irritated nod. ' . . . mentioned the delay on the insurance. He had meat stored with you, I gather.'

Miles looks at his mother, but it's his father who answers, very sharply. 'Told you. Brussels are holding it up.'

'Can we help expedite things?' asks Hazel.

Thorne flicks his head at his wife while looking at me. 'She does the admin.'

'A query over the value of the stock,' she says, giving nothing away. No one helps her, so she has to go on. 'Some EC meat. Been there years. A batch was released recently. Some mercy mission airlift to Bosnia. It was a bit off.'

'Past its sell-by date, you mean?' Hazel interrupts.

Stella nods and continues, 'So it's just a question of what the rest of their stock is worth in today's terms. Nothing in it for us. Just more inconvenience.'

'Bloody Brussels,' Thorne growls.

'It will be sorted out soon,' says Stella evenly.

I need confirmation. 'Nothing to do – this insurance delay, I mean – with the meat Mr Powers had stored with you then?'

'Lord, no,' says Mrs Thorne. 'Only the EC stuff.'

'Ours and Combined were A1,' adds her husband. 'So was the EC's. Sure of it. Bloody cheek.'

Anita approaches, trailed by Rodney Montgomery. Stella speaks to her, rather loudly, from some distance away. 'How is she?'

There is no reply until Anita comes to a halt before us, then, softly, 'Resting.'

Stella turns to me. 'All too much for her.' For Mrs Knight, I gather, who went indoors soon after the chief constable left. She looks back at Anita. 'Will she be fit to travel?'

'Fine, fine,' says Anita soothingly. 'The doctor has given her something for the journey.'

I groan inwardly, fearing that I will not be able to take Mrs Knight aside for even the briefest and gentlest of words.

'Should have flown,' Stella says rather bossily.

'We need a car at the other end.'

Brian nods agreement. 'Quite right, with ours on the bloody blink again.' He grumbles a bit about breaking down in St Malo right in the middle of a traffic jam near a church. 'You know these Catholics and their days of obligation.'

He shakes his head. 'Just got it fixed and, bugger me . . .' Now he inclines towards his wife, grinning maliciously. 'Pranged it, she did, on the main drag outside the post office at the Doll.' He shakes his head, highly amused.

'Wasn't my fault,' says Stella, irritated. She looks at me for support. 'You know these Continental drivers on roundabouts.'

So, both Brian and Stella Thorne had been in France. I make a mental note to check with the postal authorities to find out just when and where that plain postcard was mailed. Sooner or later, I'm going to have to tie down each member of this family as to where they were and what they were doing when Hicks posted his card and Knight kept his appointment at Red Gutter. I have no enthusiasm for the task now; not here at a funeral.

The Thornes are heading for a bit of a public spat, she complaining that her husband should have accompanied her, he protesting it would have been rude to miss a lunch barbecue being thrown by an American ex-pat neighbour.

There's a lot of tension between this couple, caused, no doubt, by (or maybe the cause of) Brian's boozing. They are an ill-matched pair – she sharp and quite sophisticated, he fifteen years older and lacking county style.

On our travels this morning, Hazel and I rehearsed a variety of openings for this occasion. She uses one now to end this squabble. She gestures to me again. 'He's going with his crew –' now she nods at Rodney – 'this evening.' She smiles at me warmly. 'Send me a card.'

'Hardly worth it on a day trip,' I protest, going through the motions.

'Of course it is,' she insists. 'For the kitchen cork board.' She looks dazzlingly at Miles. 'Isn't it?'

A smiling shrug. 'I always send a couple to my mates, certainly.'

Hazel looks puzzled. 'You didn't, by any chance, send your uncle one to the force's local, the Fairways Hotel, when you were there?'

Now he's puzzled. 'Why?'

'Oh, it was just a jokey unsigned message from Normandy we found in his in-tray. We wondered if it had anything to do with his last case.'

'Not guilty,' says Miles with an innocent face. 'Haven't had a day off for months. Not like him here.' He flicks his head towards his father, who grumbles about having nothing better to do.

Hazel improvises, turning to Thorne senior. 'You didn't send it, by any chance?'

Stella answers. 'We don't bother with cards on a long weekend.'

'Well, there you are then,' mumbles her husband, not making much sense. Either he's acting dumb or the whisky is getting to him.

'I've never been to Normandy,' Hazel lies effortlessly. 'Nice, is it?'

'Prefer Brittany myself,' Brian interjects. 'Don't we?' Stella nods. Anita chips in. 'They've a nice place there.'

'Good weather last week?' I ask, conversationally.

'Fair,' says Brian. 'Only had a few days there, though. Why not? Can't do much here, can I, till the store's rebuilt?'

While he rants about the inefficiency of his builders, I am racking my brains for a way to bring Miles back into the conversation. Rodney does it for me. 'That chill-down equipment wasn't up to speed, I gather.'

Miles goes into a technical explanation as to why he didn't order what Combined Counties have installed. Despite his duties at the

140

club, he's clearly still very much involved in the cold store business.

Stella urges a quick decision on the replacement machinery but her husband tells her there's no hurry until the rebuilding work is complete.

Miles wanders off. I stroll after him, leaving Hazel to keep the rest talking. 'A private word,' I say when I catch him up. 'Do you stock Pestine at your club?'

'Why?' He's cautious, cute.

'Because we've evidence that Alan Hicks was in possession of a tin of it.'

'Yes,' he finally answers. 'Pinched it, did he, like the nitrogen? What did he want it for?'

'Is there any missing?'

'I'll run a stock check.' He groans as he belatedly answers his own question with another. 'Do you think he poisoned our bull, too?'

'I'll ask him when I find him.'

'He's up to his eyes in it, isn't he?'

I shrug, non-committal.

'The treacherous little bastard. Why did Uncle Andy let him go?'

I don't answer that either. Instead, I yank my head back in the direction of the family group. 'That business about the meat going off . . .'

'Oh, take no notice of dad,' he says with an annoyed wave of his hand. 'Of course, some stuff had deteriorated. It's been in there yonks. Freezer burn. You know these Common Market mountains. More surplus than they know what to do with. The equipment had become out-of-date over the years. It would have to have been replaced soon.'

A motive, of sorts, I suppose. New gear on insurance rather than out of profits. 'Yes, but what happened?'

'Some people in Sarajevo got gippy stomach.'

'Not read that in the papers,' I say.

'No, thank God. UN doctors suspected it was the EC meat a charity picked up from us.' He shrugs uncertainly. 'I mean, no one can be sure.'

I raise my eyebrows to ask: Why?

He shrugs: 'The cold store was destroyed before they could inspect the rest, wasn't it?'

'When was this?'

'Five or six weeks ago. Dad said that the EC had released some old stock and donated it to a charity. Then they phoned up mum a week or so later and said they'd have to run lab tests on the rest because there'd been some food poisoning scare.'

More of a motive, I think, excitedly, then calm as I can: 'What charity?'

He looks hard into a bed of cream lupins where bees are busy as if he'd find the answer there. 'Ask Rod. He'll know. His firm ferried it.'

The Thornes have drifted off separately to mingle, leaving the Montgomerys with Hazel, by the time I start to stroll back across the lawn to rejoin them.

'A word, Sweeney.' Carole Malloy waylays me, taking an arm, guiding me towards a shaded, fern-covered corner of the garden. Her other arm has her jacket draped over it. Her hand holds a glass of lager. The black linen dress is sleeveless as well as collarless; sexy. Her blue eyes, normally icy cool, have thawed through drink. 'Is there anything amiss about Silent Knight's death?'

No point in a flat 'No' or a 'Why?' Someone has tipped her off that I'm asking questions. Can't be Jacko. He knows nothing. Has to be the pathologist.

I brief her, but far from fully. 'Silent dispatched an informant after the bombers to Normandy to try to ID their whereabouts and next target. His mole set up a meeting at Red Gutter on Saturday noon, presumably to pass on the inside info. So he's back, but we can't find him. We need to know what he knows.'

I'm going to hint that I've rumbled her tipster; always an unnerving experience. 'I was trying to work out whether the shock of something Silent was told at that meeting brought on his heart attack, that's all. I don't doubt it was natural.'

She holds me with a steady look. 'You will let me know, won't you, if it becomes more than natural?'

She's pulling rank on me, letting me know that, if it's murder, she, as CID chief, wants the inquiry back. No chance, I vow, now that I'm experiencing that thrill of making progress even if I can't quite define it yet. 'Of course,' I say.

Jacko wanders up, trying to organise a drinking school from the fast-dwindling crowd into a trip to the local pub up on the main road, the Pauncefote. Carole accepts. I turn him down, pleading a prior appointment, but I don't say what.

Irritatingly, a grey-suited solicitor I haven't seen for a long time, senior partner in an old-established firm, full of old-world charm, has got to the Montgomerys ahead of me. His welcoming handshake is Masonic.

Clearly the family's lawyer, he's wanting to know how long Mrs Knight will be away. 'Up to her,' says Anita defensively.

It could be a long wait before I get to talk to her, I fret.

'Send anything needing urgent signature to auntie's post office box,' she adds, businesslike. She writes the details on an envelope with a pen the solicitor proffers. As she does so, she says, 'You, too, Mr Todd, if it's important.' She reads out what she's writing – a box number at the post office in a place called Doll de Bretagne. I jot it down in my notebook. She looks over my shoulder and corrects me, 'Only one "l" in Dol.'

Time is running out for me, so I go straight in as soon as the solicitor bows out. 'This duff meat on your mercy –'

Rod's expression is startled. 'How did you know that?'

'Miles just told me.'

'How does he know?'

'Haven't you discussed it with him?'

'No.'

'Or Mr and Mrs Thorne?'

He looks quickly at his frowning wife. 'Or anyone. Andy told me not to.'

'But you did tell Mr Knight?'

'Of course, and he told me not to discuss it with anyone.'

I smile. 'I'm sure he didn't mean me.'

He begins to talk softly, anxious not to be overheard. Arc Air had volunteered its plane at cut price to a relief organisation for a day trip to Bosnia in April. They thought it might be good PR in case news of their livestock flights leaked out. The cargo was delivered to the airport by the charity he names. Some boxed-up meat was among it. The plane had no freezer equipment. Since the meat was likely to be cooked and eaten within hours of landing, it didn't really matter.

A few days later, the charity came on with the disturbing news that several refugees had gone down ill. Health inspectors turned up and the plane missed a scheduled flight while they carried out on-board checks. 'They thought the livestock we've carried might have left a bovine bug behind. We only heard yesterday that we've been cleared.'

'Did you know the meat came from Thorne's cold store?'

'Good God,' gasps Anita. She exchanges fraught glances with her husband.

Rodney is looking away guiltily. 'Yes, I did.'

'You never told me,' huffs Anita.

'Your father told me not to tell anyone.'

'Yes,' says Hazel, 'but who told you?'

Knight himself, he answers. On a free afternoon, he'd brought the children round to see their grandfolks. 'I mentioned our trouble with the health inspector. Why not?' He nods at his wife. 'Her mum's a shareholder in Arc, after all, and a cancelled trip means money.'

I nod him on.

'He said the meat had come from the EC stock at Thorne's depot. That's all. Except to keep quiet about it.'

'And you told no one?' Hazel double checks.

'Well, if I'm not going to tell her . . .' He looks briefly towards his wife. '. . . I'm not going to tell anyone, am I?' Both expressions are annoyed; Anita with her husband, for holding back, Rod with me for dropping him in it. I seem to be causing a few family rifts here today.

I'm not going to tell him that, through his air firm, he's been implicated in the coded card Hicks sent to Knight.

'How did Miles know?' Hazel resumes.

'His father told him,' I report.

'Yes – but who told him?' asks Hazel.

Knight, I suspect immediately. A favour to someone who's a brother in more than law. To warn him to expect an inquiry into the state of his stored meat. 'When did you have this chat with Mr Knight?'

He thinks out loud, eyes skyward, working out where he was on what day according to his air trips. 'First Tuesday in May.'

Two days before the arson, I calculate. But by then, Brussels would have had the news from UN medics of the outbreak of food poisoning. And the next port of call for the health inspectors would be Thorne's cold stores. Only before they could visit and carry out an inspection, it had been burned down. Convenient that. No wonder Knight was privately questioning whether the job was connected with the boat bombing.

Anita looks at me quizzically. Quite bluntly she comes out with a question that must have preoccupied her late father. 'Do you think there's something untoward about Uncle Brian's fire?'

I still can't come out with 'Yes – and so did your late father'. So: 'Do you?'

Her face sets. 'I'm asking you.'

'I don't know. Did your father?'

She looks severely at Rod, calling on him for an answer. 'He never expressed any doubts to me.' A shrug. 'Honestly.'

'Me either,' says Hazel.

My eyes catch and hold Anita's. 'Would he have discussed it with your mother?'

She looks uncertain. 'Bits of it, perhaps. He sometimes did. If it was a family, well . . .' Her voice trails. Yes, he would, she's all but saying.

'Listen.' I take a chance now. 'I get the impression that he may have taken her some way at least into his confidence. I can't push it, certainly not now.'

Her expression sets aggressively.

'But when she's settled down a bit,' I hurry on, 'you know . . . is ready . . . will you tell her I'm interested in a chat?'

The thought of an outsider prying into family matters fills her face with undisguised disgust, making me feel like a tabloid reporter digging for dirt.

I shrug, embarrassed. 'I've already told you I'm a bit puzzled about her words "Beware imposters". Did your father think his informant had been turned or substituted or something?'

'I . . .' A fraction of a second's pause from Anita so the word rings out its capital letter. '. . . will talk to her when the time is right.'

Now she's coming the protective daughter. I fear I have made a mess of this. 'Of course. I mean . . .' I feel myself backing off. '. . . it may not be necessary. If we find Hicks, we may get all the answers.'

'Talking of which,' says Rod, seemingly anxious to break up what had become a tense encounter, 'you'd best be off soon.'

'Us, too,' says Anita stiffly. 'We really ought to thank a few more people.' She turns, looking at me over her shoulder. 'Have a good trip.'

Somehow I don't think she really means it.

16

Not a good trip this.

I'm in one of three seats in a roomy cockpit, behind Charlie Disney on the left and the third partner to my right.

Ahead and each side are blue skies and thinning clouds and, below, sweeping countryside in variegated greens – a spectacular overview of rural England, farming England.

Behind us, though, is that other rural England – the crewyard smells from calves crammed into their arched metal cages made to measure for the contours of the wide fuselage.

The containers stretch out in a line towards the tail on duckboards covered with plastic sheeting to catch their droppings.

They'd been loaded before I climbed the steep steps into a door at the front of the plane. The hold was already steaming up from the humidity they create.

A brief sight of them only as Charlie tested a safety net, straps of brown leather spoking out from a centre circle. '9G,' he'd said. In the event of an emergency stop, it would prevent them finishing up in the cockpit or us in a cage, I suppose. Not that there was any room in any cage. No zoo would get away with packing them so tightly.

A grey door was shut to deaden their low, plaintive calls, but I can still hear their cries echoing in my head above the steady sound of the four turbo-prop engines.

Cargo planes, I was forewarned in the crew room, are more noisy than passenger airliners because much of the insulation is stripped away to maximise every cubic inch of room, so engine noise is increased; just as well with this cargo.

Lacking insulation, they're colder, too, Charlie had added. Not noticed that. I can feel the heat from the hold at my back – heat from the animals, the heat of fear.

A smooth, if rather loud, take-off, Charlie working his way

146

through the controls at his right hand, the partner next to him reading out loud from so many dials in front and to each side that they were impossible to take in without head movement.

For ten minutes I have been ignored while they go through their drill. A minute or two is spent studying the airline-type ticket for insurance cover and to get me past security. Handguns, I noted, were prohibited baggage; just as well that I'm not tooled up. Another few seconds go by craning my neck but managing to see only the tips of each wing a long way behind.

Only now, when we've levelled out and all the reds and greens on the panels are oranges, does the second officer turn. Raising his voice, he looks up at the ceiling above me. 'Take that headset.'

I release a four point harness, stand and pull the set down on a long cable. The earpieces have silver, lightweight padding; a comfortable fit.

'OK?' he asks, speaking normally.

'Fine. Thanks.'

He tells me we're flying at 19,000 feet and 360 miles an hour. I try to work out how far, at 1000 air hours a year for thirty-five years, this plane has travelled, give up. Further than my old Cavalier, now our runabout, and I wonder if Em's gone to Sainsbury's shopping in it.

Eventually Charlie asks how Old Man Knight's funeral went, presenting me with an opening.

'Very moving. Had a long chat with Rod. He was telling me over a drink about your bit of bother with the health inspectorate. You're in the clear, I gather.'

'Too bloody true.' Pause. 'You were there, weren't you?' Another pause. 'When they phoned yesterday.'

I remember him being on the phone, I tell him, but don't add that he sounded shirty.

'Took bloody weeks to complete the lab tests,' he complains.

He runs through the story again – their offer of a flight to Sarajevo, the arrival at the airport of the charity's lorry with a load that included crates of boxed-up meat, and, soon afterwards, the examination of the plane by health inspectors who only phoned yesterday with the all-clear while I was in the crew room with Hazel.

A casual, very gentle probe follows, disguising the questions with a feigned interest in the logistics of the aviation business. Did

147

the boxes of meat come in separate transport? One job lot. Did Rod help with the loading or unloading? Airport handlers both ends. Did Charlie know the name of the cold store the consignment came from? Haven't a clue.

I move on to the joyrides members of Knight's family have made in the seat I'm now occupying, but all I get is confirmation that both Thorne senior and Anita came when they claimed they did, and Miles hadn't made a trip at all.

Switching the subject to sport, which everyone joins in, I mention I've recently bumped into Geoff Powers, the old rugger star.

The second pilot, a rugger man, has heard of him but never met him, and the topic dribbles out.

'Still coming back tomorrow night?' Charlie asks.

'If that's OK.'

'Sure.' He wonders if I'll complete my business in twenty-four hours. Yes, I assure him. The dossier they had delivered last night would save a lot of time.

'Well, if not, come back on Friday. The seat's free.' Rod had planned to return on Friday, he goes on, but had been talked into taking the weekend off. 'Only fair.' He worked last weekend, so the co-pilot could watch the rugger on TV. 'Unfortunate, really.'

'Where was he when his father-in-law died?' I ask.

'Day trip, special delivery to Dublin.' He breaks off to talk to Control.

So – I run it past my mind again – Rod kept his word to Knight. He hadn't even told his partners the source of the meat. If you believe his story, of course.

He'd been out of the country when Knight died. What do you make of that? Well, if I was plotting with the Stones or Lynch or Hicks or anybody to put the fatal frighteners on my sick father-in-law, I'd arrange an alibi too. He can't get round the fact that Hicks named this firm, his firm, in that card.

Nothing's what I'm going to make of it – yet. I stay silent, brooding on my lack of progress. A wild-goose flight this, I'm certain of it. There's no way I can place any member of the family, Rod apart, or Powers in Cherbourg at the same time as Hicks wrote and posted that card.

The only answer is to find Hicks and, more important, the trio from the *Tyke* and ask them point-blank: Have you done two jobs or three?

Or . . . Suddenly I feel sick. Not air sickness; the nausea of anxiety and foreboding. Come on, face it. Well, if they've scored a new hit today, is it No. 3 or No. 4?

Should never have gone to that funeral, I rebuke myself. Should have made this trip last night. Should already be there, searching for the bombers, not pissing about, getting absolutely nowhere on a side issue. My mind stands still, viewing yet again that other funeral, seeing those widows, all those orphans.

An age passes – or so it seems – and I am craning my neck again looking down on blue-grey sea and an armada of tiny boats, praying that the *Lindum Castle* is among them and isn't already at the bottom of it.

The plane appears to hang like a helicopter in mid-air and I will it to go faster.

Think positive, I urge myself, and I wonder how Hazel is getting on back at headquarters contacting the UN in Sarajevo, the EC in Brussels and local insurance assessors, checking Rod's story.

She'd volunteered to phone Powers' daughter, too, to confirm the stuff in the Co-op bag Hicks dropped off at Powers' place reached her. I'd added the task of finding out just what Powers did in his days in the army when, according to the custody sergeant, he played for the Combined Services.

The conversations over my headphones are in French now and every time Control comes on I wait with heart in mouth for the crew to translate the message: 'You're too bloody late.'

The descent is gentle. Yachts with billowing sails, more wind in them than I feel in mine, grow bigger. The green decks of a large car ferry ahead are getting closer. Soon, green coastline and masts and water towers on a wooded hill. At its foot, trapped in the evening sun, is Cherbourg; chimneys, cranes, pylons and the colourful roofs of warehouses with staider brickwork.

I concentrate on the landing, always do. It's perfect, and, with headphones on, not much of an engine whine, plenty of runway to spare. We turn left rather sedately, no more than 20 miles an hour, on to an apron towards the main terminus, a Lego-type building in pale-coloured blocks next to a taller control tower on which a red and white wind sock flies taut on its pole.

I wonder if Dubal is waiting, imagine his face – his funereal face that policemen the world over wear when they're breaking tragic news, hear those word again, 'Too late.'

In an airliner half the passengers would be standing up, collecting their hand luggage, wanting to be first off and away. The calves behind won't be in such a hurry.

I think of the 9G safety net between us, mercifully not needed, and realise with shame I've not thought of something for some time: K2, still unresolved.

We turn left again away from the terminus towards twin half-moon huts with rusting metal roofs that look more like wartime relics than hangars.

On a wide verge of grass between them and us is a double-decker livestock transporter. Ready to manoeuvre into position, I guess, when we've come to a stop, to off-load our cargo and take them to their tiny pens where they're fed on a diet of milk and darkness to keep their meat nice and white.

Oh, sod 'em. I've got my own problems. Think positive. Come on, now. OK then. K2 is unresolved. It's not cropped up anywhere again in the inquiry.

So what, I ponder, does . . .

The private query never gets completed as I gaze absently out my window. What's that? That vehicle beside the transporter?

I stare now, long and hard at a battered truck with the words 'Arc Air' painted rather amateurishly in plain white capitals on a green door, no rainbow above them. I note the colour of the vehicle. Green. Green!

My eyes stay on it, my brain racing. Well? I snap. Well what?

Arc is spelt correctly, I see. Can't be Hicks' handiwork then, but . . .

Well? The back is sheeted down with roped blue covering. What did Hazel say this morning? Where's that stolen fertiliser?

Another sense takes over, clamouring for attention, begging me to scent the diesel fumes that docks patrolman smelt from the hold-all in the *Lindum Castle*.

Well, is that a vehicle bomb, or just a clapped-out truck? Make up your mind. A third sense hears the c-r-u-m-p that thundered along the river on election night.

Come on. Is that a bomb or not? You wanted the top job, the big time. This is what it means. Making life or death decisions. Wrong and you're a panic-stricken fool. Right and you're still an idiot for missing a clue.

I taste again the smoke-laden fall-out from the cold store fire, see the blood flowing down the drain.

Is it or isn't it? Come on. I don't know. Compromise then, at the very least, you dithering duffer. Raise the question.

Charlie speaks first. 'Same time here tomorrow then. There's –'

I break in. 'Have you got ground crew here, handlers perhaps?' I am speaking in a voice I have only used once before and can't immediately place.

'No,' replies Charlie. 'Why?'

'Take a look at that green truck beside that long transporter.' There's a distant drone in my voice, but not the sound that comes with hearing impaired by landing.

He turns his head left, not locating it immediately.

'See it?' I point. Now I know where I've heard this strangled voice before. On the railway line. With my leg hanging half off. Thinking I was going to die. 'Keep going.' It's my own voice again, in command.

'What?' His is slightly raised.

'Keep going. Right away from it.'

'But –'

I am sweating like the calves behind me. Fear of death? Fear of making a mistake? Don't know, don't care. 'Tell Control: "Bomb alert." '

'But –'

'Just do it.' Finally I shout, have to. '*Now*.'

He does something with the controls. The engines thrust us faster forward. Simultaneously he says, incredibly calmly, '*Attention. Attention.*' He adds a sentence I don't understand apart from one phrase: '*une alerte à la bombe*'. He is describing what he is seeing, repeating the word '*vert*'.

He gives my name and the police force I'm from, presenting me another opening. 'Tell them to inform Chief Inspector Dubal who's awaiting this flight's arrival.' I add, 'Immediately.'

All the time we are picking up ground speed, the co-pilot looking around, then at me, grim-faced. Charlie translates into his microphone, turning at the same time, heading back the way we came, then announces, 'We've got a new parking slot.'

Finally we slow and stop four or five hundred yards from the transporter and green truck. The plane turns slowly again to give us a head-on view.

Down a perimeter road in front of the terminus speeds a police jeep, blue lights twirling. I can't hear any sirens above the sound of the throbbing engines. The vehicle bumps on to the grass verge and halts some distance short of the two stationary trucks.

A flak-jacketed man jumps out, loud-hailer in hand, and mouths something into it. His colleague emerges from the other door, crouching behind it, training a handgun ahead of him.

Out of the lorry jump two men who run, stumbling, towards the policemen, hands clasping the back of their necks. From this distance neither looks much like Richard Stone. No one vacates the green truck.

The men are manhandled into the jeep which backs away faster than seems possible in reverse.

Overhead a yellow plane with a third engine on its tail swoops low, then rises again, waving its wings as it straightens out.

'They're closing the airport,' groans Charlie, white-faced. 'I hope we're right about this.'

The only two planes on the ground, both smaller than ours, start to taxi slowly away from parking places facing the terminus. A fuel tanker departs more swiftly.

Hope? I query privately. It's time for prayers.

Across the space they have vacated lumbers an armoured vehicle that looks as though it's missed its turning to a war zone – four-wheeled, gun metal grey and a turret from which a stubby barrel points. Each side are viewing slits.

As the vehicle turns off the concrete on to the grass verge the barrel revolves. From it comes a thick spurt of white liquid which sprays the truck's bonnet, cab, then canvas-covered back.

Quickly the truck begins to disappear in a bubbling balloon of foam, which is expanding all the time like some scene in a sci-fi film.

Then . . . a flash, yellowy-green, outshines the sun.

C-r-u-m-p. That now familiar crump.

The runway seems to rock the wheels beneath us. Reds, blacks, greys, yellows and bits of green tinge the white balloon, disintegrating upwards and outwards. Fragments fly, one bit of black, twisted metal landing only a hundred yards or so from us.

The armoured vehicle is engulfed as grey foam floats and debris falls silently like feathers all around it.

My heart is about to explode, too. Oh Christ, we've lost the fire crew. You've lost the fire crew because you didn't figure things out soon enough.

This was the target. This plane, you berk. And Hicks said so in code on his card. Zip. Ark. You and your one-track mind. He wasn't naming Rod as a bomber. He was naming him as a target. You stupid, stupid bastard. You had the connection. And you missed it.

I can't bear to think any more, just look.

Out of the tangle of half a dozen different colours, nothing like a rainbow, backs the armoured truck agonisingly slowly, caked with dripping grey suds.

Charlie is talking again into his mike, his face and voice joyful. 'Fantast-eke. Fantast-eke.' He looks at me. 'No casualties.'

I close my eyes and blow out hot air. A cooling feeling of overwhelming, overpowering relief courses through me – as much for myself as the fire crew, I have to admit.

17

'*Bienvenue.*' A moustachioed man, not quite as tubby as Claude from Fraud, is beaming and pumping my hand that's frozen despite the warmth of a sunny evening. 'Wonderful.'

He'd been waiting inside the terminal to which the pilots and myself, all shocked speechless, were ferried in a convoy of police cars.

He looks like a departing holidaymaker in a cotton jacket the colour of bleached straw and light grey flannels. He introduces himself. 'Dubal.'

'Chief inspector,' I manage.

'Michel, please.'

'Phil,' I say.

'Come. Please. Tell me about it.' Dubal half turns and issues instructions to three or four men and one woman around him. 'We will use an office above.' He turns fully, shepherding me with

153

an arm across my shoulder through a cool foyer with the flags of several nations, including the Union Jack, hanging from a high ceiling. Climbing a wide set of stairs, he tells me the crew will go to the gendarmerie HQ on the other side of the airfield to make statements while safety experts examine their plane for damage.

The two men who escaped from the transporter were livestock handlers, not the bombers from the houseboat *Tyke*, he adds. Shit, I fret, they are still on the loose.

Opening a door to a small office with a wall map in a glass frame, he asks, 'You are married?' When I reply 'Yes' he points me to a desk, empty apart from a lime green phone. 'First, call home.'

First, in fact, I phone HQ after he dictates the international code. I ask for Hazel, but her line is busy. I wonder whether to brief Dale, but don't want him shouting the odds about this cock-up along the flight deck. I give the switchboard operator my number and extension, again at Dubal's prompting, and tell him to ask Hazel to call back.

Dubal has perched on the corner of the desk, looking away, pretending not to listen. On closer inspection, he's shorter than Claude at five-nine and a year or two older. His fair hair is long at the back with an unruly quiff at the front, nothing other than rather red skin in between. There is a prominent wart on his right cheek. His stomach is more pronounced than Em's will be at nine months. Even with a pipe and a waltzing accordion in the background he'd never have made a Maigret.

I dial again and reach Em. 'Missing me this badly?' she asks mischievously. I tell her briefly what's happened and not to worry if she hears anything on the radio. 'Are you all right?' she asks, worried.

The strain in my voice must be audible. 'Fine,' I fib.

I answer a few of her questions, trying to resist the temptation to seek an interpretation from her on Mrs Knight's selection from Shakespeare for the funeral. It's too difficult to explain right now, especially in front of a stranger; do it later, I half decide, when no one can hear. I don't want people to know I'm scraping the barrel this low for clues. Shortly he's going to find out I'm incompetent enough as it is. Somehow all my confidence has been blown away by the blast.

Come on, I urge myself. Don't be too proud to make a fool of yourself. Fishing the order of service from an inside pocket, I give her the play, act and scene and the opening and closing lines. 'See what you can make of it.'

'I'll try,' she replies, unsure.

If Dubal does regard it as a bizarre request by someone who's just walked away from an inferno, his round, rosy face isn't changing expression.

I ask her to pat her stomach goodnight for me. 'OK,' she laughs. Goodbye kisses are smacked.

'Ça va?' Dubal asks.

Even I know he's asking me if everything is all right. The truthful answer – 'Anything but' – escapes me, so I force a weak smile. 'Ça va, merci.'

I brief him fairly fully. 'Your information was good.' He sums it all up. 'Wonderful.'

I shake my head, facing up to it. 'Not so wonderful, I'm afraid.'

'Why so?' he asks, with a heavy frown.

I have given him bum info, the wrong target, I confess, shamefaced. While his team has been lying in wait at the sea port for the *Lindum Castle*, the terrorists had Arc Air in their sights at the airport.

Lincsline, I explain, not only owned the boat but were major investors in the aviation company. Richard Stone, working on admin at the shipping company's head office, would have known that. He and his gang had been here long enough to monitor Arc Air's regular timetable of trips. I feel miserable. 'I should have worked it out.'

'But you did,' he comforts me, 'and in time to save lives.' He shrugs expressively. 'They will not strike twice on the same day. You have given us time to find them.'

I feel lightened, a pack-horse which has shed its load.

The phone rings and Dubal gestures for me to answer. The switchboard operator I spoke to at HQ announces himself. 'Connecting you.'

There's a click, then: 'Dale.'

I moan to myself. It's late for him to be hanging about the office and I can only assume the chief must still be around, catching up on time lost at the funeral.

'Where are you?' he demands.

155

I tell him.

'What the devil are you doing there? Who cleared it?'

'What's the problem?' I ask.

The chief wanted a word, he explains. I permit myself a small smile, right about something. He'd asked Dale to find me. He'd phoned my and Hazel's extensions, got no reply, called the switchboard and obtained the number I'd just phoned in.

I ask to be connected, but he says in a tone that's irritatingly airy that he's got a message from him for me. 'He's had Knight's daughter on, in effect, complaining at your persistence. Go easy on Mrs Knight, that's all. She has enough troubles, don't you think?'

I think I might explode, but Dubal's presence is a calming influence and I grit my teeth. 'She'd have a lot more if her son-in-law's business in which she has a quarter of a million invested had gone up in flames.'

I go through the story again, boring Dubal into a blank expression. 'So just tell the chief that, will you?' I conclude.

'Have you caught the offenders?' he asks.

'Any moment now,' I lie breezily.

'Oh.' Disappointment dampens his tone.

I ask to go back to the switchboard. Hurriedly he offers to pass my message to the chief. And a highly censored account it will be, I privately wager. It's Sergeant Webster I want to speak to, I tell him.

The operator comes back on to inform me that Hazel is out. He volunteers to raise her on a two-way radio and, after a short delay, relays her progress report.

The medics in Sarajevo were certain that the outbreak of illness – 'hepatitis, as a matter of fact' – came from the EC meat Arc Air flew in. They alerted Brussels who informed the charity.

It told Environmental Health, but she hadn't yet been able to contact the inspector in charge of their inquiries.

Powers' daughter Dawn is proving elusive, too, so she'd taken a radio car and is doorstepping her home as we speak.

'And', the operator gabbles on, almost mimicking Hazel, 'Powers' unit in the army was Ordnance.'

Neither he nor she has to add that the corps' duties include expertise in bombs.

'She wants to know how you are doing,' the operator says.

Time for the truth, I decide, at least for Hazel. 'Not as well as her, by the sounds of it.'

He passes the message on and her response. 'Any fresh instructions?'

I decide to cover my back. 'Take Surveillance off the waterfront and put them on Powers.'

'So let's find the bombers,' says Dubal with Hazel-like enthusiasm, rubbing his chubby hands.

So far, easier said than done, he continues. As well as forming a reception party for the *Lindum Castle* at the docks, his men had searched all the bars and boarding-houses where the flotsam of any port like Cherbourg wash up. 'Nothing,' he says regretfully. He looks at me pleadingly. 'Is there anything, anything new, we can examine?'

Nothing new at all, but something old dredges itself up from the churning mud in my mind, something I mentioned to that MoD Intelligence colonel, but not Dubal, something that was beginning to resurface as we taxied in the plane before that fake Arc Air truck mercifully distracted me.

'The only loose end is something with a letter and a number – K2.'

'K2,' he repeats, pronouncing it slightly differently, clipping the 'K', half adding an 'e' and rounding the 'two'.

He heaves himself up, lands lightly on his feet and strolls to the map, motioning me to follow. He studies it briefly, then places his index finger on the airport, runs it east along a red road and south down a yellow route to a name in small, black print. He is smiling across his shoulder. 'K2.'

It's spelt very differently from the way either of us has been pronouncing it.

A relaxed and informal affair is Dubal's council of war at the gendarmerie headquarters, a collection of modern cream buildings, some no bigger than bungalows, just beyond the eastern perimeter fence of the airport.

Half a dozen officers, casually dressed, lounge in chairs in an airy ground-floor office with 'Commandant' on the door. They often break out into laughter at things he says, incomprehensible to me, in a deep, musical voice.

Others in uniform stroll in and out, bringing up-to-date reports, which he reads through metal-framed spectacles that hang on a chain round his bull neck.

After friendly introductions, I have spoken only when spoken to in answer to questions put by or through Dubal.

It would, he explained in English, be a joint operation because, geographically, the sabotage occurred next door, outside the city police force's borders in gendarmerie territory. 'Anyway . . .' He shrugged. 'We co-operate on important inquiries.' A good deal more happily than some neighbouring forces back home, I decided, feeling the warmth of a good team spirit.

The commandant, a tall man with steel grey hair, three stripes on the shoulder of his blue open-necked shirt, had welcomed us, then listened intently to Dubal's briefing.

Almost immediately, he departed, Dubal translating his orders to make ourselves at home in an office with primrose wallpaper on which group photos and a portrait of General de Gaulle hang. In one corner a glass cabinet displays collections of berets, belts, badges – and bullets in clips.

'The media,' Dubal announced answering a black telephone on the commandant's walnut desk. 'They are aware of our incident. We cannot control them. Is this a problem?'

'It could be if someone back home reads Arc Air was the target and we're seeking a gang of Brits,' I'd pointed out.

He nodded and is now issuing instructions I don't understand. I gaze out of the window. Behind a red barrier to the gatehouse, a tricolour at full stretch on its pole, drab-coloured jeeps are being lined up.

Another phone call makes my eyes follow my ears back to the desk. Replacing the receiver, Dubal announces, 'There are fragments of blue plastic in the debris. Is this of use?'

I reveal the suspected source and the colour of the bags of nitrogen at a golf club where Hicks, the missing informant, worked which he interprets for his team. All look very impressed with me.

The commandant returns with a revolver on a belt round his dark blue trousers. There's much gabbled conversation, then Dubal beckons me out of my chair.

Leisurely, he leads me outside where a dirty white Citroën is waiting. There's a 'Taxi' sign on its roof. A dark, stocky driver, very hairy, in an open-necked blue check shirt, squeezes his foot on a half-smoked untipped cigarette as he opens the back door for us. I didn't have to be told he was no civilian cabbie. He'd earlier been in and out of the office.

Once we and the driver are settled, Dubal introduces us. 'Paul Février. February in your language.' Both laugh.

He swings round to reach over the back of his seat to take my hand in a strong grip. 'Hallo,' he says, surprisingly softly.

In the back, Dubal tells me where we are headed is not far. 'It is well signposted on the main roads that run down the spine of our peninsula, so, therefore, your Mr Knight's informant Hicks may have seen the signs on his way to pick grapes further south, perhaps. If, as you say, he speaks good French, well, the name might be known to him. Yes?'

Before I can reply he goes on, 'And if, in his presence, Richard Stone mentioned the village in conversation, say, with his sister, Hicks may well have given a hint of the name when striking his bargain with your chief. Yes?'

I get out 'Perhaps' this time, but question how we are going to locate them.

'Oh,' he says airily, 'it is a *petite* place. Three or four bars. We have their photos and, with Stone's description . . .' He leans forward, hands crossed at the wrists to hunch his back. ' . . . *pas difficile. Oui*?'

Slowly, he sits upright again in his corner seat, letting his crossed hands flop on to his lap and, smiling, closes his eyes.

Monsieur Sang-Froid all right, I think, looking away from him over rolling countryside, small fields hiding behind high hedges, many mainly yellow gorse. I hope I'm this cool when I'm . . .

Forget it. Concentrate. Work it out.

I had been quick to spot that fake Arc Air truck, true enough, I console myself, but much slower to appreciate its significance.

If Stone and Hicks are in league with each other, getting pissed over here and taking the piss out of Knight, setting up that meeting at Red Gutter, planting false leads about Arc Air, then there's something wrong with the postcard.

Stone knew the correct spelling of Arc. He'd seen it in writing while working at Lincsline. That's how he knew the shipping company had invested in the air firm, making it a target. Hicks may not have known the spelling, but Richard Stone did. Getting the spelling right on the green truck at the airport proves it.

If and when they had got their heads together cooking up a ruse to mislead Knight, Stone would have corrected Hicks' spelling, surely?

So, at whose dictation did Hicks write the card? Where – here or back home? And, if it was back home, who posted it from here?

'Quettehou,' February announces only fifteen minutes into the trip, so quietly that it actually comes out as K2.

18

Dubal struggles out of the back of the Citroën, which comes to a halt in a sunlit square.

He lowers his head to speak through the opened window to February who nods and makes a show of keeping on the '*Occupé*' sign, so no one will try to hire him.

Dubal turns and views the square, dominated by two large civic-looking buildings facing each other across a line of mature, heavily pruned lime trees.

'A beer, *peut-être*?' He is throwing in the odd simple word to encourage French replies.

'*Très bon*,' I say with more embarrassment for my accent than enthusiasm for the idea, but both Richard Stone and Alan Hicks like their drink, so a bar is as good a place as any to start.

The sun at our backs, we stroll beyond the corner of the market place on which stands another smart, stone building with 'La Poste' in blue letters on yellow glass and emerge in a wide street. There are shops on either side, one a taxidermist. It is too far away to make out what's on display, but I visualise Dale, stuffed and with an apple in his mouth.

We glance in passing inside one double-fronted bar. Dubal looks across the road at another, walks into the third which has a small counter for cigarette sales and a longer one for drinks. *'Deux bières, s'il vous plaît.'*

While they are being drawn from a pot pump, he puts his hand on my shoulder. *'Mon ami cherche . . .'*

Though he is speaking slowly for a Frenchman, I can only identify a couple of words a sentence, if that. Hazarding a guess at the rest, I am looking for four English friends – three men and a woman – whose address I have lost.

Recognition dawns on the dark attractive face of the young barmaid as Dubal tilts slightly forward, twists an arm behind his back and places a hand between his shoulder blades.

He pulls four photos from an inside pocket and places them on the elbow-height fawn counter. *'Mais oui,'* nods the barmaid looking with brown eyes down in turn on Stone, his sister Zoe and Lynch. *'Non,'* she says as she studies the face of Hicks, shaking her head so firmly that her long ear-rings sway.

They talk quietly for some time, Dubal and me sipping our cold, lager-type beers, the barmaid gesticulating in the direction we walked. There are references to a *bateau*, the barmaid pointing in the other direction.

We finish our beers, Dubal settles up on a plate and leaves with hearty thanks to which I add, *'Merci beaucoup.'*

Outside, we stroll back the way we came. 'We have them,' says Dubal, with a quiet, satisfied smile. 'Three of them, at least.'

Stone, his sister and Lynch are renting a cottage which an Englishman owns in a terraced street beyond the square. A yacht in a harbour a couple of kilometres east goes with the letting.

'They are regular frequenters of the bar,' Dubal relays, 'Richard Stone in particular. None of them speak much French.' He shakes his head heavily. 'There is no sighting or information regarding Alan Hicks or anyone resembling him. Are we sure he is here?'

'No' is the honest reply.

In the market square, we get back into the Citroën. While we were having our beers, two other cars have joined the dozen or so that were already parked here.

February doesn't start the engine until he has radioed on orders Dubal gives him. Then we pull away, into the main street, passing the bar we've just left.

The road narrows into a long, very straight stretch, sloping gently after a couple of miles into another grey stone village, and dramatically opens up again on to a breathtaking sight. The car stops. We get out.

St Vaast smells just as much of money as it does of the sea. Its harbour is packed with yachts, a forest of masts, hundreds of them.

'We do not know the name of the boat,' sighs Dubal, the lowering sun shining over his left shoulder.

'I could phone their landlord in England,' I volunteer, wondering if he's holding something back.

He gives my idea some thought, looking across the harbour to a newish building with sharp, slate roofs on the northern wall. 'We could go to the club and ask.' He gives his own idea longer thought. 'We are doing remarkably well. Let us not rush things.' Then, 'You have eaten?'

Not since a snack after Mr Knight's funeral, I reply.

He beams. 'Just time, I think, for a small *repas*.' He has a longish conversation with February while I try to identify the metallic melody all around us, finally deciding it is the sound of cables being blown against the multitude of masts.

We don't head for the café in whose car-park we have stopped, but down the front in the shade. Behind us February pulls away.

Just a short walk takes us to a restaurant with green umbrellas over pavement tables. He leads the way inside where an expensively dressed middle-aged blonde, very chic, holds his hands, kisses both his cheeks and shakes my hand more formally.

She sits us at a table with a starched white cloth, Dubal on a leather bench below a ship's wheel in the window, me with a view of the harbour and an almost cloudless blue sky over it.

He doesn't ask for the menu, just orders *fruits de mer* and a bottle of Muscadet *sur lie*. '*D'accord?*'

Agreed, I agree, explaining, not in too much detail, where I was this morning. 'Hope I never get caught up in any of these EC fishing disputes or I'll finish up a veggie.'

'Ah, you animal-loving English,' he smiles.

Emboldened by a gulp of cold wine on an empty stomach, I ask point-blank if the English landlord is called either Powers or Thorne. He gives a name which is neither.

Shamed at my distrust, I tell him all I think I know – how and why Powers and someone in the Thorne family copied the terrorist trio's *modus operandi* from the original boat bombing to cover their crime. Suddenly, I confess, I feel at the wrong end of the inquiry.

He assures me that catching the conspirators in the attack on the plane is reason enough for my being here. 'Relax and enjoy your short stay.'

The meal arrives on a two-tier plate overflowing with crabs, oysters, shrimps, prawns, whelks and cockles with dips of mayonnaise and vinegar with onions and a basket of chunkily sliced bread.

Dubal operates the shell crackers and pin-like pickers deftly. I fiddle as I try to follow his technique, at times making a messy job of it. Some meat is chewy, hardly worth all the effort, but the crab is succulent and the prawns juicy.

I begin to expand on the reason I think Hicks may be back home, about the Sunday sighting of him in Newark and the call he made to his girlfriend's neighbour.

Without guilt at being disloyal to a dead chief, I speculate that Knight, for all his experience, may have been fatally wrong to put his trust in Hicks as an informant when he might have been a leading player in the plotting.

I can understand, I tell him, Knight not asking Dubal to stake out a zoo here last Friday. The initial Z was part of the code which really stood for A. He'd have known, anyway, that the rendezvous was the next day at Red Gutter. 'What I can't fathom is why didn't he cross-check K2 with you. Hicks must have mentioned it to him for it to appear in the files.'

'Professional pride, perhaps,' Dubal suggests after a longish pause in which he dabs his thick moustache with a white napkin. 'Perhaps he trusted Hicks no more than you. Turning him loose might have produced all the answers. At the very least, releasing him in Powers' recognisance may have forced someone to reveal themselves. Perhaps that happened at the Saturday meeting, the truth about the middle case, the precise whereabouts of the gang responsible for the first case, their next target.'

And perhaps, I'm thinking, with the first trace of guilt, that was Knight's plan – to get the job lot, tell the chief who did what and offer his resignation because his family's involvement might harm the reputation of the force.

Dubal spreads his rather greasy hands expansively. 'It would have been a remarkable coup for a man soon to leave the police service because of ill-health – all the more remarkable if he was to provide evidence against a corrupt member of his own family; a parting testament to his own incorruptibility, a lasting example to any police officer who follows him.'

He sighs heavily. 'The tragedy is, of course, that he died before he could achieve that final ambition.'

No, it wasn't pride or ambition. It was honour, out of fashion these days. But I'm not going to argue, wish I'd kept my mouth shut.

Finally he unveils his plan. 'Février is a good man, the best.' By now he will have been to the rented cottage in Quettehou and knocked on the door, he continues. If anyone answered, he would have apologised for getting the number wrong. No reply, and he would have come away with a feeling for the place.

'What then?' I ask.

He pulls a face. 'Workmen from the gas or street lighting company will be busy in the street, repairing a non-existent fault. I leave such matters to the experts.'

I fish out the order of service at Knight's funeral and hand it over.

'Ah,' he says, studying it as he sips the last of the wine. 'Explains your puzzling inquiry of your wife.' With so much French literature still unread, he adds apologetically, he's not studied Shakespeare, and he can't help me understand it.

'*Pas problème*,' I reply sincerely. He has helped my understanding considerably already.

February, in dark blue overalls and a hard white hat, is on the square platform of a mobile lift parked alongside a concrete lamp standard in a one-way street. In slow, easy rhythm, his left hand is winding black cable into a coil, using his right thumb and elbow for a frame.

The platform is in the down position, lower than the red roof of the empty cab in front. It has just one solid side. The other three have thin chains hooked to corner posts. Two taller posts with a crossbar stand at the centre of two sides. From the crossbar dangles a stronger chain.

In an alleyway alongside one of the civic buildings (the local assembly rooms, it turns out), three men, similarly dressed, curse as they examine a black fuse box. It is taller but thinner than the yellow grit box which occupied my attention for so long and so unsuccessfully at the start of this long trail. I send up a private prayer that they have more luck than me.

On the shale surface of the alley is a metal tube, like a torpedo, fat and heavy, with hand grips. Two more teams of three are at each end of the short, narrow street of mostly pebble-dashed houses, some with opened shutters.

In the market place, we get out of the back of the police car which collected us after a meal which ended without cheese or coffee, Dubal settling the bill again. He stretches and yawns.

On the short trip back, he'd translated a couple of several messages the uniformed driver passed on to him. 'The plane is undamaged. The cattle removed. It is clear for its return. Does that meet with your approval?'

'Provided the crew don't talk about what's happened when they get back.' I explained that I planned to break the news personally to Rodney Montgomery and Mrs Knight tomorrow.

He'd smiled wickedly. 'I can make your request a condition of their release.' The driver passed a phone over his shoulder. Dubal talked on it for some time before handing it back. 'Also, one of the cars parked in the street was hired by Rex Lynch a few days ago. In Paris, not here.' He shook his head in grudging admiration.

'Lynch and the Stone woman are inside the house. There is, regrettably, no pin-pointing as yet of a second or third man. All roads in the village will be sealed at ten. They go in at one minute past.' He looked at me intently. 'And we go in after that.'

No heroics, he was telling me.

Until my leg wound finished me in Special Ops, I ran jobs like this. Capers, we called them. An unbelievable buzz when you got it right and came out unscathed. Indescribable agony on the last occasion when I got it wrong, followed by months of pain and misery fearing that I'd never be fit to return to duty.

With a grateful nod, I told him everyone back home saw his

boys in action on TV storming that hijacked plane in Marseilles, but didn't add that I was more than happy to leave it to them.

The village doesn't exactly go deathly quiet. Swifts screech in a flock. A throstle sings. Dogs bark in the distance. But suddenly Dubal is the only person in civvie clothes that I can see. 'The call of nature, I think.'

He leads the way from the car to the alley which has a line of toilets attached to the assembly hall, the men's open-aired and smelling rather ripe.

Standing shoulder to shoulder, we have a better view of a terraced house built in stones of different sorts and sizes, bonded together by thick, white pointing. There is a dormer window in a slate roof.

I answer nature's call. Dubal doesn't.

A whine drowns out the throstle's song.

February, his back to the solid side, hand on a silver lever, rises slowly. He stops after fifteen feet, just above the sill of the bedroom window. He unclips a chain to his left.

Two men in the alleyway pick up their battering ram. The third man stands at its blunt stern.

February is attaching a black weight to a hook in the chain hanging from the crossbar.

He pulls it back like Tarzan in the trees, looks down, gives a thumbs up, then lets it go. The sound of breaking glass, the crack of splintering wood echoes down the alley.

The three men run, bawling, whooping, out of the passage across the street.

Carefully, almost casually, February steps off his platform into the gap where the attic window was a second ago. At street level, the grey door collapses as if hit by a howling hurricane.

A high-pitched scream, the call of a banshee, adds soprano counterpoint to the male voice choir, all of them grotesquely out of tune.

Zoe Stone comes out first, between two boiler-suited officers. Her arms are behind her, handcuffed. A waif-like body, denim-clad, veggie thin, wriggles and writhes, dragging her bare feet every forced step towards a police jeep that skidded to a halt the second after the door and window went in.

'Keep quiet.' Over her shoulder she is shouting. 'Tell 'em nothing.' She repeats her order, adding screamed obscenities about the police.

Puzzled faces peer out of the curtained windows of neighbouring houses. Dubal tuts. 'No lady.'

For a silly second, I'm embarrassed to be English, feel like a middle-class holidaymaker observing the yobbish behaviour of travelling soccer fans in places like Dublin.

Her instructions are clearly for Lynch who follows her out, similarly manacled, in sandals, khaki shorts and dirty white T-shirt, white-faced, not struggling as he is bundled into a separate vehicle.

February stands in the gap where the front door once stood and shouts something towards us which Dubal translates.

'No one else is home.' He leads the way out of the toilet. 'Come. We will take a look.'

I follow, feeling (though it had nothing to do with me) the glow of a mission accomplished without any blood shed – my blood especially.

The half-panelled front room is small. With a front door, it would have been cosy. A three-piece suite, a polished coffee table, grey-tiled floor, with a mat on it in front of a stone fireplace in which driftwood, white with dried salt, has been stacked in the black grate. The mantelpiece above is well filled.

There's a black portable radio on a sideboard, no TV set or phone. Lots of books, mainly colourful guides, are scattered on an antique sideboard in the far corner. English papers are in an untidy heap beside the sofa. All *Guardians*.

Beyond a wooden staircase, two tiled steps up from the lounge, is a small kitchen with white sink, boiler, fridge and a clean cooker attached to a blue calor gas cylinder. Inside the fridge are eggs, cheese, stuff for salads, milk, bottles of beer and wine; no steaks, chicken legs, chops or pâté.

A sliding door leads to a cramped, windowless bathroom with a condensation problem that has made the mottled wallpaper peel at some edges. Two toothbrushes sit on the top edge of the bath between the taps. Only two? My heart misses a beat. There is no back door, no back garden.

Dubal has not followed me. He stands before the fireplace, head lowered to inspect the contents of the mantelpiece.

Wet weather clothing hangs at the bottom of a banister which runs up beside the pine stairs. I rummage through. A large man's waxed jacket, a small woman's padded Kagoul. Only two sets. Shit.

The stairs creak beneath my feet. So, too, the floorboards of a landing, just a yard square, which leads to two bedrooms with pine ceilings angling sharply down to follow the line of the roof to their windows.

The front room is windowless. Glass and wood splinters are on the stained floorboards and pink duvet. A footstool has lost two legs. Clothes, both men's and women's, are in undisturbed piles on two chairs. More hang in a wardrobe in a curtained alcove. On a bedside cabinet, on top of each other, are dark blue British passports. Three. The two Stones' and Lynch's. Thank God.

Not Hicks' – but somehow that's no surprise.

In a stiff drawer is a rolled wad of French francs. I wonder how much of it was converted out of the two thou sterling they collected as they fled south after their last ransom demand while I was on holiday. I'll not stop to work out how much might be left of the two grand snatched across the river from under my nose in the Thorne cold store job on election night. I'm sure now, absolutely certain, they were never involved.

The back bedroom is also in chaos, through no fault of February's. Men's clothes are dumped on the bed, but not too many of them. A brown bottle of beer has rolled to a halt next to a green haversack on the floor. I crouch to zip it open.

'Phil.'

I zip it to, stand and walk to the top of the stairs.

At the bottom Dubal is waving a sheet of paper. 'I do not fully understand all of this.'

I climb down, take the paper and walk on to the front window, turning, to read by what's left of the light. I suspect Dubal reads English as well as he speaks it, but wants me to feel useful.

'*Bienvenue!*' I read, stumbling over the very first word. Merci-

fully, it's the only French word in a neatly typed guide the English
landlord has left for his paying guests – where to eat, drink, shop,
change money and find his boat, *Les Pioneers*.

'And there's this.' Dubal nods to a small table in front of the
window. On it is a pot of white paste and more *Guardians*, some
headlines chopped out.

On a plain sheet of paper, the cuttings have been reassembled
in various print sizes. 'Animal Salvation' is pasted near the top.
'Next Time it will Be the plane and All who fly it unLess –'

They had still been working on their claim of responsibility and
their threat of future action when February dropped in.

Two down, two to go. Except that I have this nagging, ever
expanding feeling that we'll only find one.

19

Les Pioneers bobs a little more vigorously than its neighbours
moored to a long pontoon in the harbour at St Vaast, brightly lit
in the gathering dusk.

From within come big girls' giggles. My heart revs for take-off.
What did Mel Dexter say? 'Giggling like girls.' Both. We could
have both Hicks and Stone.

Dubal grins maliciously, drops with some effort to his knees and
places an ear to the wooden pontoon, like an Indian scout, enjoying the moment.

Still on all fours, he nods at February whose left hand holds a
long, black baton. His right hand withdraws a revolver from its
holster at his hip. He steps off the gangplank on to *Les Pioneers*, a
white sailing dinghy, its mast higher than its length of not much
more than twenty feet. He doesn't add to its gentle sway.

He stands for a second, his back to a black outboard motor. He
presses the sole of his right boot to double doors to the cabin, one
above the other, like a stable's. He screws his left firm to the
plastic fibre deck. With a loud holler, he kicks. He vanishes, right
foot first.

The gentle sway becomes violent rocking. No ecstatic
sounds from within now. A low shout and a high-pitched scream

accompany the out-of-view February's barked orders. There are a few seconds of silence. Then 'OK' is called.

With more effort Dubal pulls himself upright. He removes a black torch he took from a police jeep from his jacket pocket. In three or four long steps, he is on the boat and into the cabin, me following.

There is not the headroom inside to stand upright. February has his doubled back to us, panting slightly.

No electrics on board, just an unlit lantern; the stooping Dubal shines the torch into the pointed bow. Among ropes, yellow oars and red lifejackets are two contorted torsos, naked apart from a tangled sleeping bag across their legs.

They lie face down on a foam mattress, breathing so fast they are quivering. Both heads are angled away from us. February is pressing his long baton, gripped firmly at each end, across the backs of their necks.

The portside body is Richard Stone's. No doubt about that. He has no shoulder blades, just a lopsided paunch, not as big as Dubal's belly, very white and veined.

All I can see of his companion are slender tanned shoulders, long, matted fair hair, and a ring in a pierced ear, but it's enough to make my heart soar. Hicks. Well, well. An AC, DC Hicks. No wonder he and Stone spent nights out together back home, giggling like big girls. We've got him; got them all. Four out of four.

'OK,' says Dubal, very quietly. February lifts his baton a foot. 'Face me very slowly.'

Pivoting on his stomach, Stone raises his upper body, lifts his head slowly to look up at us. His brown eyes are wide and round, glistening, like a scared calf. His head flops down again, defeated, exhausted.

'You also, please,' says Dubal very politely. 'Let us have a good look at you.'

The body next door does not stir.

'Come on, Hicksey,' I urge over February's shoulder. 'Don't piss us about. It's all over.'

The body lies still.

Dubal speaks sharply in French. The thin shoulders rotate. The face brushes the grey, plastic mattress, then looks up.

My heart crash lands. We've got the wrong man. In fact, not a man at all. We've got a woman, if that's what you can call this shaking, spotty, skinny slip of a bare thing.

Zoe Stone pulls her thin frame up, straightening her back, in a hard chair to which she is handcuffed and fixes us defiantly with steely grey eyes.

Every detective knows when he walks into an interview if he's confronting a talker or a clammer. Zoe is going to clam.

Dubal senses it, too, sighing heavily as he sits down at a desk in a comfortable office back at the gendarmerie next to the airport. I stand behind him on a grey cord carpet, slightly to his right.

Two women officers are seated on chairs, one behind the door, one in front of a barred window beyond which night has finally fallen. Both wear sweaters a darker blue than their trousers with a red and yellow emblem on their left arms. Both are wearing guns.

Dubal asks in French if she speaks French. Zoe shakes her head dumbly. He breaks into English. 'Very well.' She will know why she's here, he tells her very politely. 'And we now also have your brother Richard.'

Her face sets impassively. 'You'll get nothing out of him, either.'

'Truthfully, mademoiselle,' says Dubal crisply, 'we do not need anything from anybody.' And he runs through the evidence he's got – the pasted-up note, the blue fragments from fertiliser bags, the ownership of the green truck.

'Do your worst then,' says Zoe, couldn't care less.

He tries a few more questions, gets nothing and gives up. 'You may, however, wish to speak to my friend.' Looking over his shoulder he formally introduces me. Even before he's finished Zoe says, 'No, I don't.'

'We are also investigating two cases of sabotage back home,' I plough on regardless. She gives her head the tiniest of shakes. 'First the sinking of the cattle boat, the *Lindum Arch*, in April after a threat to its sister ship.' Still shaking. 'Then the blowing up of Thorne Meat Depot last month.'

Her headshake is a little firmer now. 'We're confirming or denying nothing. We demand a solicitor.'

'We have the right to hold you without access to an advocate for twenty hours,' says Dubal sharply.

'We'll take our day in court.'

I take a step nearer and lean forward close to her face. No feminine fragrance greets me. 'Oh, you'll get that all right,' I promise, 'but over here where there'll be no public gallery to play to. We're not seeking extradition.'

I trot out all the questions that have been growing within me for the past three days, getting no replies, her thin lips tighter.

Only when I ask, 'How can you, an animal lover, justify poisoning a bull?' do they open to release one word. 'Bollocks.'

'No,' I smile, enjoying the moment, 'not a bullock, a bull.'

A mistake, that. Zealots like Zoe have no sense of humour. All we get for the next minute is an abusive tirade against the trade in meat and all who eat it.

'So long, Vegelante,' I say cheerily, turning my back on her.

Rex Lynch folds his arms when we walk into another office down a long corridor with potted palms. Here we go again, I think, all humour gone.

He is not handcuffed. Two officers stand guard over him with guns drawn.

Every question the seated Dubal asks is met with headshakes or 'Nothing to say'.

When I do my stand-up piece, all I get is 'Shouldn't this be taped?'

'You are not in England now, my friend,' says Dubal evenly.

I look around me to bait a trick question. 'You've got to admit . . .'

He breaks in. 'I'm admitting nothing.'

'. . . that these are more comfortable surroundings than the Detained Room at Combined Counties.'

He stares at me blankly. 'Don't know what you're talking about.'

I don't doubt that, but when I try to explain, I am faced with headshakes and no comments. 'Well,' I tell him, giving up, rising, 'you're in the soft and smelly, but, as a dilly man, you'll know all about that, won't you?'

'Piss off,' he hisses.

Soon we do.

'We have interviewed your sister and Mr Lynch . . .' After a tactics talk, I am batting first against Richard Stone.

Dressed in a borrowed white overall, Stone breaks into my rehearsed opening line, smirking. 'Bet you got nothing.'

172

I continue, '. . . and Mr Alan Hicks.'

His smirk goes.

I pull out my notebook and place it on the desk in a third office in which two more officers stand guard. 'We have statements . . .'

'Not from Zoe and Rex, you haven't.'

'. . . which inform us that the nitrogen used in the bomb this evening was stolen by you, with Hicks' admitted complicity, from Trentside Golf Club.'

'Bastard,' he hisses.

'Further,' I go on formally, 'we are informed that you personally opened an account at the Southwell branch of –'

'The bastard.' He almost shouts it, wriggling in the chair to which he is handcuffed. 'The shit.'

I look up from my notebook, say nothing.

His face is as twisted as his back. 'Done a deal, has he? For his freedom?'

The room goes silent for what seems a long time as he fidgets. Finally, 'What about my girl?' His face has become anxious. 'What will happen to her?'

Dubal speaks for the first time. 'She's also being interviewed, *naturellement*.' Pause. 'What do you want to happen to her?'

'Nothing.' Stone looks at him with pleading eyes. 'She knows nothing about any of this.'

She's a runaway, he explains. He'd met her in a bar in Cherbourg. They'd been shacking up in the boat for a week or more. He repeats two or three times that she knows nothing about what happened at the airport, wasn't there.

'In which case nothing will happen to her,' says Dubal softly.

'On your word?'

'I promise.'

All the hostility in his eyes evaporates.

Well, he begins, stretching out one leg, he was upset, like, cross, when he was fired by Lincsline because he didn't deserve it. Zoe became even more angry when the company airily dismissed claims for financial compensation.

She was already heavily into animal lib, and Lincsline was into cattle transporting, so they decided, all three of them, to teach them a lesson.

173

Lynch drove up north in his green truck to buy the fertiliser, posing as a playing-fields groundsman. Not being farmers, entitled to subsidies, they had to pay the full price. Half was used as a warning in the hold of *Lindum Castle* – 'a shot across the bows,' Zoe called it.

The demand for fifty thou was to finance future operations. They were sure the pay-out would be covered by insurance. Lynch plotted the route via the sewer to the sand box at Southwell and made the collection.

He and Zoe were enraged when all they got was cut-up pieces of newspaper. They used the rest of the fertiliser for real on the *Lindum Castle*'s twin, the *Arch*, in the Wash. They told the papers because they felt it would put pressure on both the company and the police to co-operate next time.

They had no fertiliser left and no cash to buy any more. Stone knew Hicks, his drinking mate from college days, worked at a golf club with access to nitrogen. 'So I tapped him. "Sure," he said. "For a ton." He's in on every fiddle that's going.'

Lynch, following Hicks' directions, collected it from the club's stores. They stacked it in the houseboat while they plotted their next move.

Zoe felt the animal rights campaign had gone as far as it could in Britain and was for spreading the word by dramatic example to the Continent where security would be less tight than at picket-plagued points of departure in England.

They'd already decided that Arc Air would be the target. Stone knew that Lincsline had money in it. He'd seen and photocopied details of their investment document before he left.

His sister and Lynch had been across here on a seventy-two-hour recce, to plan the escape route, double check the plane's movements and book a house.

To twist the knife still further, they decided on their return that Lincsline would finance the move, phoned again. 'You know we mean business.'

This time it worked – or seemed to. They found there was cash in the account they opened. 'I wanted Hicks to come with us, told him where we'd be based. Is that how you found us? Did the bastard tip you?'

'In a roundabout way,' I say cautiously.

'He knows the lingo. We could have left Zoe and Rex to it and gone off fruit- and veg-picking, but, no, he said, he'd got a soft touch going with his current girl. "Just give me my money." I had no readies because we decided to draw out on the way, so I gave him a spare cash card and told him to use it just the once and well away from Southwell.' He claims not to have seen or heard from Hicks since, and I don't push it – not yet.

They loaded up the green truck with the stolen nitrogen and headed south, using their cards at cash points on the journey. At Newbury the card was rejected. They realised they had been short-changed again.

In Cherbourg, they monitored again the plane's movements and decided that Wednesday, when it always made two trips, would be the day. Zoe got the idea of phoning the company with the 'D-Day plus one' message because she and Lynch had toured the Normandy beaches on their previous trip.

They took a train to Paris to hire a car, well away from Cherbourg, because they knew they'd need a getaway vehicle once they'd blown up the truck. The idea, he insists, was not to blow up the plane – 'not with calves on board. Defeats the object.'

They planned to destroy the transporter before the plane arrived, using remote control from the car-park where they'd posed as plane-spotters. 'Just to show Lincsline we were capable of it, so next time we made a demand they would pay up in full.'

The trouble was that the transporter's driver and his mate stayed in the cab. They decided to hold their fire and recover the green truck for a second go later. 'But then we saw the fire brigade haring towards it. The blokes ran out the big wagon. We knew our truck was a goner. The plane was a safe distance away. I had a good line of vision. So . . .'

He cocks his head. End of story.

'So,' says I, after a thoughtful pause, 'if blowing up calves defeats Zoe's object, why poison the bull?'

'What bloody bull?'

'The bull on Brian Thorne's farm . . .'

'Never heard of him.'

'. . . with poison stolen by Hicks from the club . . .' He is looking lost for words. '. . . where you later blew up Thorne's cold store on May 4th . . .'

An amused smile. 'Now that is bullshit.'

'. . . after escaping with two thou of your ransom demand.'

'Crap.' Not amused now. 'We're not carrying that can. None of us. Never. No. We know nothing about it. If that's what Hicksey claims, he's lying. Was he pissed when he talked? Or has he done it himself and is shifting the blame on to us? Ask him that.'

The names of all the Thornes, the Montgomerys, Powers and Knight are tried on him. Only Knight does he admit recognising, and only then because they'd seen him squirming on TV trying to explain away the events surrounding the bombing of the boat on the Wash. 'A good laugh, that,' he adds pleasurably.

I ask, 'What about the coded card . . .'

A confused look at Dubal. 'What card? What code?'

'. . . which you and Hicks sent to my chief?'

'Has he been on the vino or something?' He looks from Dubal at me, challengingly. 'When?'

'From here on May –'

'Here? Hicks has never been here. Not that I know of. I wanted him to come, but he wouldn't.' He leans forward threateningly. His guards follow suit. 'If you see him, tell him from me that calves have a better time of it than he'll get, the bastard, when me and Rex catch up with him.'

'And where will I find him to tell him?'

'Buggered if I know. Haven't seen him since I gave him that cash card.'

'I think he's telling the truth,' says Dubal as we walk back to the commandant's office.

So do I, I tell him.

20

D-Day plus two

Slept like a log with no early morning awakening.

Dubal took me to his home, a large stone detached house with white shutters in a quiet street in the old part of Cherbourg beyond a swing bridge. His wife didn't greet me. At three in the morning, that was no surprise.

His dog, a liver and white spaniel, did welcome us in a well-equipped kitchen where, bushed, I turned down offers of coffee and a nightcap. I was shown up steep, thickly carpeted stairs to a room with heavy old furniture and a bed that was a bit too soft.

At nine, he called me and, after a shower and a shave, I have come downstairs to hot croissants with salted butter and black coffee in a big room, massive – yet hardly any room in it. Round three walls cabinets are filled to overflowing with family photos, ornaments and books. On top of one is an animal, a bit like a stoat, glaze-eyed and stuffed.

The long table where Dubal waits, in a grey lightweight suit today, is lace-covered. Between it and a window overlooking a small shaded garden is a three-piece suite with a sheepskin rug on the couch on which the dog lies.

It uncurls itself, jumps down on to a brown and white calfskin mat, pads across to lick the back of my proffered hand and, on Dubal's quiet command, goes back to base again.

Dubal takes his chained spectacles off his chest to read out the story about last night's explosion from his morning paper, which doesn't disclose an English connection.

Mrs Dubal, pleasantly plump, proudly shows me a tapestry of the dog, the colours of its coat exactly caught, which she is sewing on a metal frame.

It is clear that the dog – Freedo by name – has replaced their departed children in their hearts. On days off, Dubal tells me, he takes him hunting – anything from rabbits to wild boar. The stuffed stoat, which turned out to be a pine marten, is one of their bags.

Ten o'clock now (an hour less back home) and I call Hazel on a grey phone Mrs Dubal brought to the table on a long cable.

She'd spoken to Em last night and knew about the airport bomb, she says. It has made a few of the heavier English papers, but they haven't linked it with Arc Air and no mention is being made of a hunt for any Brits.

According to Surveillance, Powers had stayed in all night at his humble terraced home where he'd lived alone since the break-up of his marriage. He'd been tailed to work.

'I caught up with his daughter,' she goes on. 'She's not taken delivery of old college books from Hicks via her dad. And . . .' She still hasn't finished. '. . . I finally got that health inspector.'

The Thornes were told that a stop was being put on any further shipments out of their cold store, pending the outcome of tests on the plane.

The next step would have been to examine the meat mountain. 'Before they could . . .' She lets it hang there. 'All this they told Knight two weeks ago, by the way.'

So, I'm thinking, Rod hadn't tipped off the Thornes about the inquiry. The health inspector had told them officially. But had Knight shown his hand to one of the family, someone who had been running a racket with Powers going back years?

Condemned meat in Combined Counties was transferred to Thorne's to replace good stuff which was put on the market at top prices to get Powers out of hock with the bank.

Worked well while the unwanted surplus built up, but as soon as the EC released a consignment as an act of charity the racket was about to be exposed. The meat that made those refugees sick wasn't just past its sell-by date. It had been condemned as jaundiced and unfit for human consumption.

So the store – and all the frozen evidence – had been destroyed under the guise of animal lib sabotage.

Knight had worked all this out. Once he'd got his hands on Hicks he'd rightly decided his priority was to bag the terrorists first, then worry about the fraud in his family.

'I'm concerned about Powers,' says Hazel, sounding it.

She wants me to order his arrest. There's reasonable grounds for suspicion, but I aim to be at that interrogation. This is my case and, after what I went through last night, I'm not handing it over to Carole Malloy or, worse still, Dale. 'Let's see what we can dig up this end first,' I say.

'OK,' she replies, with a dissenting sigh.

I get on to Em. 'Been up half the bloody night,' she complains, not unhappily.

Shakespeare's words, she reports, came out of the mouth of Richard, but there was an interesting aside immediately before the funeral service extract in which the late king's widow complained Richard killed her husband and her son.

'As well as the babes in the tower?' They're the only victims I ever remember.

' "A murderous villain and so still art," opines the queen,' she adds gaily. 'He began his ascent to the throne by bumping off his brother, didn't he?'

Did he? I ask only myself. We chat a little longer, me telling her that if I do make it home tonight, I'll be very late, so don't cook for me or wait up.

'Your plans today – what are they?' asks Dubal when I replace the receiver.

'Mrs Knight,' I reply.

Before I can beg transport, Dubal volunteers to accompany me to act as interpreter. Hadn't he lots of loose ends on the airport job? I query. He gives me a little lecture on the art of delegation. As everyone I want to see speaks English, the real reason is obvious. He's become intrigued, absorbed.

I tell him I'd be delighted. I might need him to flash his card at the post office in Dol de Bretagne to extract the holiday address. Mrs Dubal takes my hand as I take my leave. Freedo gives me a big, wet kiss.

All the way down, chauffeured by a plainclothes man, not February, at the wheel of a large red Peugeot, we talk; so much talk that I see little of the countryside on each side of a fast, flat road.

'*Donc*,' Dubal says and I've heard it so often I can translate it into 'So . . . what about your Shakespeare?' he asks.

'The hint could be in the choice of play itself,' I conjecture, 'the fact that it starts with one brother killing the other.'

'Had your Mr Knight a brother?'

'No,' I concede, 'but Brian Thorne is more than a brother-in-law.' I tell him both were in the Brotherhood of Freemasonry, secure in the knowledge, having shaken his hand on arrival, that Dubal himself is not in some French lodge.

'This Geoffrey Powers,' he asks, 'is he one, too?'

That I don't know, never having been formally introduced.

We bounce thoughts and theories off each other for so long that we finally run out of ideas and, grinning, he changes the subject somewhat dramatically. 'Roast beef,' he says, then stops and laughs. 'You know, of course, we French call you English Roast Beef. Oh, yes. You call us Frogs' Legs. We call you Roast Beef.'

He becomes serious. 'It would be a shame if you English spoilt a perfectly good name by all becoming vegetarians like Lynch and the dreadful Stone woman. Most people, ninety-seven per cent, eat meat and fish. They do it for pleasure. They don't have to, not to survive. They do it because they enjoy it. Therefore they cannot without being hypocrites object to the killing of animals for pleasure because animals are killed for their pleasure.'

It's a long debate, not much argument from me, a country boy, but I do play the devil's advocate over fox-hunting.

'A shot or gassed fox can live on in agony for days, a slow death. At least, when it is hunted, it is caught and killed or it is not.'

He returns to his main theme with such passion that he is gesticulating. 'When fifty-one per cent of the population don't eat meat and stop wearing clothes from animal products, then so will I. Meantime I will go on hunting and eating. *D'accord*, Roast Beef?'

D'accord, I reply sheepishly.

To our right in distant blue haze is a sight which he tells me with a grin was named after him – St Michel on his Mount – and there'll be other sights to see where we are headed in Dol de Bretagne – an old cathedral, ramparts running round the town and a lovely main street with half-timbered shops.

At journey's end, more than a hundred miles in under two hours, I don't get to see the promised sights, only an ordinary dual carriage road which runs by a post office, bigger and more modern than K2's.

Dubal makes no move to order his driver to stop. Instead, he suggests Mrs Knight and the Montgomerys be allowed more time 'to find their land legs' after their overnight ferry crossing. 'Lunch, perhaps?' he adds.

'My turn and pleasure to pay,' I insist.

We drive a short distance round a flower-filled roundabout and up a gentle slope, pulling in at a restaurant with a glass-encased conservatory.

Seated in comfortable old chairs at a round table, I defer to him the task of ordering from the leather-bound menu. For the main

180

among four courses, he decides on veal chops with an Alsace wine. 'OK?' he asks.

I nod. It is more than OK; tasty and tender. Half-way through, the chef appears at our table, white smock failing to hide a stomach as big as Dubal's. We compliment him. As he departs, Dubal gives me more advice. 'Never eat at a restaurant with a thin chef.'

Over the cheese board, Dubal asking for a slice of each from a selection of five, me settling for two, we swap a few of our past cases.

Dubal reveals himself as a cop of the old school, loathes account-ants and administrators – and, above all, computers. I argue for new tech, pointing out that, but for street surveillance cameras, we'd never have got on to Hicks in the first place.

Returning to the subject of work prompts a sudden thought. '*Merde.*' I'm into the lingo now. 'I forgot to ask the postal authorities in Cherbourg if they could pin-point where and when that card was mailed.'

'We will do that for you,' he offers. Then he lapses into thought-ful silence, looking down the busy road towards the roundabout and post office. 'Let us stroll down there and get them to fax the query to Cherbourg, as well as give us the address of Mrs Knight.'

For the first time, his expression is distracted, something else on his agile mind that he's not yet sharing.

Mrs Knight and the Montgomerys must have been well rested when we arrive, so long did we spend at Dol de Bretagne.

It took another twenty minutes through flatlands, towards St Malo, to reach the address we were given.

Thorne's Doll's House is, in fact, a white stucco bungalow half-way up a rocky hill with a view of a muddy beach, the tide miles out.

They are sitting in the sun round a table in a walled garden that has none of the French formality, all box hedges and straight lines. Its shaggy lawn is infested with buttercups and dandelions. Well-advanced bedding plants thrive in front of a lovely show of yellow floribundas. It is impossible to detect if they are scented, so strong is a seaweedy smell coming in on a stiffish breeze from the bay.

They have not dressed to receive visitors. Mrs Knight is in a belted lime green dress, creased from packing. Her daughter Anita wears a sleeveless grey-blue dress over a cream T-shirt. Both their faces, with the merest traces of make-up, look washed out.

Anita's expression is more than unwelcoming, hostile, simmering as I introduce Dubal. He smiles warmly down at Rodney, who defiantly doesn't stand. 'I am here to inform you that an attempt was made last night to blow up your plane.'

There's a gasped 'Gosh' from Anita and a groaned 'Oh God' from Rod. Only Mrs Knight asks the humane question: 'Are the crew all right?'

'Perfectly,' beams Dubal. 'Thanks to our friend here.' He launches into a highly exaggerated hymn of praise for my speed of thought and action; so fulsome that I might ask for it in writing to accompany my application for Knight's vacant post.

Now, of course, we're more than welcomed. 'Sit down, please,' says Rodney, rising from his cane chair. 'Join us for a drink,' says Anita, also getting up.

Rodney pulls back his chair for Dubal and transfers to a low patio wall. Dressed all in creamy white, like a cricketer, he can afford to ignore seagulls' droppings on the coping stones. I replace Anita who goes inside with an order for lemon tea all round.

Rodney grumbles about not being on the phone, frets about getting in touch with his partners. Dubal assures him the plane, as well as the crew, is unscathed and back in the air and in business. Then he offers his condolences to Mrs Knight and says what a charming man he'd found her husband on the phone.

I ask after her two grandchildren and am informed that they are napping after a sleepless night on the ferry.

Only when Anita has returned with a heavily laden tray and is sitting on a cushion by her husband does Dubal reveal, 'We have in custody the three people responsible.'

Anita and Rod ask lots of questions. Dubal holds nothing back, naming names. Mrs Knight looks away, doesn't say a word. 'Phil here has more information.' He gestures to me.

'They are also responsible for the blowing up of the boat, the *Lindum Arch*, on the Wash and the more recent extortion of further money from the same shipping company.' I pause and look directly at Mrs Knight. 'However, they were in no way involved in the crimes at Thorne Meat Depots.' Another pause. 'But then you knew all about that, didn't you, Mrs Knight?'

She looks back at me. The beginnings of a nod are quickly still. 'Not exactly all, no.'

I broaden my fixed smile. 'Well, can you tell us exactly everything you do know?' She tells it so well, softly, fluently, with such loving attention to detail that I can imagine myself back in their intimate lounge with the red and white roses outside the front window.

Knight didn't really bring home many worries from work on the boat-sinking in April; just another job, and he'd tackled far bigger in Belfast.

He became irritated, of course, by all the publicity Animal Salvation's calls to the media attracted, mainly with himself, because he didn't think he'd performed well on TV and it reflected badly on him and the force. 'He was his own sternest critic.'

They discussed the destruction of the Thorne cold store, obviously. So would anyone if such a shocking incident had happened within their family. And, because of that domestic connection, he really did distance himself from that inquiry.

'If he picked up any information from you,' she goes on, looking directly at me, 'he certainly didn't repeat it at home. My sister was on to me a time or two, wanting to know if there was any progress. I was able to tell her, hand on heart, that I knew nothing and to direct her questions to you as the officer in charge. Did she?'

I shake my head.

Then came case No. 3 while I was away – the second threat to Lincsline and the two thousand pounds that was, in effect, siphoned via cash points out of police funds. 'He was a value-for-money stickler, concerned about not having anything to show for it; so worried that I knew there had to be more to it than that.'

'Come on,' she'd urged. 'You've lost more than that buying false information in Belfast in your time. It's the nature of the job. Everyone understands that. What's really troubling you? Don't bottle it up. Remember what the doctor said. It's bad for you.'

Only then did he open up about Thorne's job. 'He said that you had already raised the matter of the poisoned bull, questioning how Animal Salvation could, as animal welfare campaigners, justify it.

'At first he thought, perhaps they were keeping quiet about it, not claiming responsibility, for that very reason. Then last week, while you were away, Hazel Webster trapped Hicks.'

The following night he came home late for the birthday party. 'He seemed cock-a-hoop, made no secret of the break-through, told anyone who cared to listen. For him, it was very strange behaviour, but then, I told myself, Stella and Brian had been temporarily put out of business. They'd kept harping on about lack of progress. Now they knew things were moving.'

Alone at last, as they stacked the dishwasher, Knight lost all his zest. Without prompting, he said, 'I'm afraid a scandal close to home is pending. I may be retiring a little earlier than we antici-pated.'

Knight didn't identify to his wife the characters involved, just referred to his informant and the bombers, but, knowing them, it's easy to put names to them as she goes along.

In his cell, Knight recounted to her, Hicks had denied any in-volvement in the *Lindum Arch* explosion, but claimed that Richard Stone in drink had openly bragged about it.

Hicks, however, did admit his part in the theft of the fertiliser but insisted the load was going to be used here in France on, he assumed, another boat.

The Stones and Lynch knew nothing about Thorne's cold store, Hicks was sure of it.

'Who did?' asked Mrs Knight, fearing the worst.

'Well, Geoff Powers for certain,' her husband replied, naming his first name.

Five years ago, Powers was in trouble with the bank, Knight had discovered. He'd over-extended himself by building the new slaughterhouse.

About this time, Hicks, still at college, had joined Combined Counties as Saturday delivery boy. Powers started to accompany Hicks on his regular run from Combined Counties to Thorne Meat Depots. According to Hicks, they were transferring twice the normal loads.

The extra boxes of jointed meat were differently marked. Powers always handled them. At Thorne's, they were stacked in a special corner. Out of the same corner Powers would carry boxes marked 'EC'.

Hicks knew there was a fiddle, but said nothing because, not having parents to support him through college, he needed the job.

He finally landed a greenkeeping post at Trentside Golf Club in the trade he'd been trained for and left Combined Counties, but still popped in now and then to see old workmates for a drink.

Powers approached him last month. 'I need some poison,' he said. Hicks provided Pestine in a Co-op bag, got thirty pounds for it.

Mrs Knight continues, 'Andy knew that by then some of the transferred meat released from the cold store as charity aid to Bosnia had been found to be contaminated.'

Rodney, listening intently, nods gravely, and so do I. Knight didn't really have to be in Intelligence to work out that Powers had been switching condemned, worthless meat for good EC stuff which he then sold for top prices on the market to get himself out of the red at his bank. When the UN and the EC started making inquiries about the Bosnia bug, the crates of condemned meat still in there would not pass inspection.

Knight told his wife that he didn't know for sure – but the assumption had to be – that Powers copied Animal Salvation's well-publicised drill: phoned threat, reprisal when the demand wasn't met.

It was a big bomb, a hundred-pounder, but, as a regular visitor, he'd be able to go in and out of Thorne's depot without attracting suspicion with the explosive packed in the heavy cardboard boxes used for meat.

He followed other aspects of the MO too – a cunning getaway across the river with the advance on the ransom and the blowing-up of the cold store which would be seen as an act of reprisal when the real intention was to destroy all the incriminating evidence inside.

Very clever, Knight pronounced, and I'm agreeing.

Hicks insisted to him that he was not the source of the fertiliser for that explosion. Knight reasoned that Powers would have access to as much nitrogen as he needed through his farming contacts.

'Why didn't dad order the arrest of Powers immediately?' asks Anita, a question that disturbs me.

Her mother gives her a bland smile. 'I'm sure he had his reasons.'

So am I – because he judged that Hicks had a more urgent role to play in locating Animal Salvation's cell and preventing another bombing. Powers would keep. Besides, Hicks had no proof, apart from the stolen poison for which Powers may have had a ready-made excuse; vermin on the premises, for instance.

OK, Hicks could testify to shipping extra crates from Combined to Thorne's, but Claude from Fraud had found all the paperwork in order. The real proof – the condemned meat – had been burnt to a cinder. Catch the Animal Salvation gang and eliminate them from Thorne's job and Knight had the answers. I'd followed the same route.

Anita won't give up. 'But why did he make such a song and dance to this Powers man, and, before that, Miles and Uncle Brian at your party, that he was releasing his informant on bail?'

Mrs Knight looks rather crossly at her daughter. 'I'm sure I don't know.'

I do. He wanted the Thornes to know he had Hicks. When Miles couldn't be raised to stand bail, he roped in Powers who was bound to tell his fellow conspirator in the family. It was a classic destabilisation ploy, the cat among the pigeons.

'Why resign?' Anita demands.

'He was ill.'

'But why now?'

'He thought it the right thing to do; for the good of the force.'

Anita looks crossly back. 'Oh, come on, mum, Powers can't have been in this business on his own. You don't just walk in and out –'

'You can on a Saturday,' Mrs Knight protests vainly.

'Nonsense. You know why. Someone in the family's involved. That's it, isn't it?'

'I don't know.' Mrs Knight tries but fails to pass it off but everyone keeps quiet and she has to add, 'Perhaps.' Silence still, so: 'He was certainly worried that Powers might heap all the blame on him.'

Everyone lapses into another silence that's too long for comfort, so I smile at Anita and then at Mrs Knight. 'Why at your home, on Monday, did you say "Beware the imposter"?'

'Silly that.' She makes a flustered movement with a hand. 'Sorry. I never saw the card before you showed it to me. Andy said information had been received. That's all. He was very, very worried about it.

'He wondered if Hicks had backed out of their arrangement to locate Animal Salvation and was playing a double game or was even fielding a substitute.' She adds, looking at Anita to make sure she knows it is for her benefit, 'Some informants do, you know.'

And, I'm thinking, Knight believed Hicks had told Powers all (for a promised price, perhaps) and he got Hicks to write the card which set up a secret meeting at Red Gutter.

Maybe Knight thought he'd be meeting the bent member of the family, hearing a confession and giving advice on how to limit the fall-out. Or he'd issue an ultimatum: 'I have an appointment with my chief on Monday and will tell him all. Get yourself a good lawyer.'

Instead, he met up with Powers, the main man, the secret service handler's ultimate nightmare, a fatal nightmare.

And where is Hicks? I ponder gloomily. Where every two-timing agent winds up. Either well paid and well out of it. Or dead, jointed and boxed in Combined Counties' cold store.

I daren't tell Mrs Knight any of this, can hardly bear to think of it myself. Instead, 'Why didn't you tell me all of this, instead of picking that bit of Shakespeare for the service about trouble in the family?'

'How could I?' She looks extremely sad. 'Think what it will do to Stella. It's bad enough for her without me, her sister, being a witness for the prosecution. I just wanted you to look further, not accept the obvious. That's all. Andy had great faith in you.'

I try not to blush, go silent, more shamed than shy.

'Who is it then, mummy?' asks Anita gamely. 'Uncle Brian or Miles?'

Mrs Knight looks at me, a begging look, close to tears. 'Need I really answer?'

I shake my head.

I know the answer already.

An even faster journey back up the spine of Normandy, Dubal dozing part of the way, a contented smile on his face.

With Mont St Michel more than an hour behind us, a road sign points the way to Utah Beach. It's not the spot where grandad landed all those years ago, and, with Arc Air's Merchantman waiting, there's no time anyway for a visit.

But I see him in my mind and tell him: 'Did as you said, grandad. Found my old sweat of a foot soldier and followed him. And here I am, still in the battle.'

No time for long farewells at the airport, so Dubal doesn't get out, just takes my hand through the opened back door. '*Au revoir*, Roast Beef.'

21

I'd like to claim that instinct, something subliminal, brings me back to HQ, instead of driving straight home from the airport.

I kidded myself that Em wasn't really expecting me, wouldn't worry if I was late. The truth is I planned to type a memo into the computer for the overnight log, required reading for the chief constable, reporting how two out of the three blackmail-cum-bombings had been cleared up, but requesting no publicity till the third is resolved.

I've leap-frogged well clear of Dale now. Chief super and soon acting ACC; the desk is mine.

The phone rings as I am keying in. 'Station sergeant, Newark here, sir. Something I think you ought to know about.'

'What's that?' I inquire sharply, distracted from mental composition.

'You were asking about Mr Powers on Tuesday. Well, his daughter's here.'

'What's she want?'

'None too sure. Either to report him missing or file a complaint about Sergeant Webster. A high old state she's in. Speak to her, will you?'

Heavy footsteps echo away from the mouthpiece. Lighter ones approach. The cradle scrapes on hard surface as it is picked up. 'Hallo. To whom am I speaking?' A woman's voice, tight, agitated.

I tell her and ask how I can help.

Her name is Dawn Powers and she was trying to reach Sergeant Webster. According to a note on my desk, Hazel's joined Surveillance outside Combined Counties, but I don't tell her that, just that she's unavailable. Again I offer my help.

'I don't know whether you know this but Sergeant Webster has been in touch with me twice over the last couple of days.'

I throw in the first of several 'yeses' as she rushes through her story. Hazel asked over the phone if she'd seen or heard from Alan Hicks, an old college chum. 'Hadn't seen him in months,' she'd answered.

Later that day, she called in on Powers – she often popped over to make sure he was all right living on his own – and she mentioned the call to him.

Worry not, he'd replied easily. Hicks had apparently skipped bail he'd put up, but it was only a hundred and wouldn't break the bank, a favourite phrase of his.

'Why do that?' she demanded. 'You're not his employer any more. And I'm not his date. You owe him no obligation.'

'He's in a fix over a bank card. It was that or the remand wing.'

Last night brought a personal visit from Hazel wanting to know, 'Did Hicks recently return to you via your father a Co-op carrier bag full of college books?'

'Don't know what you're talking about,' she'd replied.

This afternoon she'd phoned her father again, puzzled and a bit angry this time. 'What the devil's going on?'

'Oh, my God,' her father groaned when she told him.

Then, uncharacteristically, he exploded. 'If you hadn't brought him home in the first place, none of this would have happened.'

Dawn flew into a paddy. 'Don't you tell me who I should or shouldn't be seeing. Then or now. Not with your track record. What's wrong, for goodness sake?'

'I bought some material off him and he delivered it here in a carrier bag. The police found out. They tackled me completely unawares. All I could think of saying was the first thing that came into my head – that it was old books for you. Sorry.'

'What material?'

'Never you mind.'

'Don't tell me to mind my own business. You've made it my business. Without a by-your-leave, you've involved me with the police.'

'It's all Hicks' fault.'

'I didn't ask you to find him a bloody job or stand his bail. That's nothing to do with me.'

Her father didn't appear to be listening. 'The blackmailing little swine.'

Now Dawn became concerned. 'What blackmail?'

No reply.

'Dad, is there something wrong?'

'Everything's wrong.'

'What? Tell me. Please.'

'Can't talk. Not here. Not over the phone.'

'Tonight then. Seven o'clock. My place. Over a bite to eat. And you'd better have a decent explanation.' She slammed down the phone.

Seven o'clock came. No dad. Eight. Still no sign. She phoned his home. No reply. His works. No reply. She'd driven to his home. No answer. On to his office. 'His car's there. The store doors are locked, but the office lights are on. I can't raise anybody. I'm worried sick. He's never been like that before. He sounded beside himself. What's happening?'

I promise to find out, get handed back to the sergeant and instruct him to give her a cup of tea and keep her there. I don't answer her question, though I fear I know what's happened.

All Dubal's string-pulling, the media manipulation, to keep the progress we made in Cherbourg from him and the Thorne family had been to no avail. The secret has been inadvertently blown because our inquiries have been too diligent.

I take the late-shift Forensics team with me. It will save time later on.

Hazel is sitting, sipping tea from a flask, in the back of a grey van, antique bodywork, souped-up engine, in the communal car-park that serves the industrial estate on which Combined Counties stands.

Lights from the office window shine brightly through the gloom cast by grey clouds I've just flown through all the way from the south coast. I pull alongside, wind down the window, put my head out, feeling spits of rain on it.

Had we been alone, she'd have made some flip remark like,

'Welcome home, the conquering hero' but she's circumspect in front of non-branch officers. All she says is, 'Well done, sir.' Twenty minutes ago I might have accepted that accolade; not now.

She wants to know what Dubal was like. I'm not going to spoil her illusion by telling her he's a ringer for Claude from Fraud. Enough illusions are about to be shattered. 'A smashing man,' I say truthfully. Then, nodding at the yellow-topped building, 'What's he been up to?'

The driver, a senior surveillance operative, takes over. 'Went to a solicitor's office off the market square at four. Was there three-quarters of an hour. Returned and hasn't been out since.'

Oh, Christ, I think, he's been putting his affairs in order.

'Any visitors?'

'Two. One left on foot in a bit of a hurry, carrying white paper, looked like an envelope.'

'Description?'

Oh, God, I groan privately when I hear it. I've misread this completely. 'Half an hour ago, a woman, early twenties, arrived by car, rang the bell, but the door didn't open. She drove off again.'

I don't ask for a description of Dawn Powers. Hazel and her team are told to stay put. I drive on to the front door with the scene-of-crime specialists, gut bubbling.

A humane killer had been placed at Geoffrey Powers' temple and triggered. The impact had blown him off his chair on to the lino where his head lies in a lake of blood so large that it's lapping slowly against the skirting boards. The gun, bolt extended four inches, has dropped into the blood.

Guilt flows through me. Should have ordered his arrest last night, I rebuke myself, instead of having him watched till I got back to claim the glory. What I've got now is gore, not glory.

I steady myself and look around. On the desk, the phone as its paperweight, is a letter and a sealed white envelope addressed 'To Whom It May Concern'.

One of the Forensics men pulls on transparent gloves and lifts the phone.

The writing is in a strong firm hand. The letter reads:

Darling Dawn,
  Please, please forgive me for the continuing heartbreak I have
caused you – not just by my actions now but for splitting up our
family and my subsequent neglect.
  Do not in any way blame yourself. The fault is all mine.
  God watch over you.
  Blessings, too, to your mother whose forgiveness I also ask.
  Peace and happiness to you both.
                    Very much love.
                       Daddy

  Inside the envelope is another letter, same hand, bright blue, the
paper slightly smudged, a carbon copy. 'To Whom It May
Concern' is repeated at the top, then:

  I, Geoffrey Powers, being of sound mind, wish to state that I,
and I alone, am responsible for the scandal that is about to
engulf me and destroy all I have achieved.
  I, single-handed, carried out the destruction of Thorne's
cold store in order to prevent the exposure of previous mis-
deeds – namely the exchange of best for inferior quality meat.
It was done at a time when I was under extreme financial
pressure.
  I wish to exonerate my former employee, Mr Alan Hicks, from
complicity in an offence.
  I also want it to be known that he was not involved in the
unfortunate death of Mr Andrew Knight which was completely
accidental and natural.

  Both letters are read several times, but it takes paper and pencil
to work something out.

Outside, I assign Hazel to break the news to daughter
Dawn at the station, a ghastly task, down to me really. I
could and should have had her father safely under lock
and key. Not unnaturally, she demands, 'Where are you
going?'

192

'A place I should have gone yesterday.' I look at the surveillance driver. 'Got a nice thin, black torch?'

22

The days of kicking in locked and bolted doors *à la* February ended for me when the blast of a shotgun left one leg a bit shorter and stiffer than the other.

So I hammer on the varnished brown door that leads from the rounded stern deck into the living quarters of the *Tyke*, illuminated by the floodlights on the walls of the ruined castle. 'Dilly man,' I call.

A befuddled 'What?' comes from inside.

'Dilly man,' I repeat. 'Night soil collection.'

'I'm just lodging here.'

'Makes no difference.'

'Piss off.'

'Your chemical bog's leaking.'

'Nowt to do with me.'

'It's causing pollution, killing fish.'

'Come back tomorrow.'

'I'll come back with a load of policemen in five minutes unless I get in to fix it. Now. We're legally liable. Come on. It's a health risk.' I raise my voice. 'Now please.'

Something creaks. A bolt is scraped on the other side of the door. The lock clicks. The door opens an inch.

Now I do kick.

The door is thrown back wide. I catch only the tail end of Hicks' fall to the floor. I am on him as he hits it, rolling him face down. Knees on his neck, I twist an arm up the back of his stained white T-shirt till it touches his long, matted blond hair. He screams with fear and pain. 'What the –'

'Todd's my name,' I say. Prematurely, I promote myself. 'The late Assistant Chief Constable Knight's deputy.'

I have both wrists crossed now and gripped firmly in my right hand. My left takes the surveillance man's torch from my jacket pocket. I flash it very quickly in front of his face, cheek on the carpet, golden ear-ring visible. 'Seen one of these before, haven't you, when you worked in the pens at Combined Counties? Seen what they can do to a thick-skinned beast, how they jump in shock, haven't you? Think what it will do when I stick it up your arse.'

All my weight is on my knees in the small of his back. 'I'm going to ask you some questions and if I don't like the answers that's where it's going. Up yours.' Pause. 'Now.' I steady my breathing. 'Tell me about your little talk with Mr Knight?'

'I told him . . .' He gasps, starts again. '. . . I told him all I knew. The truth. Honest.'

'Now you're going to tell me.'

'About Stone and his loony sister and that boyfriend of hers. Is that what you mean?'

'Why did you grass them?'

'Why not? They owed me a hundred, the bastards, and got me arrested instead. They stitched me. I stitched them.'

'What else did you tell him?'

'About the meat runs with Powers years back and the poison I pinched for him last month. Stuff like that, you mean?'

'And you came to a deal?'

'Sort of, like. I mean, I knew where Stone and Co. would be. I knew exactly because they'd told me. In here. One night.'

'K2?'

He repeats it, correcting my pronunciation.

'And you told Mr Knight?'

'Not exactly. No. 'Cos I wanted out. So I kept vague about that, the location, I mean, somewhere in Normandy, I said, but I could track 'em down. Anything to get out of that nick.'

'Then how come it's in his records?'

He twists. 'Can't be.'

'It is. Capital K, then 2.'

He goes rigid. 'Oh.' He untenses slightly. 'He asked me for a code for the operation. He's into codes. Was. So I suggested that.'

I tighten my grip. 'Taking the piss, were you?'

'No.' It jolts out. 'No. Not really. It was easy to remember. To carry in my head. If I had to contact him by phone.'

'And he released you on bail?'

'Only on condition that I followed them – he put up the money, three hundred – and sent back a message identifying their next target before they killed someone. And I would have. Did do in a way.'

'And he taught you a code so you could communicate the info from K2 without being detected as a nark?'

'Right.' He tries to nod his head, can't.

'What got in the way?'

'Powers. That's who. After I got out the cop shop, he offered to follow me back to the club in the truck, wait up the road, pick me up, call to collect some gear and drop me off at the station. Instead, he drove back to Combined Counties.'

'What did he want?'

'What was happening, like. To know all about it. He was a bundle of nerves. I told him what I told Knight. Not all of it, like. Not the bit about the meat runs and nicking some poison for him. All the rest. About the crackpots from here. Just them.'

'What did he do?'

'Offered me two grand to stay – half down and half when the coast was clear. "Won't work," I said. "Knight's expecting a message in code from France from me." "Write it here," he said. "I'll see it gets posted over there." '

'And you agreed?'

No response.

I brush the seat of his dirty jeans with the torch.

'No. No. Please.' He whimpers it. 'Yes. I mean, yes. It was a better offer, wasn't it? More money.'

So he just broke his contract, I think, like a soccer star walking out on his club when another waves a bigger cheque. 'And?'

'Took loads of goes to get it right. We went through a pack of postcards he bought.' He tries to look up at me, fails again. 'But I did what I promised, didn't I? I got the message through that the plane was the target. Zip, I wrote, before the code. That means Ark.'

'How did you know?'

'They talked about it in here. Mentioned the airline. That's got to be worth three hundred, hasn't it? They didn't get any plane last night, did they? Says so in the paper.'

'How did you know Arc Air was the target?'

'Stone told me. Here. Pissed one night. Showed me a photocopy of a brochure with the plane's data – range and load and things. The shipping company that fired him owned it or had money in it or some tie-up. Right? That was their next target. Right? Always knew that.'

'Why didn't you tell Mr Knight that when you were inside?'

'Held that bit back, didn't I? Had to. Or there'd have been no bail or deal, no money. Anyway he wanted the date as well as the target so they'd be nicked red-handed.'

'So you never went to France?'

'Powers said the card would, but not me. He told me to lie low. I knew this place was empty, knew how to get in through the toilet window, 'cos Rich and me came in that way once when he lost his key.'

'So who kept the date you set up in the coded card with Mr Knight at Red Gutter?'

'Me and Powers.'

'What happened?'

'Powers pleaded with him. "Let's square this," he said.'

Masonic code, that, for let's cover this up. Powers, I belatedly realise, was in the Brotherhood, too.

Hicks gabbles on. 'He pointed at me and said, "You gave him a deal. Now give me one. Stick Thorne's explosion against Animal Salvation or someone in your family goes to jail with me." '

'Did he say who?'

'No chance to. Your gaffer went spare, blue in the face and said, "Don't try to compromise me. I'm arresting you both." Powers pushed him away. He was already out of breath, buggered from the walk. He just wobbled, sagged, passed out, collapsed down the hill. Honest to God. Powers went after him, said he was a goner and we did a runner. I've been laying low here ever since.'

'What happened tonight?'

'Told him I couldn't hide away for ever. I wanted the rest of my dough and away, out of it before it all comes out.'

'What did he say?'

'Not much. He looked like death. Worse than old Knight afore he croaked. He said things had gone badly wrong, everything. The police were bound to find that he had done the Thorne's job. He'd been to see his solicitor to confess, lost his bottle, wrote a new will instead. He was going to sleep on it and, if he still felt the same way in the morning, he'd go to the police.'

'What did you say?'

'Well, wot you think? "For christsake, don't." I was in deep –

you know, the meat run, the poison for him, the fertiliser for Stoney, double-crossing you lot, being there when your boss died. Really deep.'

'So what did you do?'

'Got him to write a letter.'

'Saying what?'

'Clearing me.'

'Come on. He's an ex-rugger star. He'd make mincemeat out of you. Did you persuade him?'

'Sort of.'

'How?'

'He wouldn't give me my money . . .'

I roll one knee on his neck. 'How?'

'There was a humane killer there on the window sill. I asked him why. He said he'd been considering his options. There was a half-finished letter in front of him. I knew what it all meant. He was going to shoot himself, leave me to face the music.'

Powers' dilemma I can appreciate. He was off to jail. No more after-dinner speeches, no more entertaining at big matches in his sponsors' tent. Risking the health of refugees to get yourself out of hock with the bank is bad PR.

'So what did you do?'

'Snatched it up, the gun, I mean, held it to him, made him hand over my money and write a letter clearing me. He gave it to me, kept a copy himself. Mine's in the post to the local cop shop. Then he said, "May as well finish this to Dawn." He sucked on his pen for ages, but only wrote a few more lines.'

'What did you do?'

'Put the gun back and pissed off, didn't I? Left him to it. Why? Has he done it? Have you found him?' His voice goes up a note. 'It wasn't me, you know. I'm no killer. You believe that, don't you?'

What I believe doesn't matter. What the pathologist and Forensics find will prove it, one way or another. I pocket the torch and use both hands to pull him to his feet. Over his shoulder, he says, 'I was going to do a bunk tomorrow. France, fruit-picking. How the hell did you know where I'd be?'

Because Hicks had passed on Knight's code to Powers when they cobbled up the message on the card and, with a humane killer at his temple, Powers had added four lines to his last letter to his daughter. Short sentences that began with GBPV which decodes into *'Tyke'*.

But I can't be bothered to explain.

'So how long had this business been going on?' asks Hazel, behind me as I drive through steady rain back to HQ from Thorne's house, a big, modern place, not very homely.

'The business with the meat?' comes the reply from beside her.

I doubt that was what Hazel had in mind, but I'm not going to interrupt. It's her interview, her pinch, the least I can do.

'Lasted a year. The switch-overs, I mean. It was in our store, tons of it, I'm afraid, for five years.'

'Why didn't you get rid of it a bit at a time?' asks Hazel.

'We couldn't. We had nothing to put in its place for the annual EC audit.'

'How did it start?'

'He was on the financial brink. Couldn't help out myself. Not then. We were struggling before we came into money.'

'When did you realise you were in trouble?'

'When the health inspector phoned and said there'd have to be an examination after what had happened with the charity consignment.'

'So you phoned Powers?'

'At home. He said we'd have to do something, get rid of the evidence.'

'Do you know what he had in mind?'

'No, but as soon as the explosion happened I knew it was him, trying to make it look like that other case of Andy's, the boat bombing. And he admitted as much when I next saw him.'

'What happened on that occasion?'

'Very tense, it was. He told me he'd stolen a car so you couldn't trace tyre marks on the track from the river back to him after he'd towed the money across. He didn't need or want it; burned it, in fact, in case it was marked and traceable.'

A deep sigh. 'Told me not to worry. He'd never involve me. But I have been, all the time, for a month now, worried out of my mind, wondering what I'd let myself in for.'

'What about the postcard?'

'We were going away, anyway, for a long weekend, all planned. He told me to make sure I checked our post office box every day in case of developments, to warn me.'

'And you did?'

'Yes. He wrote, registered express, to say that Andy was on to the boat saboteurs but he could control the situation, provided I posted a card he enclosed. It had to be mailed from Normandy, not Brittany.'

'Was that difficult?'

'Not really. I hared up from the gite on Monday while our American neighbours were throwing a Memorial Day party. They drink so much, all of them, that they lose track of time. I told them I'd had a shunt on a roundabout in the main street to explain the long absence and backed into a post on the way home to make it look real.'

Made a mistake there, I think, thankfully. The signature for the recorded letter from England gave Dubal the time the collection was made at Dol de Bretagne's post office. The street cameras showed no accident outside on the roundabout.

Now Hazel repeats and expands on her opening question. 'How long was this business going on, Mrs Thorne – your affair, I mean?'

'Ten years,' Stella says with a catch in her throat. 'A bit more. Ever since we met at a rugger do. We managed to keep everything secret.'

Not half, I am brooding. Even Mrs Knight hadn't rumbled her sister's involvement. Knight had suspected Thorne, but then he'd never been to Brittany to see that traffic video for himself and the second clue was perhaps too close to home.

His poor widow. She'd tried to do the honourable thing, point me in what she believed to be the right direction. The irony, the tragedy, was that her secretive sister had all the answers all the time.

'I just didn't have the courage to join him,' Stella is explaining, 'even when his marriage broke up. I mean, my husband needs me, doesn't he? You've seen the state of him. Hopeless.'

Duty before love, I'm thinking. And, oh, she loved Powers all right. Filled her garden in France with yellow roses, his team's

199

colour, to be reminded of him when they were apart, letting flowers talk for her, the way her sister did.

Em said this morning it will be veal cutlets washed down with Bull's Blood tonight, but I know she was kidding as soon the lemony smell of Thai food follows her out of the kitchen.

'Well?' she asks, wiping her hands on an Irish linen tea towel. A floaty red dress with tiny white floral sprigs and a waist that comes up to just under the bust only partially hides the fact that she's very large now.

I shake my head.

'You mean to say you spent two hundred on that . . .' She nods at my dark brown suit, making its debut. '. . . and you didn't land it?'

Another shake.

'So it's no chauffeured Roller, still a self-drive Volvo.' She doesn't look too unhappy.

Me, neither. Somewhere, I've lost a bit of confidence. Anyway, I put my hat in the ring, so, as gran said, I'm qualified to criticise when things go wrong.

'Who did?' Em asks.

'You'll never guess.'

'Not Dale, surely?'

A third shake. 'His post's been abolished and he's been transferred' – i/c Community Affairs, sadly, not point-duty.

'Who then?'

'Carole Malloy.'

Now she looks distinctly happy. If I'm not going to make ACC, Em would want the CID chief, a close pal, to have it.

'A woman!' she says with an evil glint. 'Well, you can't blame a Masonic conspiracy for that either, can you?'

ALLISON & BUSBY CRIME

Jo Bannister
A Bleeding of Innocents
Sins of the Heart
Burning Desires

Brian Battison
The Witch's Familiar

Simon Beckett
Fine Lines
Animals

Ann Cleeves
A Day in the Death of
Dorothea Cassidy
Killjoy

Denise Danks
Frame Grabber
Wink a Hopeful Eye
The Pizza House Crash

John Dunning
Booked to Die

John Gano
Inspector Proby's Christmas

Bob George
Main Bitch

T. G. Gilpin
Missing Daisy

Russell James
Slaughter Music

J. Robert Janes
Sandman

H. R. F. Keating
A Remarkable Case of
Burglary

Ted Lewis
Billy Rags
Get Carter
GBH
Jack Carter's Law
Jack Carter and the
Mafia Pigeon

Ross Macdonald
Blue City
The Barbarous Coast
The Blue Hammer
The Far Side of the Dollar
Find a Victim
The Galton Case
The Goodbye Look
The Instant Enemy
The Ivory Grin
The Lew Archer Omnibus
Volume 1
The Lew Archer Omnibus
Volume 2
The Lew Archer Omnibus
Volume 3
Meet Me at the Morgue
The Moving Target
Sleeping Beauty
The Underground Man
The Way Some People Die
The Wycherly Woman
The Zebra-Striped Hearse

Priscilla Masters
Winding Up The Serpent

Jennie Melville
The Woman Who Was Not There

Margaret Millar
Ask for Me Tomorrow
Mermaid
Rose's Last Summer
Banshee
How Like An Angel
The Murder of Miranda
A Stranger In My Grave
The Soft Talkers

Frank Palmer
Dark Forest

Sax Rohmer
The Fu Manchu Omnibus
Volume 1
The Fu Manchu Omnibus
Volume 2
The Fu Manchu Omnibus
Volume 3

Frank Smith
Fatal Flaw

Richard Stark
The Green Eagle Score
The Handle
Point Blank
The Rare Coin Score
Slayground
The Sour Lemon Score
The Parker Omnibus
Volume 1

Donald Thomas
Dancing in the Dark

I. K. Watson
Manor
Wolves Aren't White

Donald Westlake
Sacred Monsters
The Mercenaries
The Donald Westlake Omnibus